P. G. Wodehouse

'The ultimate in comfort reading because nothing bad ever happens in P.G. Wodehouse land. Or even if it does, it's always sorted out by the end of the book. For as long as I'm immersed in a P.G. Wodehouse book, it's possible to keep the real world at bay and live in a far, far nicer, funnier one where happy endings are the order of the day' *Marian Keyes*

'You should read Wodehouse when you're well and when you're poorly; when you're travelling, and when you're not; when you're feeling clever, and when you're feeling utterly dim. Wodehouse always lifts your spirits, no matter how high they happen to be already' *Lynne Truss*

'P.G. Wodehouse remains the greatest chronicler of a certain kind of Englishness, that no one else has ever captured quite so sharply, or with quite as much wit and affection' *Julian Fellowes*

'Not only the funniest English novelist who ever wrote but one of our finest stylists. His world is perfect, his stories are perfect, his writing is perfect. What more is there to be said?' *Susan Hill*

'One of my (few) proud boasts is that I once spent a day interviewing P.G. Wodehouse at his home in America. He was exactly as I'd expected: a lovely, modest man. He could have walked out of one of his own novels. It's dangerous to use the word genius to describe a writer, but I'll risk it with him' *John Humphrys*

'The incomparable and timeless genius – perfect for readers of all ages, shapes and sizes!' *Kate Mosse*

'A genius . . . Elusive, delicate but lasting. He created such a credible world that, sadly, I suppose, never really existed but what a delight it always is to enter it and the temptation to linger there is sometimes almost overwhelming' *Alan Ayckbourn*

'Wodehouse was quite simply the Bee's Knees. And then some' *Joseph Connolly*

'Compulsory reading for anyone who has a pig, an aunt – or a sense of humour!' *Lindsey Davis*

'I constantly find myself drooling with admiration at the sublime way Wodehouse plays with the English language' *Simon Brett*

'I've recorded all the Jeeves books, and I can tell you this: it's like singing Mozart. The perfection of the phrasing is a physical pleasure. I doubt if any writer in the English language has more perfect music' *Simon Callow*

'Quite simply, the master of comic writing at work' *Jane Moore*

'To pick up a Wodehouse novel is to find oneself in the presence of genius – no writer has ever given me so much pure enjoyment' *John Julius Norwich*

'P.G. Wodehouse is the gold standard of English wit' *Christopher Hitchens*

'Wodehouse is so utterly, properly, simply funny' *Adele Parks*

'To dive into a Wodehouse novel is to swim in some of the most elegantly turned phrases in the English language' *Ben Schott*

'P.G. Wodehouse should be prescribed to treat depression. Cheaper, more effective than valium and far, far more addictive' *Olivia Williams*

'My only problem with Wodehouse is deciding which of his enchanting books to take to my desert island' *Ruth Dudley Edwards*

The author of almost a hundred books and the creator of Jeeves, Blandings Castle, Psmith, Ukridge, Uncle Fred and Mr Mulliner, P.G. Wodehouse was born in 1881 and educated at Dulwich College. After two years with the Hong Kong and Shanghai Bank he became a full-time writer, contributing to a variety of periodicals including *Punch* and the *Globe*. He married in 1914. As well as his novels and short stories, he wrote lyrics for musical comedies with Guy Bolton and Jerome Kern, and at one time had five musicals running simultaneously on Broadway. His time in Hollywood also provided much source material for fiction.

At the age of 93, in the New Year's Honours List of 1975, he received a long-overdue knighthood, only to die on St Valentine's Day some 45 days later.

P. G. WODEHOUSE

Young Men in Spats

arrow books

Published by Arrow Books 2009

5 7 9 10 8 6 4

First published in the United Kingdom in 1936 by Herbert Jenkins Ltd

Arrow Books
The Random House Group Limited
20 Vauxhall Bridge Road, London, SW1V 2SA

www.randomhouse.co.uk

www.wodehouse.co.uk

Addresses for companies within The Random House Group Limited can be
found at: www.randomhouse.co.uk/offices.htm

The Random House Group Limited Reg. No. 954009

A CIP catalogue record for this book
is available from the British Library

ISBN 9780099514039

The Random House Group Limited supports The Forest Stewardship
Council (FSC®), the leading international forest certification
organisation. Our books carrying the FSC label are printed on FSC®
certified paper. FSC is the only forest certification scheme endorsed by
the leading environmental organisations, including Greenpeace.
Our paper procurement policy can be found
atwww.randomhouse.co.uk/environment

Printed and bound by CPI Group (UK) Ltd, Croydon, CR0 4YY

Young Men in Spats

CONTENTS

I⊤ was the hour of the morning snifter, and a little group of Eggs and Beans and Crumpets had assembled in the smoking-room of the Drones Club to do a bit of inhaling. There had been a party of sorts overnight, and the general disposition of the company was towards a restful and somewhat glassy-eyed silence. This was broken at length by one of the Crumpets.

'Old Freddie's back,' he observed.

Some moments elapsed before any of those present felt equal to commenting on this statement. Then a Bean spoke.

'Freddie Who?'

'Freddie Widgeon.'

'Back where?'

'Back here.'

'I mean, back from what spot?'

'New York.'

'I didn't know Freddie had been to New York.'

'Well, you can take it from me he has. Or else how,' argued the Crumpet, 'could he have got back?'

The Bean considered the point.

'Something in that,' he agreed. 'What sort of a time did he have?'

'Not so good. He lost the girl he loved.'

'I wish I had a quid for every girl Freddie Widgeon has loved and lost,' sighed an Egg wistfully. 'If I had, I shouldn't be touching you for a fiver.'

'You aren't,' said the Crumpet.

The Bean frowned. His head was hurting him, and he considered that the conversation was becoming sordid.

'How did he lose his girl?'

'Because of the suitcase.'

'What suitcase?'

'The suitcase he carried for the other girl.'

'What other girl?'

'The one he carried the suitcase for.'

The Bean frowned again.

'A bit complex, all this, isn't it?' he said. 'Hardly the sort of stuff, I mean, to spring on personal friends who were up a trifle late last night.'

'It isn't really,' the Crumpet assured him. 'Not when you know the facts. The way old Freddie told me the story it was as limpid as dammit. And what he thinks – and what I think, too – is that it just shows what toys we are in the hands of Fate, if you know what I mean. I mean to say, it's no good worrying and trying to look ahead and plan and scheme and weigh your every action, if you follow me, because you never can tell when doing such-and-such won't make so-and-so happen – while, on the other hand, if you do so-and-so it may just as easily lead to such-and-such.'

A pale-faced Egg with heavy circles under his eyes rose at this point and excused himself. He said his head had begun to throb again and he proposed to step round to the chemist on the corner for another of his dark-brown pick-me-ups.

'I mean to say,' resumed the Crumpet, 'if Freddie – with the best motives in the world – hadn't carried that suitcase for that girl, he might at this moment be walking up the aisle with a gardenia in his buttonhole and Mavis Peasemarch, only daughter of the fifth Earl of Bodsham, on his arm.'

The Bean demurred. He refused to admit the possibility of such a thing, even if Freddie Widgeon had sworn off suitcases for life.

'Old Bodders would never have allowed Mavis to marry a bird of Freddie's calibre. He would think him worldly and frivolous. I don't know if you are personally acquainted with the Bod, but I may tell you that my people once lugged me to a week-end at his place and not only were we scooped in and shanghaied to church twice on the Sunday, regardless of age or sex, but on the Monday morning at eight o'clock – eight, mark you – there were family prayers in the dining-room. There you have old Bodders in a nutshell. Freddie's a good chap, but he can't have stood a dog's chance from the start.'

'On the contrary,' said the Crumpet warmly, 'he made his presence felt right from the beginning to an almost unbelievable extent, and actually clicked as early as the fourth day out.'

'Were Bodders and Mavis on the boat, then?'

'They certainly were. All the way over.'

'And Bodders, you say, actually approved of Freddie?'

'He couldn't have been more all over him, Freddie tells me, if Freddie had been a Pan-Anglican Congress. What you overlook is that Bodsham – living, as he does, all the year round in the country – knew nothing of Freddie except that one of his uncles was his old school-friend, Lord Blicester, and another of his uncles was actually a Bishop. Taking a line through them, he undoubtedly regarded Freddie as a pretty hot potato.'

The Bean seemed shaken, but he put another point.

'What about Mavis, then?'

'What about her?'

'I should have thought Freddie would have been the last bloke she would have considered hitching up with. I've seen her in action down at Peasemarch, and you can take it from me that she is very far from being one of the boys. You needn't let it get about, of course, but that girl, to my certain knowledge, plays the organ in the local church and may often be seen taking soup to the deserving villagers with many a gracious word.'

The Crumpet had his answer to this, too.

'She knew nothing of Freddie, either. She liked his quiet, saintly manner and considered that he had a soul. At any rate, I can assure you that everything went like a breeze. Helped by the fact that the sea was calm and that there was a dashed fine moon every night, old Freddie shoved his nose past the judge's box at 10.45 p.m. on the fourth day out. And when next morning he informed old Bodsham that he had now a son to comfort his declining years, there was not a discordant note. The old boy said that he could wish no better husband for his daughter than a steady, respectable young fellow like Freddie, and they arrived in New York a happy and united family.'

The only thing in the nature of a flaw that Freddie found in New York, he tells me, was the fact that the populace, to judge from the daily papers, didn't seem to be so ideally happy in its love-life as he was. What I mean to say, he wanted smiling faces about him, so to speak, and it looked to him as if everybody in the place were cutting up their wives and hiding them in sacks in the Jersey marshes or else putting detectives on to them to secure the necessary evidence.

It saddened him, he tells me, when he opened his illustrated tabloid of a morning, to have to try to eat eggs and bacon while gazing at a photograph of Mae Belle McGinnis, taken when she was not looking her best because Mr McGinnis had just settled some domestic dispute with the meat-axe.

Also, there seemed to him far too much of all that stuff about Sugar-Daddies being Discovered In Love Nest As Blizzard Grips City.

However, when you are the guest of a great nation, you have to take the rough with the smooth. And there appears to be no doubt that, despite all the marital unrest around him, Freddie at this juncture was indisputably in the pink. I've never been engaged myself, so I know nothing of the symptoms at first hand, but Freddie tells me that the way it takes a fellow is to make him feel as if he were floating on a fleecy cloud, high up in the air, and only touching the ground at odd spots.

Most of the time, he says, he just hovered over New York like some winged thing. But occasionally he would come down and emerge from the ether, and on one of these rare occasions he found himself wandering in the neighbourhood of Seventy-Second Street, somewhere on the West Side.

And just in front of him was a girl lugging a dashed great heavy suitcase.

Now, I want you to follow me very closely here. This is where Freddie stands or falls. He was pretty eloquent at this point, when he told me the story: and, as far as I am concerned, I may say fearlessly that I dismiss him without a stain on his character. I consider his motives to have been pure to the last drop.

One of the things that being engaged does to you, you must remember, is to fill you to the gills with a sort of knightly chivalry. So Freddie tells me. You go about the place like a Boy Scout, pouncing out on passers-by and doing acts of kindness to them. Three times that day Freddie had chased seedy-looking birds up side-streets and forced cash on them. He had patted four small boys on the head and asked them if they meant to be President some day. He had beamed benevolently on the citizenry till his cheeks ached. And he was still full of the milk of human kindness and longing to assist some less fortunate fellow-traveller along the road of Life, when he saw this girl in front of him, staggering under the weight of the suitcase.

Now, although the impulse to help her with her burden was intense, he tells me that, if she had been a pretty girl, he would have resisted it. His sense of loyalty to Mavis was so great that he was right off pretty girls. They were the only persons he had excluded from his beaming operations. Towards them, in spite of all that milk of human kindness, he had been consistently aloof and austere. The cold face. The unwobbly eye. Something seemed to tell him that Mavis would prefer it so.

But this girl before him was not pretty. She was distinctly plain. Even ugly. She looked as if she might be a stenographer selected for some business magnate by his wife out of a number of competing applicants. And, such being so, he did not hesitate. Already the suitcase seemed to be giving the poor little thing a crick in the back, and it was as if he heard Mavis's voice in his ear, whispering: 'Go to it!'

He ambled up like a courtly mustang.

'Excuse me,' he said. 'May I help you with that apparatus of yours?'

The girl gave him a keen look through her spectacles, and either thought he was thoroughly to be trusted, or didn't. At any rate, she passed over the bag.

'And now where?' asked Freddie.

The girl said she lived in Sixty-Ninth Street, and Freddie right-hoed, and they set off. And presently they came to a brownstone building, in which she had Flat B on the fourth floor.

Well, of course, you may say that, having deposited female and suitcase at their destination, old Freddie should have uttered a brief, courteous 'Pip-pip!' and legged it. And very possibly you are right. But consider the facts. The flat, as I have indicated, was four flights up. There was no lift, so he had to hoof it up all those stairs. It was a warm day. And the suitcase appeared to be packed with sheet-iron or something.

I mean to say, by the time he had reached Journey's End, he was in sore need of a spot of repose. So, rightly or wrongly, he didn't biff off, but sort of collapsed into a chair and sat there restoring his tissues.

The girl, meanwhile, prattled in friendly vein. As far as Freddie can recall her remarks, her name was Myra Jennings. She was employed in the office of a wholesale silk importer. She had just come back from the country. The photograph over the sideboard was her mother's, who lived in Waterbury, Connecticut. The girlfriend with whom she shared the flat was away on her vacation. And all that sort of thing, don't you know. I mean, pleasant gossip from the home.

She had just begun to tell him that, though she yielded to no one in her admiration for Ronald Colman, she couldn't help saying that William Powell had a sort of something that kind of seemed to place him sort of even higher in a girl's estimation, when there occurred one of those interruptions which, I understand, are always happening in New York.

If you're a native, you hardly notice them. You just look over your shoulder and say 'Oh, ah?' and go on trying to get Los Angeles on the radio.

But Freddie, being new to the place, was a little startled. Because you see, what happened was that just as they were sitting there, chatting of this and that, there was a sudden crash. The door of the hallway which opened on to the landing outside was burst open. And in surged an extraordinarily hefty bloke with a big moustache. He wore a bowler hat. Behind him came a couple of other birds, also hefty and similarly bowler-hatted.

'Ah!' said Bloke A, in a satisfied sort of voice.

Freddie did a bit of gaping. He was a good deal on the nonplussed side. He supposed, as his head began to clear, that this was one of those cases of 'Bandits Break Into Home and Rob Two'.

'Seems to me,' said the Bloke, addressing his associate Blokes, 'this case is open and shut.'

The other two nodded.

'That's right,' said one.

'Open and shut,' said the other.

'Yes,' said the Bloke, summing up. 'That's about what it is. Open *and* shut.'

Miss Jennings, who had been dusting the photograph of her mother, now appeared to notice for the first time that she had visitors. She spoke as follows:

'What in the world do you think you're doing?'

The Bloke lit a cigar. So did his associates. Two cigars.

'That's all right, Mrs Silvers,' he said.

'Sure it's all right,' said the other two.

'You boys are witnesses,' said the Bloke.

'Sure, we're witnesses,' said the other two.

'You can give evidence that we found Mrs Silvers alone in her apartment with this pie-faced cluck.'

'Sure, we can give evidence that we found her alone in her apartment with this pie-faced cluck.'

'Then that's all right,' said the Bloke contentedly. 'That is all her husband will want to know. It makes the thing open and shut.'

And it came home to Freddie with a sickening thud that these fellows were not, as he had supposed, a hold-up gang, but detectives. He ought to have recognized them from the start, he tells me, by the bowler hats. What had misled him was the fact that at the outset they weren't smoking cigars. When they started smoking cigars, the scales fell from his eyes.

He gulped a bit. In fact, he gulped rather more than a bit. He realized now what his mistaken sense of knightly chivalry had made him stumble into. The soup, no less. With the best intentions, meaning only to scatter light and sweetness on every side, he had become a Sugar-Daddy Surprised In Love Nest.

The female of the species, however, appeared unwilling to take this thing lying down. Her chin was up, her shoulders were squared, she had both feet on the ground, and she looked the troupe steadily in the eye through her spectacles.

'Just for fun,' she said, 'tell me where you fellows think you are?'

'Where do we think we are?' said the Bloke. 'That's all right where we think we are. We're in Flat 4A. And you're Mrs Silvers. And I'm from the Alert Detective Agency. And I'm acting under instructions from your husband. Laugh that off!'

'I will,' said the girl. 'I'm not Mrs Silvers. I haven't a husband. And this isn't Flat 4A, it's Flat 4B.'

The Bloke gasped. He reminded Freddie of his uncle Joseph, the time he swallowed the bad oyster. The same visible emotion.

'Don't tell me we've busted into the wrong flat?' he said, pleadingly.

'That's just what I am telling you.'

'The wrong flat?'

'The wrong flat.'

There was a pause.

'I'll tell you what it is,' said one of the assistant blokes, a pretty acute chap, quick in the uptake. 'We've been and busted into the wrong flat.'

'That's it,' said the other. 'The wrong flat.'

Well, they were very decent about it, Freddie tells me. They didn't take off their hats, and they went on smoking their cigars, but they paid for the door. And presently the party broke up, the Bloke protesting to the last that this was the first mistake he had made in twenty years.

Having had a hearty laugh with the Jennings over the whole amusing episode, Freddie hopped into a taxi and started off for Forty-Sixth Street, for he was lunching with old Bodsham and Mavis at the Ritz-Carlton and a bit late already. All the way down there, he was chuckling to himself at the thought of what a capital story he had to tell them. Put him one up, he thought it would.

You see, if there was a snag in the wholehearted joy of being engaged to Mavis Peasemarch, it was the fact that, when in the society of herself and father, he occasionally found the going a bit sticky as regarded conversation.

Freddie, as you know, is a bird who, when the conditions are right, can be the life and soul of the party. Shoot a few stiffish cocktails into him and give him his head in the matter of sprightly anecdotes and the riper kind of Limerick, and he will hold you spellbound. But, cut off from these resources, he frequently found himself a trifle tongue-tied when taking a bite with old Bodsham.

And, as no fellow likes to feel that his future father-in-law is beginning to regard him as a loony deaf-mute, he welcomed the opportunity of showing himself a gay and gifted raconteur.

If the story of his morning's adventure, told as he proposed to tell it, didn't have the old boy hiccoughing and wiping the tears from his eyes, he would be jolly well dashed.

And the same applied to Mavis.

'Capital! Capital! Ah, Van Sprunt, this is my son-in-law-to-be, Frederick Widgeon. A most entertaining young fellow. Get him to tell you his story about the detectives in the wrong flat. You'll die laughing. We all think very highly of Frederick Widgeon.'

And all that sort of thing, I mean. What? I mean to say, you follow his reasoning.

Well, he didn't get a chance to spring the story over the melon and powdered ginger, because old Bodsham was rather holding the floor a bit on the subject of iniquitous Socialist attacks on the House of Lords. Then, with the *côtelettes* and mashed, Mavis started to haul up her slacks about the Soul of America. In fact, it wasn't till the coffee had arrived that he secured a genuine opening.

'I say,' said Freddie, catching the Speaker's eye at this juncture, 'a most awfully funny thing happened to me this morning. Make you scream. You'll burst your corsets.'

And, lighting a carefree cigarette, he embarked upon the narrative.

He told it well. Looking back, he says, he can't remember when he has ever done more justice to a yarn, squeezed the last drop of juice out of it with a firmer hand, if you know what I mean. The grave, intent faces of his audience, he tells me, only spurred him on to further efforts. He approved of their self-restraint. He realized that they realized that a story like this was not the sort of story to fritter away with giggles. You saved yourself up for the big howl at the finish.

And then suddenly – he couldn't tell just when – there stole over him a sort of feeling that the *conte* wasn't getting across quite so big as he had hoped. There seemed to him to be a certain definite something in the atmosphere. You know how it is when you strike a cold audience. Old Bodsham was looking a little like a codfish with something on its mind, and there was an odd kind of expression in Mavis's eye.

When he had finished, there was a longish silence. Mavis looked at old Bodsham. Old Bodsham looked at Mavis.

'I don't quite understand, Frederick,' said Mavis at length. 'You say this girl was a stranger?'

'Why, yes,' said Freddie.

'And you accosted her in the street?'

'Why, yes,' said Freddie.

'Oh?' said Mavis.

'I was sorry for her,' said Freddie.

'Oh?' said Mavis.

'In fact, you might say that my heart bled for her.'

'Oh?' said Mavis.

Old Bodsham let his breath go in a sort of whistling sigh.

'Is it your practice, may I ask,' he said, 'to scrape acquaintance in the public streets with young persons of the opposite sex?'

'You must remember, Father,' said Mavis, in a voice which would have had an Esquimaux slapping his ribs and calling for the steam-heat, 'that this girl was probably very pretty. So many of these New York girls are. That would, of course, explain Frederick's behaviour.'

'She wasn't!' yipped Freddie. 'She was a gargoyle.'

'Oh?' said Mavis.

'Spectacled to bursting-point and utterly lacking in feminine allure.'

'Oh?' said Mavis.

'And when I saw her frail form bowed down by that dashed great suitcase ... I should have thought,' said Freddie, injured, 'that, having learned the salient facts, you would have fawned on me for my big-hearted chivalry.'

'Oh?' said Mavis.

There was another silence.

'I must be going, Father,' said Mavis. 'I have some shopping to do.'

'Shall I come with you?' said Freddie.

'I would prefer to be alone,' said Mavis.

'I must be going,' said old Bodsham. 'I have some thinking to do.'

'Thinking?' said Freddie.

'Thinking,' said old Bodsham. 'Some serious thinking. Some extremely serious thinking. Some very serious thinking indeed.'

'We will leave Frederick to finish his cigarette,' said Mavis.

'Yes,' said old Bodsham. 'We will leave Frederick to finish his cigarette.'

'But listen,' bleated Freddie. 'I give you my honest word she looked like something employed by the Government for scaring crows in the cornfields of Minnesota.'

'Oh?' said Mavis.

'Oh?' said old Bodsham.

'Come, Father,' said Mavis.

And old Freddie found himself alone, and not feeling so frightfully good.

Now, it was Freddie's practice – and a very prudent practice, too – to carry on his person, concealed in his hip pocket, a small but serviceable flask full of the true, the blushful Hippocrene. Friends whom he had made since his arrival in New York had advocated this policy, pointing out that you never knew when it would come in useful. His first act, accordingly, after the two Vice-Presidents of the Knickerbocker Ice Company had left him and he had begun to thaw out a bit, was to produce this flask and take a quick, sharp snort.

The effect was instantaneous. His numbed brain began to work. And presently, after a couple more swift ones, he saw daylight.

The whole nub of the thing, he perceived clearly, was the personal appearance of the girl Jennings. In the matter of her loved one's acts of chivalry towards damsels in distress, a fiancée holds certain definite views. If the damsels he assists are plain, he is a good chap and deserves credit. If they are pretty, he is a low hound who jolly well gets his ring and letters back by the first post.

Obviously, then, his only course was to return to Sixty-Ninth Street, dig up the Jennings, and parade her before Mavis. Her mere appearance, he was convinced, would clear him completely.

Of course, the thing would have to be done delicately. I mean to say, you can't just go to a comparatively strange female and ask her to trot round to see a friend of yours so that the latter can ascertain at first hand what a repellently unattractive girl she is. But Freddie, now full of the juice, fancied he could work it all right. All it wanted was just a little tact.

'Yoicks!' said Freddie to himself. 'Hark for'ard!' And, in his opinion, that about summed it up.

It was a lovely afternoon as Freddie got into his taxi outside the Ritz and tooled off up town. Alighting at Sixty-Ninth Street, he braced himself with a visible effort and started the long climb up the four flights of stairs. And presently he was outside the door of Flat 4B and tootling on the bell.

Nothing happened. He tootled again. He knocked. He even went so far as to kick the door. But there were no signs of human occupation, and after a bit he was reluctantly forced to the conclusion that the Jennings was out.

Freddie had not foreseen this possibility, and he leaned against the wall for a space, thinking out his next move. He had just come to the conclusion that the only thing to do was to edge away for the nonce and have another pop later on, when a door opposite opened and a female appeared.

'Hullo,' said this bird.

'Hullo,' said Freddie.

He spoke, he tells me, a little doubtfully, for a glance had shown him that this woman was not at all the kind of whom Mavis would have approved. A different species altogether. Her eyes were blue and totally free from spectacles. Her teeth were white and even. Her hair was a beautiful gold.

Judging by her costume, she seemed to be a late riser. The hour was three-thirty, but she had not yet progressed beyond the negligee and slippers stage. That negligee, moreover, was a soft pink in colour and was decorated throughout with a series of fowls of some kind. Love-birds, Freddie tells me he thinks they were. And a man who is engaged to be married and who, already, is not any too popular with the bride-to-be, shrinks –

automatically, as it were – from blue-eyed, golden-haired females in pink negligees picked out with ultramarine love-birds.

However, a fellow has to be civil. So, having said 'Hullo!' he threw in a reserved, gentlemanly sort of smile for good measure.

He assures me that it was merely one of those aloof smiles which the Honorary Secretary of a Bible Class would have given the elderly aunt of a promising pupil: but it had the effect of encouraging the contents of the negligee to further conversation.

'Looking for someone?' she asked.

'Why, yes,' said Freddie. 'I suppose you couldn't tell me when Miss Jennings will be in?'

'Miss Who?'

'Jennings.'

'What name?'

'Jennings.'

'How do you spell it?'

'Oh, much in the usual way, I expect. Start off with a J and then a good many "n"s and "g"s and things.'

'Miss Jennings, did you say?'

'That's right. Jennings.'

'I'll tell you something,' said the female frankly. 'I've never seen any Miss Jennings. I've never heard of any Miss Jennings. I don't know who she is. She means literally nothing in my life. And I'll tell you something else. I've been breaking my back for half an hour trying to open my living-room window, and do you think I can do it? No, sir! What do you advise?'

'Leave it shut,' said Freddie.

'But it's so warm. The weather, I mean.'

'It *is* warm,' agreed Freddie.

'I'm just stifling. Yes, sir. That's what I am. Stifling in my tracks.'

At this point, undoubtedly, old Freddie should have said 'Oh?' or 'Well, best o' luck!' or something of that order, and buzzed off. But once a fellow drops into the habit of doing acts of kindness, he tells me, it's dashed difficult to pull up. The thing becomes second nature.

So now, instead of hoofing it, he unshipped another of those polished smiles of his, and asked if there was anything he could do.

'Well, it's a shame to trouble you . . .'

'Not at all.'

'I hate to impose on you . . .'

'Not – a – tall,' said Freddie, becoming more *preux* every moment. 'Only too pleased.'

And he trotted after her into the flat.

'There it is,' said the female. 'The window, I mean.'

Freddie surveyed it carefully. He went over and gave it a shake. It certainly seemed pretty tightly stuck.

'The way they build these joints nowadays,' observed the female, with a certain amount of severity, 'the windows either won't open at all or else they drop out altogether.'

'Well, that's Life, isn't it?' said Freddie.

The thing didn't look any too good to him, but he buckled to like a man, and for some moments nothing was to be heard in the room but his tense breathing.

'How are you getting on?' asked the female.

'I've a sort of rummy buzzing in my head,' said Freddie. 'You don't think it's apoplexy or something?'

'I'd take a rest if I was you,' said his hostess. 'You look warm.'

'I *am* warm,' said Freddie.

'Take your coat off.'

'May I? Thanks.'

'Your collar, too, if you like.'

'Thanks.'

The removal of the upholstery made Freddie feel a little better.

'I once knew a man who opened a window in a Pullman car,' said the female.

'No, really?' said Freddie.

'Ah, what a man!' sighed the female wistfully. 'They don't make 'em like that nowadays.'

I don't suppose she actually intended anything in the way of a slur or innuendo, if you know what I mean, but Freddie tells me he felt a bit stung. It was as if his manly spirit had been challenged. Setting his teeth, he charged forward and had another go.

'Try pulling it down from the top,' said the female.

Freddie tried pulling it down from the top, but nothing happened.

'Try wiggling it sideways,' said the female.

Freddie tried wiggling it sideways, but his efforts were null and void.

'Have a drink,' said the female.

This seemed to old Freddie by miles the best suggestion yet. He sank into a chair and let his tongue hang out. And presently a brimming glass stole into his hand, and he quaffed deeply.

'That's some stuff I brought away from home,' said the female.

'From where?' said Freddie.

'Home.'

'But isn't this your home?'

'Well, it is now. But I used to live in Utica. Mr Silvers made this stuff. About the only good thing he ever did. Mr Silvers, I mean.'

Freddie pondered a bit.

'Mr Silvers? Don't I seem to know that name?'

'I wish I didn't,' said the female. 'There was a palooka, if you want one.'

'A what?'

'A palooka. Mr Silvers. Slice him where you like, he was still boloney.'

The rather generous nature of the fluid he was absorbing was making Freddie feel a bit clouded.

'I don't altogether follow this. Who is Mr Silvers?'

'Ed. Silvers. My husband. And is he jealous? Ask me!'

'Ask who?'

'Ask *me*.'

'Ask you what?'

'I'm telling you. I left him flat, because he didn't have no ideals.'

'Who didn't?'

'Mr Silvers.'

'Your husband?'

'That's right.'

'Ah!' said Freddie. 'Now we've got it straight.'

He quaffed again. The foundation of the beverage manufactured by Mr Silvers seemed to be neat vitriol, but, once you had got used to the top of your head going up and down like the lid of a kettle with boiling water in it, the effects were far from unpleasant. Mr Silvers may not have had ideals, but he unquestionably knew what to do when you handed him a still and a potato.

'He made me very unhappy,' said the female.

'Who did?'

'Mr Silvers.'

'Mr Silvers made you unhappy?'

'You're dern tooting Mr Silvers made me unhappy. Entertaining his low suspicions.'

Freddie was shocked.

'Did Mr Silvers entertain low suspicions?'

'He certainly did.'

'Mr Ed. Silvers?'

'That's right.'

'I bet that made you unhappy.'

'You never said a truer word.'

'You poor little thing,' said Freddie. 'You poor little Mrs Silvers.'

'Mrs Ed. Silvers.'

'You poor little Mrs Ed. Silvers. I never heard anything so dashed monstrous in my life. May I pat your hand?'

'You bet your lavender spats you may pat my hand.'

'I will,' said Freddie, and did so.

He even went further. He squeezed her hand. His whole attitude towards her, he tells me, was that of a brother towards a suffering sister.

And at this moment the door flew open, and a number of large objects crashed in. Without any warning the air had suddenly become full of bowler hats.

Freddie, gazing upon them, was conscious of an odd feeling. You know that feeling you sometimes feel of feeling you're feeling that something has happened which has happened before. I believe doctors explain it by saying that the two halves of the brain aren't working strictly on the up-and-up. Anyway, that was how Freddie felt at this point. He felt he had seen those bowler hats before – perhaps in some previous existence.

'What ho!' he said. 'Callers, what?'

And then his brain seemed to clear – or the two halves clicked together, or something – and he recognized the Bloke who had interrupted his *tête-à-tête* with Miss Myra Jennings that morning.

Now the last time Freddie had seen this Bloke, the latter had been bathed in confusion. You pictured his embarrassment. He was now looking far cheerier. He had the air of a bloke in a bowler hat who has won through to his objective.

'We're in, boys,' he said.

The two subsidiary Blokes nodded briefly. One of them said: 'Sure, we're in.' The other said: 'Hot dog!'

The head Bloke scrutinized Freddie closely.

'Well, I'm darned!' he exclaimed. 'If it isn't you again! Boys,' he said, a note of respect creeping into his voice, 'take a good slant at this guy. Eye him reverently. The swiftest worker in New York. Mark how he flits from spot to spot. You can't go anywhere without finding him. And he hasn't even got a bicycle.'

Freddie saw that it was time to draw himself up to his full height and put these fellows in their place. He endeavoured to do so, but something seemed to prevent him.

'Let me explain,' he said.

The Bloke sneered visibly.

'Are you going to tell us we are in the wrong flat again?'

'My answer to that,' said Freddie, 'is yes – and no.'

'What do you mean, yes and no? This is Flat 4A.'

'True,' said Freddie. 'That point I yield. This *is* Flat 4A. But I assure you, on the word of an English gentleman, that this lady is a complete stranger to me.'

'Stranger?'

'A complete and total stranger.'

'Oh?' said the Bloke. 'Then what's she doing sitting in your lap?'

And Freddie, with acute astonishment, perceived that this was indeed so. At what point in their conversation it had occurred, he could not have said, but Mrs Ed. Silvers was undeniably nestling on the spot indicated. It was this, he saw now, which had prevented him a moment ago drawing himself up to his full height.

'By Jove!' he said. 'She is, isn't she?'

'She certainly is.'

'Well, well!' said Freddie. 'Well, well, well!'

You could have knocked him down with a feather, and he said as much.

Mrs Silvers spoke. 'Listen,' she said. 'As Heaven is my witness I never saw this man before.'

'Then what's he doing here?'

'Opening the window.'

'It's shut.'

'I know it's shut.'

'Open *and* shut,' said the Bloke. 'Like the case. Eh, boys?'

'Ah!' said one of the boys.

'Uh-huh,' said the other.

The Bloke eyed Mrs Silvers severely.

'You ought to be ashamed of yourself, lady,' he said. 'Such goings-on. I'm shocked. That's what I am. Shocked. And the boys are shocked, too.'

Freddie was able to rise now, for the female had ceased to roost. He got up, and would have towered above the Bloke, only it so happened that the latter was about six inches taller.

'You are aspersing a woman's name,' he said.

'Eh?'

'Don't attempt to evade the issue,' said Freddie, giving him a haughty glance. 'You are aspersing a woman's name, and – what makes it worse – you are doing it in a bowler hat. Take off that hat,' said Freddie.

The Bloke stared at him blankly. He was probably on the point of explaining that detectives' hats don't take off, when Freddie – injudiciously, in my opinion – got him in the right eye with one of the nicest wallops you could wish to see.

And after that, Freddie tells me, things got a bit mixed. He is conscious of having done his best, but he thinks he must have had rather the worse of the exchanges, because some little time later he became aware that he was in a prison cell and that one of his ears had swollen to the proportions of a medium-sized cauliflower. Also the black eye and the bees swarming in the head.

And scarcely had he coughed up the fifty dollars to the Clerk of the Court next morning when, coming out into the open and buying a paper, he found the events of the previous afternoon splashed over half a column of the very periodical which, he knew, old Bodsham was in the habit of reading with his morning Java and egg.

And, to show you how overwrought the poor chap must have been, Freddie had actually omitted to take the elementary precaution of giving a false name. He had even gone to the extraordinary length of revealing his middle one – which, though I don't think we should hold it against him, is Fotheringay.

Well, that finished it. Rightly or wrongly, Freddie decided not to wait for the full returns. There was a boat starting back for England that night, and he leaped aboard it without having ascertained from a personal interview what old Bodsham and

Mavis thought of the episode. He is a pretty intuitive chap, Freddie, and he was content to guess.

So now he's back, and more or less soured and morose. He was saying some pretty harsh things about Woman this morning, some very harsh things.

And I happen to know that, as the boat docked at Southampton, an extraordinarily pretty girl standing beside him stumbled and dropped her vanity bag. And Freddie, instead of springing to her aid, just folded his arms and looked away with a sombre frown. He says that damsels in distress from now on must seek elsewhere for custom, because he has retired from business.

This fact, he tells me, cannot be too widely known.

THE annual smoking-concert of the Drones Club had just come to an end, and it was the unanimous verdict of the little group assembled in the bar for a last quick one that the gem of the evening had been item number six on the programme, the knockabout cross-talk act of Cyril ('Barmy') Fotheringay-Phipps and Reginald ('Pongo') Twistleton-Twistleton. Both Cyril, in the red beard, and Reginald, in the more effective green whiskers, had shown themselves, it was agreed, at the very peak of their form. With sparkling repartee and vigorous by-play they had gripped the audience from the start.

'In fact,' said an Egg, 'it struck me that they were even better than last year. Their art seemed to have deepened somehow.'

A thoughtful Crumpet nodded.

'I noticed the same thing. The fact is, they passed through a soul-testing experience not long ago and it has left its mark upon them. It also dashed nearly wrecked the act. I don't know if any of you fellows are aware of it, but at one time they had definitely decided to scratch the fixture and not give a performance at all.'

'What!'

'Absolutely. They were within a toucher of failing to keep faith with their public. Bad blood had sprung up between them.

Also pique and strained relations. They were not on speaking terms.'

His hearers were frankly incredulous. They pointed out that the friendship between the two artistes had always been a by-word or whatever you called it. A well-read Egg summed it up by saying that they were like Thingummy and what's-his-name.

'Nevertheless,' insisted the Crumpet, 'what I am telling you is straight, official stuff. Two weeks ago, if Barmy had said to Pongo: "Who was that lady I saw you coming down the street with?" Pongo would not have replied: "That was no lady, that was my wife," – he would simply have raised his eyebrows coldly and turned away in a marked manner.'

It was a woman, of course (proceeded the Crumpet) who came between them. Angelica Briscoe was her name, and she was the daughter of the Rev. P. P. Briscoe, who vetted the souls of the local peasantry at a place called Maiden Eggesford down in Somersetshire. This hamlet is about half a dozen miles from the well-known resort, Bridmouth-on-Sea, and it was in the establishment of the Messrs. Thorpe and Widgery, the popular grocers of that town, that Barmy and Pongo first set eyes on the girl.

They had gone to Bridmouth partly for a splash of golf, but principally to be alone and away from distractions, so that they would be able to concentrate on the rehearsing and building-up of this cross-talk act which we have just witnessed. And on the morning of which I speak they had strolled into the Thorpe and Widgery emporium to lay in a few little odds and ends, and there, putting in a bid for five pounds of streaky bacon, was a girl so lovely that they congealed in their tracks. And, as they stood staring, she said to the bloke behind the counter:

'That's the lot. Send them to Miss Angelica Briscoe, The Vicarage, Maiden Eggesford.'

She then pushed off, and Barmy and Pongo, feeling rather as if they had been struck by lightning, bought some sardines and a segment of certified butter in an overwrought sort of way and went out.

They were both pretty quiet for the rest of the day, and after dinner that night Pongo said to Barmy:

'I say, Barmy.'

And Barmy said:

'Hullo?'

And Pongo said:

'I say, Barmy, it's a bally nuisance, but I'll have to buzz up to London for a day or two. I've suddenly remembered some spots of business that call for my personal attention. You won't mind my leaving you?'

Barmy could scarcely conceal his bracedness. Within two minutes of seeing that girl, he had made up his mind that somehow or other he must repair to Maiden Eggesford and get to know her, and the problem which had been vexing him all day had been what to do with the body – viz. Pongo's.

'Not a bit,' he said.

'I'll be back as soon as I can.'

'Don't hurry,' said Barmy heartily. 'As a matter of fact, a few days' lay-off will do the act all the good in the world. Any pro. will tell you that the worst thing possible is to over-rehearse. Stay away as long as you like.'

So next morning – it was a Saturday – Pongo climbed on to a train, and in the afternoon Barmy collected his baggage and pushed off to the Goose and Grasshopper at Maiden Eggesford. And, having booked a room there and toddled into the saloon bar for a refresher with the love-light in his eyes, the first thing he saw was Pongo chatting across the counter with the barmaid.

Neither was much bucked. A touch of constraint about sums it up.

'Hullo!' said Barmy.

'Hullo!' said Pongo.

'You here?'

'Yes. You here?'

'Yes.'

'Oh.'

There was a bit of a silence.

'So you didn't go to London?' said Barmy.

'No,' said Pongo.

'Oh,' said Barmy.

'And you didn't stick on at Bridmouth?' said Pongo.

'No,' said Barmy.

'Oh,' said Pongo.

There was some more silence.

'You came here, I see,' said Pongo.

'Yes,' said Barmy. 'I see *you* came here.'

'Yes,' said Pongo. 'An odd coincidence.'

'Very odd.'

'Well, skin off your nose,' said Pongo.

'Fluff in your latchkey,' said Barmy.

He drained his glass and tried to exhibit a light-hearted nonchalance, but his mood was sombre. He was a chap who could put two and two together and sift and weigh the evidence and all that sort of thing, and it was plain to him that love had brought Pongo also to this hamlet, and he resented the fact. Indeed, it was at this instant, he tells me, that there came to him the first nebulous idea of oiling out of that cross-talk act of theirs. The thought of having to ask a beastly, butting-in blighter like Reginald Twistleton-Twistleton if he was fond of mutton-broth and being compelled to hit him over the head with a rolled-up umbrella when he replied 'No, Mutt and Jeff,' somehow seemed to revolt his finest feelings.

Conversation rather languished after this, and presently Pongo excused himself in a somewhat stiff manner and went upstairs to his room. And it was while Barmy was at the counter listening in a distrait kind of way to the barmaid telling him what cucumber did to her digestive organs that a fellow in plus fours entered the bar and Barmy saw that he was wearing the tie of his old school.

Well, you know how it is when you're in some public spot and a stranger comes in wearing the old school tie. You shove a hasty hand over your own and start to sidle out before the chap can spot it and grab you and start gassing. And Barmy was just doing this when the barmaid uttered these sensational words:

'Good evening, Mr Briscoe.'

Barmy stood spellbound. He turned to the barmaid and spoke in a hushed whisper.

'Did you say "Briscoe"?'

'Yes, sir.'

'From the Vicarage?'

'Yes, sir.'

Barmy quivered like a jelly. The thought that he had had the amazing luck to find in the brother of the girl he loved an old schoolmate made him feel boneless. After all, he felt, as he took his hand away from his tie, there is no bond like that of the old school. If you meet one of the dear old school in a public spot, he meant to say, why, you go straight up to him and start fraternizing.

He made a bee-line for the chap's table.

'I say,' he said, 'I see you're wearing a ...'

The chap's hand had shot up to his tie with a sort of nervous gesture, but he evidently realized that the time had gone by for protective measures. He smiled a bit wryly.

'Have a drink,' he said.

'I've got one, thanks,' said Barmy. 'I'll bring it along to your table, shall I? Such a treat meeting someone from the dear old place, what?'

'Oh, rather.'

'I think I'd have been a bit after your time, wouldn't I?' said Barmy, for the fellow was well stricken in years – twenty-eight, if a day. 'Fotheringay-Phipps is more or less my name. Yours is Briscoe, what?'

'Yes.'

Barmy swallowed a couple of times.

'Er ... Ah ... Um ... I think I saw your sister yesterday in Bridmouth,' he said, blushing prettily.

So scarlet, indeed, did his countenance become that the other regarded him narrowly, and Barmy knew that he had guessed his secret.

'You saw her in Bridmouth yesterday, eh?'

'Yes.'

'And now you're here.'

'Er – yes.'

'Well, well,' said the chap, drawing his breath in rather thoughtfully.

There was a pause, during which Barmy's vascular motors continued to do their bit.

'You must meet her,' said the chap.

'I should like to,' said Barmy. 'I only saw her for a moment buying streaky bacon, but she seemed a charming girl.'

'Oh, she is.'

'I scarcely noticed her, of course, but rather attractive she struck me as.'

'Quite.'

'I gave her the merest glance, you understand, but I should say at a venture that she has a great white soul. In fact,' said Barmy, losing his grip altogether, 'you wouldn't be far out in describing her as divine.'

'You must certainly meet her,' said the chap. Then he shook his head. 'No, it wouldn't be any good.'

'Why not?' bleated Barmy.

'Well, I'll tell you,' said the chap. 'You know what girls are. They have their little enthusiasms and it hurts them when people scoff at them. Being a parson's daughter, Angelica is wrapped up at present in the annual village School Treat. I can see at a glance the sort of fellow you are – witty, mordant, ironical. You would get off one of your devastating epigrams at the expense of the School Treat, and, while she might laugh at the wit, she would be deeply wounded by the satire.'

'But I wouldn't dream . . .'

'Ah, but if you didn't, if you spoke approvingly of the School Treat, what then? The next thing that would happen would be that she would be asking you to help her run it. And that would bore you stiff.'

Barmy shook from stem to stern. This was better even than he had hoped.

'You don't mean she would let me help her with the School Treat?'

'Why, you wouldn't do it, would you?'

'I should enjoy it above all things.'

'Well, if that's the way you feel, the matter can easily be arranged. She will be here any moment now to pick me up in her car.'

And, sure enough, not two minutes later there floated through the open window a silvery voice, urging the fellow, who seemed to answer to the name of 'Fathead,' to come out quick, because the voice did not intend to remain there all night.

So the fellow took Barmy out, and there was the girl, sitting in a two-seater. He introduced Barmy. The girl beamed. Barmy beamed. The fellow said that Barmy was anxious to come and help with the School Treat. The girl beamed again. Barmy beamed again. And presently the car drove off, the girl's last words being a reminder that the binge started at two sharp on the Monday.

That night, as they dined together, Barmy and Pongo put in their usual spot of rehearsing. It was their practice to mould and shape the act during meals, as they found that mastication seemed to sharpen their intellect. But tonight it would have been plain to an observant spectator that their hearts were not in it. There was an unmistakable coolness between them. Pongo said he had an aunt who complained of rheumatism, and Barmy said, Well, who wouldn't? And Barmy said his father could not meet his creditors, and Pongo said, Did he want to? But the old fire and sparkle were absent. And they had relapsed into a moody silence when the door opened and the barmaid pushed her head in.

'Miss Briscoe has just sent over a message, Mr Phipps,' said the barmaid. 'She says she would like you to be there a little earlier than two, if you can manage it. One-fifteen, if possible, because there's always so much to do.'

'Oh, right,' said Barmy, a bit rattled, for he had heard the sharp hiss of his companion's in-drawn breath.

'I'll tell her,' said the barmaid.

She withdrew, and Barmy found Pongo's eyes resting on him like a couple of blobs of vitriol.

'What's all this?' asked Pongo.

Barmy tried to be airy.

'Oh, it's nothing. Just the local School Treat. The vicar's daughter here – a Miss Briscoe – seems anxious that I should drop round on Monday and help her run it.'

Pongo started to grind his teeth, but he had a chunk of potato in his mouth at the moment and was hampered. But he gripped the table till his knuckles stood out white under the strain.

'Have you been sneaking round behind my back and inflicting your beastly society on Miss Briscoe?' he demanded.

'I do not like your tone, Reginald.'

'Never mind about my tone. I'll attend to my tone. Of all the bally low hounds that ever stepped you are the lowest. So this is what the friendship of years amounts to, is it? You crawl in here and try to cut me out with the girl I love.'

'Well, dash it . . .'

'That is quite enough.'

'But, dash it . . .'

'I wish to hear no more.'

'But, dash it, I love her, too. It's not my fault if you happen to love her, too, is it? I mean to say, if a fellow loves a girl and another fellow loves her, too, you can't expect the fellow who loves the girl to edge out because he happens to be acquainted with the fellow who loves her, too. When it comes to Love, a chap has got to look out for his own interests, hasn't he? You didn't find Romeo or any of those chaps easing away from the girl just to oblige a pal, did you? Certainly not. So I don't see . . .'

'Please!' said Pongo.

A silence fell.

'Might I trouble you to pass the mustard, Fotheringay-Phipps,' said Pongo coldly.

'Certainly, Twistleton-Twistleton,' replied Barmy, with equal hauteur.

It is always unpleasant not to be on speaking terms with an old friend. To be cooped up alone in a mouldy village pub with an old friend with whom one has ceased to converse is simply rotten. And this is especially so if the day happens to be a Sunday.

Maiden Eggesford, like so many of our rural hamlets, is not at its best and brightest on a Sunday. When you have walked down the main street and looked at the Jubilee Watering-Trough, there is nothing much to do except go home and then come out again and walk down the main street once more and take another look at the Jubilee Watering-Trough. It will give you some rough idea of the state to which Barmy Fotheringay-Phipps had been reduced by the end of the next day when I tell you that the sound of the church bells ringing for evensong brought him out of the Goose and Grasshopper as if he had heard a fire-engine. The thought that at last something was going to happen in Maiden Eggesford in which the Jubilee Watering-Trough *motif* was not stressed, stirred him strangely. He was in his pew in three jumps. And as the service got under way he began to feel curious emotions going on in his bosom.

There is something about evening church in a village in the summer-time that affects the most hard-boiled. They had left the door open, and through it came the scent of lime trees and wall-flowers and the distant hum of bees fooling about. And gradually there poured over Barmy a wave of sentiment. As he sat and listened to the First Lesson he became a changed man.

The Lesson was one of those chapters of the Old Testament all about how Abimelech begat Jazzbo and Jazzbo begat Zachariah. And, what with the beauty of the words and the peace of his surroundings, Barmy suddenly began to become conscious of a great remorse.

He had not done the square thing, he told himself, by dear old Pongo. Here was a chap, notoriously one of the best, as sound an egg as ever donned a heliotrope sock, and he was deliberately chiselling him out of the girl he loved. He was doing the dirty on a fellow whom he had been pally with since their Eton jacket days – a bloke who time and again had shared with him his last bar of almond-rock. Was this right? Was this just? Would Abimelech have behaved like that to Jazzbo or – for the matter of that – Jazzbo to Zachariah? The answer, he could not disguise it from himself, was in the negative.

It was a different, stronger Barmy, a changed, chastened Cyril Fotheringay-Phipps, who left the sacred edifice at the conclusion of the Vicar's fifty-minute sermon. He had made the great decision. It would play the dickens with his heart and probably render the rest of his life a blank, but nevertheless he would retire from the unseemly struggle and give the girl up to Pongo.

That night, as they cold-suppered together, Barmy cleared his throat and looked across at Pongo with a sad, sweet smile.

'Pongo,' he said.

The other glanced distantly up from his baked potato.

'There is something you wish to say to me, Fotheringay-Phipps?'

'Yes,' said Barmy. 'A short while ago I sent a note to Miss Briscoe, informing her that I shall not be attending the School

Treat and mentioning that you will be there in my stead. Take her, Pongo, old man. She is yours. I scratch my nomination.'

Pongo stared. His whole manner changed. It was as if he had been a Trappist monk who had suddenly decided to give Trappism a miss and become one of the boys again.

'But, dash it, this is noble!'

'No, no.'

'But it is! It's . . . well, dash it, I hardly know what to say.'

'I hope you will be very, very happy.'

'Thanks, old man.'

'Very, very, very happy.'

'Rather! I should say so. And I'll tell you one thing. In the years to come there will always be a knife and fork for you at our little home. The children shall be taught to call you Uncle Barmy.'

'Thanks,' said Barmy. 'Thanks.'

'Not at all,' said Pongo. 'Not at all.'

At this moment, the barmaid entered with a note for Barmy. He read it and crumpled it up.

'From Her?' asked Pongo.

'Yes.'

'Saying she quite understands, and so forth?'

'Yes.'

Pongo ate a piece of cheese in a meditative manner. He seemed to be pursuing some train of thought.

'I should think,' he said, 'that a fellow who married a clergyman's daughter would get the ceremony performed at cut rates, wouldn't he?'

'Probably.'

'If not absolutely on the nod?'

'I shouldn't wonder.'

'Not,' said Pongo, 'that I am influenced by any consideration like that, of course. My love is pure and flamelike, with no taint of dross. Still, in times like these, every little helps.'

'Quite,' said Barmy. 'Quite.'

He found it hard to control his voice. He had lied to his friend about that note. What Angelica Briscoe had really said in it was that it was quite all right if he wanted to edge out of the School Treat, but that she would require him to take the Village Mothers for their Annual Outing on the same day. There had to be some responsible person with them, and the curate had sprained his ankle tripping over a footstool in the vestry.

Barmy could read between the lines. He saw what this meant. His fatal fascination had done its deadly work, and the girl had become infatuated with him. No other explanation would fit the facts. It was absurd to suppose that she would lightly have selected him for this extraordinarily important assignment. Obviously it was the big event of the village year. Anyone would do to mess about at the School Treat, but Angelica Briscoe would place in charge of the Mothers' Annual Outing only a man she trusted . . . respected . . . loved.

He sighed. What must be, he felt, must be. He had done his conscientious best to retire in favour of his friend, but Fate had been too strong.

I found it a little difficult (said the Crumpet) to elicit from Barmy exactly what occurred at the annual outing of the Village Mothers of Maiden Eggesford. When telling me the story, he had the air of a man whose old wound is troubling him. It was not, indeed, till the fourth cocktail that he became really communicative. And then, speaking with a kind of stony look in his eye, he gave me a fairly comprehensive account. But even then each word seemed to hurt him in some tender spot.

The proceedings would appear to have opened in a quiet and orderly manner. Sixteen females of advanced years assembled in a motor coach, and the expedition was seen off from the Vicarage door by the Rev. P. P. Briscoe in person. Under his eye, Barmy tells me, the Beauty Chorus was demure and docile. It was a treat to listen to their murmured responses. As nice and respectable a bunch of mothers, Barmy says, as he had ever struck. His only apprehension at this point, he tells me, was lest the afternoon's proceedings might possibly be a trifle stodgy. He feared a touch of ennui.

He needn't have worried. There was no ennui.

The human cargo, as I say, had started out in a spirit of demureness and docility. But it was amazing what a difference a mere fifty yards of the high road made to these Mothers. No sooner were they out of sight of the Vicarage than they began to effervesce to an almost unbelievable extent. The first intimation Barmy had that the binge was going to be run on lines other than those which he had anticipated was when a very stout Mother in a pink bonnet and a dress covered with bugles suddenly picked off a passing cyclist with a well-directed tomato, causing him to skid into a ditch. Upon which, all sixteen mothers laughed like fiends in hell, and it was plain that they considered that the proceedings had now been formally opened.

Of course, looking back at it now in a calmer spirit, Barmy tells me that he can realize that there is much to be said in palliation of the exuberance of these ghastly female pimples. When you are shut up all the year round in a place like Maiden Eggesford, with nothing to do but wash underclothing and attend Divine Service, you naturally incline to let yourself go a bit at times of festival and holiday. But at the moment he did not think of this, and his spiritual agony was pretty pronounced.

If there's one thing Barmy hates it's being conspicuous, and conspicuous is precisely what a fellow cannot fail to be when he's in a motor coach with sixteen women of mature ages who alternate between singing ribald songs and hurling volleys of homely chaff at passers-by. In this connection, he tells me, he is thinking particularly of a Mother in spectacles and a Homburg hat, which she had pinched from the driver of the vehicle, whose prose style appeared to have been modelled on that of Rabelais.

It was a more than usually penetrating sally on the part of this female which at length led him to venture a protest.

'I say! I mean, I say. I say, dash it, you know. I mean, dash it,' said Barmy, feeling, even as he spoke, that the rebuke had not been phrased as neatly as he could have wished.

Still, lame though it had been, it caused a sensation which can only be described as profound. Mother looked at Mother. Eyebrows were raised, breath drawn in censoriously.

'Young man,' said the Mother in the pink bonnet, who seemed to have elected herself forewoman, 'kindly keep your remarks to yourself.'

Another Mother said: 'The idea!' and a third described him as a kill-joy.

'We don't want none of *your* impudence,' said the one in the pink bonnet.

'Ah!' agreed the others.

'A slip of a boy like that!' said the Mother in the Homburg hat, and there was a general laugh, as if the meeting considered that the point had been well taken.

Barmy subsided. He was wishing that he had yielded to the advice of his family and become a curate after coming down from the University. Curates are specially trained to handle this sort of situation. A tough, hard-boiled curate, spitting out of the corner of his mouth, would soon have subdued these mothers, he reflected. He would have played on them as on a stringed instrument – or, rather, as on sixteen stringed instruments. But Barmy, never having taken orders, was helpless.

So helpless, indeed, that when he suddenly discovered that they were heading for Bridmouth-on-Sea he felt that there was nothing he could do about it. From the vicar's own lips he had had it officially that the programme was that the expedition should drive to the neighbouring village of Bottsford Mortimer, where there were the ruins of an old abbey, replete with interest; lunch among these ruins; visit the local museum (founded and presented to the village by the late Sir Wandesbury Pott, J.P.); and, after filling in with a bit of knitting, return home. And now the whole trend of the party appeared to be towards the Amusement Park on the Bridmouth pier. And, though Barmy's whole soul shuddered at the thought of these sixteen Bacchantes let loose in an Amusement Park, he hadn't the nerve to say a word.

It was at about this point, he tells me, that a vision rose before him of Pongo happily loafing through the summer afternoon amidst the placid joys of the School Treat.

Of what happened at the Amusement Park Barmy asked me to be content with the sketchiest of outlines. He said that even now he could not bear to let his memory dwell upon it. He confessed himself perplexed by the psychology of the thing. These mothers, he said, must have had mothers of their own and at those mothers' knees must have learned years ago the difference between right and wrong, and yet... Well, what he was thinking of particularly, he said, was what occurred on the Bump the Bumps apparatus. He refused to specify exactly, but he said that there was one woman in a puce mantle who definitely seemed to be living for pleasure alone.

It was a little unpleasantness with the proprietor of this concern that eventually led to the expedition leaving the Amusement Park and going down to the beach. Some purely technical point of finance, I understand – he claiming that a Mother in bombazine had had eleven rides and only paid once. It resulted in Barmy getting lugged into the brawl and rather roughly handled – which was particularly unfortunate, because the bombazined Mother explained on their way down to the beach that the whole thing had been due to a misunderstanding. In actual fact, what had really happened was that she had had twelve rides and paid twice.

However, he was so glad to get his little troupe out of the place that he counted an eye well blacked as the price of deliverance, and his spirits, he tells me, had definitely risen when suddenly the sixteen mothers gave a simultaneous whoop and made for a sailing-boat which was waiting to be hired, sweeping him along with them. And the next moment they were off across the bay, bowling along before a nippy breeze which, naturally, cheesed it abruptly as soon as it had landed them far enough away from shore to make things interesting for the unfortunate blighter who had to take to the oars.

This, of course, was poor old Barmy. There was a man in charge of the boat, but he, though but a rough, untutored salt, had enough sense not to let himself in for a job like rowing this Noah's Ark home. Barmy did put it up to him tentatively, but the fellow said that he had to attend to the steering, and when Barmy said that he, Barmy, knew how to steer, the fellow said that he, the fellow, could not entrust a valuable boat to an amateur. After which, he lit his pipe and lolled back in the stern sheets with rather the air of an ancient Roman banqueter making himself cosy among the cushions. And Barmy, attaching himself to a couple of oars of about the size of those served out to galley-slaves in the old trireme days, started to put his back into it.

For a chap who hadn't rowed anything except a light canoe since he was up at Oxford, he considers he did dashed well, especially when you take into account the fact that he was much hampered by the Mothers. They would insist on singing that thing about 'Give yourself a pat on the back,' and, apart from the fact that Barmy considered that something on the lines of the Volga Boat-Song would have been far more fitting, it was a tune it was pretty hard to keep time to. Seven times he caught crabs, and seven times those sixteen mothers stopped singing and guffawed like one Mother. All in all, a most painful experience. Add the fact that the first thing the females did on hitting the old Homeland again was to get up an informal dance on the sands and that the ride home in the quiet evenfall was more or less a repetition of the journey out, and you will agree with me that Barmy, as he eventually tottered into the saloon bar of the Goose and Grasshopper, had earned the frothing tankard which he now proceeded to order.

He had just sucked it down and was signalling for another, when the door of the saloon bar opened and in came Pongo.

If Barmy had been less preoccupied with his own troubles he would have seen that Pongo was in poorish shape. His collar was torn, his hair dishevelled. There were streaks of chocolate down his face and half a jam sandwich attached to the back of his coat. And so moved was he at seeing Barmy that he started ticking him off before he had so much as ordered a gin and ginger.

'A nice thing you let me in for!' said Pongo. 'A jolly job you shoved off on me!'

Barmy was feeling a little better after his ingurgitations, and he was able to speak.

'What are you talking about?'

'I am talking about School Treats,' replied Pongo, with an intense bitterness. 'I am talking about seas of children, all with sticky hands, who rubbed those hands on me. I am talking ... Oh, it's no good your gaping like a diseased fish, Fotheringay-Phipps. You know dashed well that you planned the whole thing. Your cunning fiend's brain formulated the entire devilish scheme. You engineered the bally outrage for your own foul purposes, to queer me with Angelica. You thought that when a girl sees a man blind-folded and smacked with rolled-up newspapers by smelly children she can never feel the same to him again. Ha!' said Pongo, at last ordering his gin and ginger.

Barmy was stunned, of course, by this violent attack, but he retained enough of the nice sense of propriety of the Fotheringay-Phippses to realize that this discussion could not be continued in public. Already the barmaid's ears had begun to work loose at the roots as she pricked them up.

'I don't know what the dickens you're talking about,' he said, 'but bring your drink up to my room and we'll go into the matter there. We cannot bandy a woman's name in a saloon bar.'

'Who's bandying a woman's name?'

'You are. You bandied it only half a second ago. If you don't call what you said bandying, there are finer-minded men who do.'

So they went upstairs, and Barmy shut the door.

'Now, then,' he said. 'What's all this drivel?'

'I've told you.'

'Tell me again.'

'I will.'

'Right ho. One moment.'

Barmy went to the door and opened it sharply. There came the unmistakable sound of a barmaid falling downstairs. He closed the door again.

'Now, then,' he said.

Pongo drained his gin and ginger.

'Of all the dirty tricks one man ever played on another,' he began, 'your sneaking out of that School Treat and letting me in for it is one which the verdict of history will undoubtedly rank the dirtiest. I can read you now like a book, Fotheringay-Phipps. Your motive is crystal-clear to me. You knew at what a disadvantage a man appears at a School Treat, and you saw to it that I and not you should be the poor mutt to get smeared with chocolate and sloshed with newspapers before the eyes of Angelica Briscoe. And I believed you when you handed me all that drip about yielding your claim and what not. My gosh!'

For an instant, as he heard these words, stupefaction rendered Barmy speechless. Then he found his tongue. His generous soul was seething with indignation at the thought of how his altruism, his great sacrifice, had been misinterpreted.

'What absolute rot!' he cried. 'I never heard such bilge in my life. My motives in sending you to that School Treat instead of me were unmixedly chivalrous. I did it simply and solely to enable you to ingratiate yourself with the girl, not reflecting that it was out of the question that she should ever love a pop-eyed, pimply-faced poop like you.'

Pongo started.

'Pop-eyed?'

'Pop-eyed was what I said.'

'Pimply-faced?'

'Pimply-faced was the term I employed.'

'Poop?'

'Poop was the expression with which I concluded. If you want to know the real obstacle in the way of any wooing you may do now or in the years to come, Twistleton-Twistleton, it is this – that you entirely lack sex-appeal and look like nothing on earth. A girl of the sweet, sensitive nature of Angelica Briscoe does not have to see you smeared with chocolate to recoil from you with loathing. She does it automatically, and she does it on her head.'

'Is that so?'

'That is so.'

'Oh? Well, let me inform you that in spite of what has happened, in spite of the fact that she has seen me at my worst, there is something within me that tells me that Angelica Briscoe loves me and will one day be mine.'

'Mine, you mean. I can read the message in a girl's shy, drooping eyes, Twistleton-Twistleton, and I am prepared to give you odds of eleven to four that before the year is out I shall be walking down the aisle with Angelica Fotheringay-Phipps on my arm. I will go further. Thirty-three to eight.'

'What in?'

'Tenners.'

'Done.'

It was at this moment that the door opened.

'Excuse me, gentlemen,' said the barmaid.

The two rivals glared at the intruder. She was a well-nourished girl with a kind face. She was rubbing her left leg, which appeared to be paining her. The staircases are steep at the Goose and Grasshopper.

'You'll excuse me muscling in like this, gentlemen,' said the barmaid, or words to that effect, 'but I happened inadvertently to overhear your conversation, and I feel it my duty to put you straight on an important point of fact. Gentlemen, all bets are off. Miss Angelica Briscoe is already engaged to be married.'

You can readily conceive the effect of this announcement. Pongo biffed down into the only chair, and Barmy staggered against the wash-hand stand.

'What!' said Pongo.

'What!' said Barmy.

The barmaid turned to Barmy.

'Yes, sir. To the gentleman you were talking to in my bar the afternoon you arrived.'

Her initial observation had made Barmy feel as if he had been punched in the wind by sixteen Mothers, but at this addendum he was able to pull himself together a bit.

'Don't be an ass, my dear old barmaid,' he said. 'That was Miss Briscoe's brother.'

'No, sir.'

'But his name was Briscoe, and you told me he was at the Vicarage.'

'Yes, sir. He spends a good deal of his time at the Vicarage, being the young lady's second cousin, and engaged to her since last Christmas!'

Barmy eyed her sternly. He was deeply moved.

'Why did you not inform me of this earlier, you chump of a barmaid? With your gift for listening at doors you must long since have become aware that this gentlemen here and myself were deeply enamoured of Miss Briscoe. And yet you kept these facts under your hat, causing us to waste our time and experience the utmost alarm and despondency. Do you realize, barmaid, that, had you spoken sooner, my friend here would not have been subjected to nameless indignities at the School Treat....'

'Yes, sir. It was the School Treat that Mr Briscoe was so bent on not having to go to, which he would have had to have done, Miss Angelica insisting. He had a terrible time there last year, poor gentleman. He was telling me about it. And that was why he asked me as a particular favour not to mention that he was engaged to Miss Briscoe, because he said that, if he played his cards properly and a little secrecy and silence were observed in the proper quarters, there was a mug staying at the inn that he thought he could get to go instead of him. It would have done you good, sir, to have seen the way his face lit up as he said it. He's a very nice gentleman, Mr Briscoe, and we're all very fond of him. Well, I mustn't stay talking here, sir. I've got my bar to see to.'

She withdrew, and for some minutes there was silence in the room. It was Barmy who was the first to break it.

'After all, we still have our Art,' said Barmy.

He crossed the room and patted Pongo on the shoulder.

'Of course, it's a nasty knock, old man ...'

Pongo had raised his face from his hands and was fumbling for his cigarette-case. There was a look in his eyes as if he had just wakened from a dream.

'Well, *is* it?' he said. 'You've got to look at these things from every angle. Is a girl who can deliberately allow a man to go through the horrors of a School Treat worth bothering about?'

Barmy started.

'I never thought of that. Or a girl, for that matter, who could callously throw a fellow to the Village Mothers.'

'Remind me some time to tell you about a game called "Is Mr Smith At Home?" where you put your head in a sack and the younger generation jab you with sticks.'

'And don't let me forget to tell you about that Mother in the puce mantle on the Bump the Bumps.'

'There was a kid called Horace ...'

'There was a Mother in a Homburg hat ...'

'The fact is,' said Pongo, 'we have allowed ourselves to lose our sober judgment over a girl whose idea of a mate is a mere "Hey, you," to be ordered hither and thither at her will, and who will unleash the juvenile population of her native village upon him without so much as a pang of pity – in a word, a parson's daughter. If you want to know the secret of a happy and successful life, Barmy, old man, it is this: Keep away from parsons' daughters.'

'Right away,' agreed Barmy. 'How do you react to hiring a car and pushing off to the metropolis at once?'

'I am all for it. And if we're to give of our best on the evening of the eleventh *prox.* we ought to start rehearsing again immediately.'

'We certainly ought.'

'We haven't any too much time, as it is.'

'We certainly haven't. I've got an aunt who complains of rheumatism.'

'Well, who wouldn't? My father can't meet his creditors.'

'Does he want to? My uncle Joe's in very low water just now.'

'Too bad. What's he doing?'

'Teaching swimming. Listen, Pongo,' said Barmy, 'I've been thinking. You take the green whiskers this year.'

'No, no.'

'Yes, really. I mean it. If I've said it to myself once, I've said it a hundred times – good old Pongo simply must have the green whiskers this year.'

'Barmy!'

'Pongo!'

They clasped hands. Tried in the furnace, their friendship had emerged strong and true. Cyril Fotheringay-Phipps and Reginald Twistleton-Twistleton were themselves again.

Two Eggs and a couple of Beans were having a leisurely spot in the smoking-room of the Drones Club, when a Crumpet came in and asked if anybody present wished to buy a practically new copy of Tennyson's poems. His manner, as he spoke, suggested that he had little hope that business would result. Nor did it. The two Beans and one of the Eggs said No. The other Egg merely gave a short, sardonic laugh.

The Crumpet hastened to put himself right with the Company.

'It isn't mine. It belongs to Freddie Widgeon.'

The senior of the two Beans drew his breath in sharply, genuinely shocked.

'You aren't telling us Freddie Widgeon bought a Tennyson?'

The junior Bean said that this confirmed a suspicion which had long been stealing over him. Poor old Freddie was breaking up.

'Not at all,' said the Crumpet. 'He had the most excellent motives. The whole thing was a strategic move, and in my opinion a jolly fine strategic move. He did it to boost his stock with the girl.'

'What girl?'

'April Carroway. She lived at a place called Tudsleigh down in Worcestershire. Freddie went there for the fishing, and the day he left London he happened to run into his uncle, Lord Blicester, and the latter, learning that he was to be in those parts, told him on no account to omit to look in at Tudsleigh Court and slap his old friend, Lady Carroway, on the back. So Freddie called there on the afternoon of his arrival, to get the thing over: and as he was passing through the garden on his way out he suddenly heard a girl's voice proceeding from the interior of a summer-house. And so musical was it that he edged a bit closer and shot a glance through the window. And, as he did so, he reeled and came within a toucher of falling.'

From where he stood he could see the girl plainly, and she was, he tells me, the absolute ultimate word, the last bubbling cry. She could not have looked better to him if he had drawn up the specifications personally. He was stunned. He had had no idea that there was anything like this on the premises. There and then he abandoned his scheme of spending the next two weeks fishing: for day by day in every way, he realized, he must haunt Tudsleigh Court from now on like a resident spectre.

He had now recovered sufficiently for his senses to function once more, and he gathered that what the girl was doing was reading some species of poetry aloud to a small, grave female kid with green eyes and turned-up nose who sat at her side. And the idea came to him that it would be a pretty sound scheme if he could find out what this bilge was. For, of course, when it comes to wooing, it's simply half the battle to get a line on the adored object's favourite literature. Ascertain what it is and mug it up and decant an excerpt or two in her presence, and before you can say 'What ho!' she is looking on you as a kindred soul and is all over you.

And it was at this point that he had a nice little slice of luck. The girl suddenly stopped reading: and, placing the volume face-down on her lap, sat gazing dreamily nor'-nor'-east for a space, as I believe girls frequently do when they strike a particularly juicy bit half-way through a poem. And the next moment Freddie was hareing off to the local post-office to wire to London for a *Collected Works of Alfred, Lord Tennyson*. He was rather relieved, he tells me, because, girls being what they are, it might quite easily have been Shelley or even Browning.

Well, Freddie lost no time in putting into operation his scheme of becoming the leading pest at Tudsleigh Court. On the following afternoon he called there again, met Lady Carroway once more, and was introduced to this girl, April, and to the green-eyed kid, who, he learned, was her young sister Prudence. So far, so good. But just as he was starting to direct at April a respectfully volcanic look which would give her some rough kind of preliminary intimation that here came old Colonel Romeo in person, his hostess went on to say something which sounded like 'Captain Bradbury,' and he perceived with a nasty shock that he was not the only visitor. Seated in a chair with a cup of tea in one hand and half a muffin in the other was an extraordinarily large and beefy bird in tweeds.

'Captain Bradbury, Mr Widgeon,' said Lady Carroway. 'Captain Bradbury is in the Indian Army. He is home on leave and has taken a house up the river.'

'Oh?' said Freddie, rather intimating by his manner that this was just the dirty sort of trick he would have imagined the other would have played.

'Mr Widgeon is the nephew of my old friend, Lord Blicester.'

'Ah?' said Captain Bradbury, hiding with a ham-like hand a yawn that seemed to signify that Freddie's foul antecedents were of little interest to him. It was plain that this was not going to be one of those sudden friendships. Captain Bradbury was obviously feeling that a world fit for heroes to live in should contain the irreducible minimum of Widgeons: while, as for Freddie, the last person he wanted hanging about the place at this highly critical point in his affairs was a richly tanned military man with deep-set eyes and a natty moustache.

However, he quickly rallied from his momentary agitation. Once that volume of Tennyson came, he felt, he would pretty soon put this bird where he belonged. A natty moustache is not everything. Nor is a rich tan. And the same may be said of deep-set eyes. What bungs a fellow over with a refined and poetical girl is Soul. And in the course of the next few days Freddie expected to have soul enough for six. He exerted himself, accordingly, to be the life of the party, and so successful were his efforts that, as they were leaving, Captain Bradbury drew him aside and gave him the sort of look he would have given a Pathan discovered pinching the old regiment's rifles out on the North-Western Frontier. And it was only now that Freddie really began to appreciate the other's physique. He had had no notion that they were making the soldiery so large nowadays.

'Tell me, Pridgeon . . .'

'Widgeon,' said Freddie, to keep the records straight.

'Tell me, Widgeon, are you making a long stay in these parts?'

'Oh, yes. Fairly longish.'

'I shouldn't.'

'You wouldn't?'

'Not if I were you.'

'But I like the scenery.'

'If you got both eyes bunged up, you wouldn't be able to see the scenery.'

'Why should I get both eyes bunged up?'

'You might.'

'But why?'

'I don't know. You just might. These things happen. Well, good evening, Widgeon,' said Captain Bradbury and hopped into his two-seater like a performing elephant alighting on an upturned barrel. And Freddie made his way to the Blue Lion in Tudsleigh village, where he had established his headquarters.

It would be idle to deny that this little chat gave Frederick Widgeon food for thought. He brooded on it over his steak and French fried that night, and was still brooding on it long after he had slid between the sheets and should have been in a restful sleep. And when morning brought its eggs and bacon and coffee he began to brood on it again.

He's a pretty astute sort of chap, Freddie, and he had not failed to sense the threatening note in the Captain's remarks. And he was somewhat dubious as to what to do for the best. You see, it was the first time anything of this sort had happened to him. I suppose, all in all, Freddie Widgeon has been in love at first sight with possibly twenty-seven girls in the course of his career: but hitherto everything had been what you might call plain sailing. I mean, he would flutter round for a few days and then the girl, incensed by some floater on his part or possibly merely unable to stand the sight of him any longer, would throw him out on his left ear, and that would be that. Everything pleasant and agreeable and orderly, as you might say. But this was different. Here he had come up against a new element, the jealous rival, and it was beginning to look not so good.

It was the sight of Tennyson's poems that turned the scale. The volume had arrived early on the previous day, and already he had mugged up two-thirds of the 'Lady of Shalott'. And the thought that, if he were to oil out now, all this frightful sweat would be so much dead loss, decided the issue. That afternoon he called once more at Tudsleigh Court, prepared to proceed with the matter along the lines originally laid out. And picture his astonishment and delight when he discovered that Captain Bradbury was not among those present.

There are very few advantages about having a military man as a rival in your wooing, but one of these is that every now and then such a military man has to pop up to London to see the blokes at the War Office. This Captain Bradbury had done today, and it was amazing what a difference his absence made. A gay confidence seemed to fill Freddie as he sat there wolfing buttered toast. He had finished the 'Lady of Shalott' that morning and was stuffed to the tonsils with good material. It was only a question of time, he felt, before some chance remark would uncork him and give him the cue to do his stuff.

And presently it came. Lady Carroway, withdrawing to write letters, paused at the door to ask April if she had any message for her Uncle Lancelot.

'Give him my love,' said April, 'and say I hope he likes Bournemouth.'

The door closed. Freddie coughed.

'He's moved then?' he said.

'I beg your pardon?'

'Just a spot of persiflage. Lancelot, you know. Tennyson, you know. You remember in the "Lady of Shalott" Lancelot was putting in most of his time at Camelot.'

The girl stared at him, dropping a slice of bread-and-butter in her emotion.

'You don't mean to say you read Tennyson, Mr Widgeon?'

'Me?' said Freddie. 'Tennyson? Read Tennyson? Me read Tennyson? Well, well, well! Bless my soul! Why, I know him by heart – some of him.'

'So do I! "Break, break, break, on your cold grey stones, oh Sea..."'

'Quite. Or take the "Lady of Shalott".'

'"I hold it truth with him who sings..."'

'So do I, absolutely. And then, again, there's the "Lady of Shalott". Dashed extraordinary that you should like Tennyson, too.'

'I think he's wonderful.'

'What a lad! That "Lady of Shalott"! Some spin on the ball there.'

'It's so absurd, the way people sneer at him nowadays.'

'The silly bounders. Don't know what's good for them.'

'He's my favourite poet.'

'Mine, too. Any bird who could write the "Lady of Shalott" gets the cigar or coconut, according to choice, as far as I'm concerned.'

They gazed at one another emotionally.

'Well, I'd never have thought it,' said April.

'Why not?'

'I mean, you gave me the impression of being...well, rather the dancing, night-club sort of man.'

'What! Me? Night clubs? Good gosh! Why, my idea of a happy evening is to curl up with Tennyson's latest.'

'Don't you love "Locksley Hall"?'

'Oh, rather. And the "Lady of Shalott".'

'And "Maud"?'

'Aces,' said Freddie. 'And the "Lady of Shalott".'

'How fond you seem of the "Lady of Shalott"!'

'Oh, I am.'

'So am I, of course. The river here always reminds me so much of that poem.'

'Why, of course it does!' said Freddie. 'I've been trying to think all the time why it seemed so dashed familiar. And, talking of the river, I suppose you wouldn't care for a row up it tomorrow?'

The girl looked doubtful.

'Tomorrow?'

'My idea was to hire a boat, sling in a bit of chicken and ham and a Tennyson . . .'

'But I had promised to go to Birmingham tomorrow with Captain Bradbury to help him choose a fishing-rod. Still, I suppose, really, any other day would do for that, wouldn't it?'

'Exactly.'

'We could go later on.'

'Positively,' said Freddie. 'A good deal later on. Much later on. In fact, the best plan would be to leave it quite open. One o'clock tomorrow, then, at the Town Bridge? Right. Fine. Splendid. Topping. I'll be there with my hair in a braid.'

All through the rest of the day Freddie was right in the pink. Walked on air, you might say. But towards nightfall, as he sat in the bar of the Blue Lion, sucking down a whisky and splash and working his way through 'Locksley Hall', a shadow fell athwart the table and, looking up, he perceived Captain Bradbury.

'Good evening, Widgeon,' said Captain Bradbury.

There is only one word, Freddie tells me, to describe the

gallant C.'s aspect at this juncture. It was sinister. His eyebrows had met across the top of his nose, his chin was sticking out from ten to fourteen inches, and he stood there flexing the muscles of his arms, making the while a low sound like the rumbling of an only partially extinct volcano. The impression Freddie received was that at any moment molten lava might issue from the man's mouth, and he wasn't absolutely sure that he liked the look of things.

However, he tried to be as bright as possible.

'Ah, Bradbury!' he replied, with a lilting laugh.

Captain Bradbury's right eyebrow had now become so closely entangled with his left that there seemed no hope of ever extricating it without the aid of powerful machinery.

'I understand that you called at Tudsleigh Court today.'

'Oh, rather. We missed you, of course, but, nevertheless, a pleasant time was had by all.'

'So I gathered. Miss Carroway tells me that you have invited her to picnic up the river with you tomorrow.'

'That's right. Up the river. The exact spot.'

'You will, of course, send her a note informing her that you are unable to go, as you have been unexpectedly called back to London.'

'But nobody's called me back to London.'

'Yes, they have. I have.'

Freddie tried to draw himself up. A dashed difficult thing to do, of course, when you're sitting down, and he didn't make much of a job of it.

'I fail to understand you, Bradbury.'

'Let me make it clearer,' said the Captain. 'There is an excellent train in the mornings at twelve-fifteen. You will catch it tomorrow.'

'Oh, yes?'

'I shall call here at one o'clock. If I find that you have not gone, I shall ... Did I ever happen to mention that I won the Heavyweight Boxing Championship of India last year?'

Freddie swallowed a little thoughtfully.

'You did?'

'Yes.'

Freddie pulled himself together.

'The Amateur Championship?'

'Of course.'

'I used to go in quite a lot for amateur boxing,' said Freddie with a little yawn. 'But I got bored with it. Not enough competition. Too little excitement. So I took on pros. But I found them so extraordinarily brittle that I chucked the whole thing. That was when Bulldog Whacker had to go to hospital for two months after one of our bouts. I collect old china now.'

Brave words, of course, but he watched his visitor depart with emotions that were not too fearfully bright. In fact, he tells me, he actually toyed for a moment with the thought that there might be a lot to be said for that twelve-fifteen train.

It was but a passing weakness. The thought of April Carroway soon strengthened him once more. He had invited her to this picnic, and he intended to keep the tryst even if it meant having to run like a rabbit every time Captain Bradbury hove in sight. After all, he reflected, it was most improbable that a big heavy fellow like that would be able to catch him.

His frame of mind, in short, was precisely that of the old Crusading Widgeons when they heard that the Paynim had been sighted in the offing.

*

The next day, accordingly, found Freddie seated in a hired row-boat at the landing-stage by the Town Bridge. It was a lovely summer morning with all the fixings, such as blue skies, silver wavelets, birds, bees, gentle breezes and what not. He had stowed the luncheon basket in the stern, and was whiling away the time of waiting by brushing up his 'Lady of Shalott', when a voice spoke from the steps. He looked up and perceived the kid Prudence gazing down at him with her grave, green eyes.

'Oh, hullo,' he said.

'Hullo,' said the child.

Since his entry to Tudsleigh Court, Prudence Carroway had meant little or nothing in Freddie's life. He had seen her around, of course, and had beamed at her in a benevolent sort of way, it being his invariable policy to beam benevolently at all relatives and connections of the adored object, but he had scarcely given her a thought. As always on these occasions, his whole attention had been earmarked for the adored one. So now his attitude was rather that of a bloke who wonders to what he is indebted for the honour of this visit.

'Nice day,' he said, tentatively.

'Yes,' said the kid. 'I came to tell you that April can't come.'

The sun, which had been shining with exceptional brilliance, seemed to Freddie to slip out of sight like a diving duck.

'You don't mean that!'

'Yes, I do.'

'Can't come?'

'No. She told me to tell you she's awfully sorry, but some friends of Mother's have phoned that they are passing through and would like lunch, so she's got to stay on and help cope with them.'

'Oh, gosh!'

'So she wants you to take me instead, and she's going to try to come on afterwards. I told her we would lunch near Griggs's Ferry.'

Something of the inky blackness seemed to Freddie to pass from the sky. It was a jar, of course, but still, if the girl was going to join him later . . . And, as for having this kid along, well, even that had its bright side. He could see that it would be by no means a bad move to play the hearty host to the young blighter. Reports of the lavishness of his hospitality and the suavity of his demeanour would get round to April and might do him quite a bit of good. It is a recognized fact that a lover is never wasting his time when he lushes up the little sister.

'All right,' he said. 'Hop in.'

So the kid hopped, and they shoved off. There wasn't anything much in the nature of intellectual conversation for the first ten minutes or so, because there was a fairish amount of traffic on the river at this point and the kid, who had established herself at the steering apparatus, seemed to have a rather sketchy notion of the procedure. As she explained to Freddie after they had gone about half-way through a passing barge, she always forgot which of the ropes it was that you pulled when you wanted to go to the right. However, the luck of the Widgeons saw them through and eventually they came, still afloat, to the unfrequented upper portions of the stream. Here in some mysterious way the rudder fell off, and after that it was all much easier. And it was at this point that the kid, having no longer anything to occupy herself with, reached out and picked up the book.

'Hullo! Are you reading Tennyson?'

'I was before we started, and I shall doubtless dip into him again later on. You will generally find me having a pop at the bard under advisement when I get a spare five minutes.'

'You don't mean to say you like him?'

'Of course I do. Who doesn't?'

'I don't. April's been making me read him, and I think he's soppy.'

'He is not soppy at all. Dashed beautiful.'

'But don't you think his girls are awful blisters?'

Apart from his old crony, the Lady of Shalott, Freddie had not yet made the acquaintance of any of the women in Tennyson's poems, but he felt very strongly that if they were good enough for April Carroway they were good enough for a green-eyed child with freckles all over her nose, and he said as much, rather severely.

'Tennyson's heroines,' said Freddie, 'are jolly fine specimens of pure, sweet womanhood, so get that into your nut, you soulless kid. If you behaved like a Tennyson heroine, you would be doing well.'

'Which of them?'

'Any of them. Pick 'em where you like. You can't go wrong. How much further to this Ferry place?'

'It's round the next bend.'

It was naturally with something of a pang that Freddie tied the boat up at their destination. Not only was this Griggs's Ferry a lovely spot, it was in addition completely deserted. There was a small house through the trees, but it showed no signs of occupancy. The only living thing for miles around appeared to be an elderly horse which was taking a snack on the river bank. In other words, if only April had been here and the kid hadn't, they would have been alone together with no human eye to intrude upon their sacred solitude. They could have read Tennyson to each other till they were blue in the face, and not a squawk from a soul.

A saddening thought, of course. Still, as the row had given him a nice appetite, he soon dismissed these wistful yearnings and started unpacking the luncheon basket. And at the end of about twenty minutes, during which period nothing had broken the stillness but the sound of champing jaws, he felt that it would not be amiss to chat with his little guest.

'Had enough?' he asked.

'No,' said the kid. 'But there isn't any more.'

'You seem to tuck away your food all right.'

'The girls at school used to call me Teresa the Tapeworm,' said the kid with a touch of pride.

It suddenly struck Freddie as a little odd that with July only half over this child should be at large. The summer holidays, as he remembered it, always used to start round about the first of August.

'Why aren't you at school now?'

'I was bunked last month.'

'Really?' said Freddie, interested. 'They gave you the push, did they? What for?'

'Shooting pigs.'

'Shooting pigs?'

'With a bow and arrow. One pig, that is to say. Percival. He belonged to Miss Maitland, the headmistress. Do you ever pretend to be people in books?'

'Never. And don't stray from the point at issue. I want to get to the bottom of this thing about the pig.'

'I'm not straying from the point at issue. I was playing William Tell.'

'The old apple-knocker, you mean?'

'The man who shot an apple off his son's head. I tried to get one of the girls to put the apple on her head, but she wouldn't, so I went down to the pigsty and put it on Percival's. And the silly goop shook it off and started to eat it just as I was shooting, which spoiled my aim and I got him on the left ear. He was rather vexed about it. So was Miss Maitland. Especially as I was supposed to be in disgrace at the time, because I had set the dormitory on fire the night before.'

Freddie blinked a bit.

'You set the dormitory on fire?'

'Yes.'

'Any special reason, or just a passing whim?'

'I was playing Florence Nightingale.'

'Florence Nightingale?'

'The Lady with the Lamp. I dropped the lamp.'

'Tell me,' said Freddie. 'This Miss Maitland of yours. What colour is her hair?'

'Grey.'

'I thought as much. And now, if you don't mind, switch off the childish prattle for the nonce. I feel a restful sleep creeping over me.'

'My Uncle Joe says that people who sleep after lunch have got fatty degeneration of the heart.'

'Your Uncle Joe is an ass,' said Freddie.

How long it was before Freddie awoke, he could not have said. But when he did the first thing that impressed itself upon him was that the kid was no longer in sight, and this worried him a bit. I mean to say, a child who, on her own showing, plugged pigs with arrows and set fire to dormitories was not a child he was frightfully keen on having roaming about the countryside at a time when he was supposed to be more or less in charge of her. He got up, feeling somewhat perturbed, and started walking about and bellowing her name.

Rather a chump it made him feel, he tells me, because a fellow all by himself on the bank of a river shouting 'Prudence! Prudence!' is apt to give a false impression to any passer-by who may hear him. However, he didn't have to bother about that long, for at this point, happening to glance at the river, he saw her body floating in it.

'Oh, dash it!' said Freddie.

Well, I mean, you couldn't say it was pleasant for him. It put him in what you might call an invidious position. Here he was, supposed to be looking after this kid, and when he got home April Carroway would ask him if he had had a jolly day and he would reply: 'Topping, thanks, except that young Prudence went and got drowned, regretted by all except possibly Miss Maitland.' It wouldn't go well, and he could see it wouldn't go well, so on the chance of a last-minute rescue he dived in. And he was considerably surprised, on arriving at what he had supposed to be a drowning child, to discover that it was merely the outer husk. In other words, what was floating there was not the kid in person but only her frock. And why a frock that had a kid in it should suddenly have become a kidless frock was a problem beyond him.

Another problem, which presented itself as he sloshed ashore once more, was what the dickens he was going to do now. The sun had gone in and a nippy breeze was blowing, and it looked to him as if only a complete change of costume could save him from pneumonia. And as he stood there wondering where this change of costume was to come from he caught sight of that house through the trees.

Now, in normal circs. Freddie would never dream of calling on a bird to whom he had never been introduced and touching him for a suit of clothes. He's scrupulously rigid on points like that and has been known to go smokeless through an entire night at the theatre rather than ask a stranger for a match. But this was a special case. He didn't hesitate. A quick burst across country, and he was at the front door, rapping the knocker and calling 'I say!' And when at the end of about three minutes nobody had appeared he came rather shrewdly to the conclusion that the place must be deserted.

Well, this, of course, fitted in quite neatly with his plans. He much preferred to nip in and help himself rather than explain everything at length to someone who might very easily be one of those goops who are not quick at grasping situations. Observing that the door was not locked, accordingly he pushed in and toddled up the stairs to the bedroom on the first floor.

Everything was fine. There was a cupboard by the bed, and in it an assortment of clothes which left him a wide choice. He fished out a neat creation in checked tweed, located a shirt, a tie, and a sweater in the chest of drawers and, stripping off his wet things, began to dress.

As he did so, he continued to muse on this mystery of the child Prudence. He wondered what Sherlock Holmes would have made of it, or Lord Peter Wimsey, for that matter. The one thing certain was that the moment he was clothed he must buzz out and scour the countryside for her. So with all possible speed he donned the shirt, the tie, and the sweater, and had just put on a pair of roomy but serviceable shoes when his eye, roving aimlessly about the apartment, fell upon a photograph on the mantelpiece.

It represented a young man of powerful physique seated in a chair in flimsy garments. On his face was a rather noble expression, on his lap a massive silver cup, and on his hands boxing-gloves. And in spite of the noble expression he had no difficulty in recognizing the face as that of his formidable acquaintance, Captain Bradbury.

And at this moment, just as he had realized that Fate, after being tolerably rough with him all day, had put the lid on it by leading him into his rival's lair, he heard a sound of footsteps in the garden below. And, leaping to the window, he found his worst fears confirmed. The Captain, looking larger and tougher than ever, was coming up the gravel path to the front door. And that door, Freddie remembered with considerable emotion, he had left open.

Well, Freddie, as you know, has never been the dreamy meditative type. I would describe him as essentially the man of action. And he acted now as never before. He tells me he doubts if a chamois of the Alps, unless at the end of a most intensive spell of training, could have got down those stairs quicker than he did. He says the whole thing rather resembled an effort on the part of one of those Indian fakirs who bung their astral bodies about all over the place, going into thin air in Bombay and reassembling the parts two minutes later in Darjheeling. The result being that he reached the front door just as Captain Bradbury was coming in, and slammed it in his face. A hoarse cry, seeping through the woodwork, caused him to shoot both bolts and prop a small chair against the lower panel.

And he was just congratulating himself on having done all that man could do and handled a difficult situation with energy and tact, when a sort of scrabbling noise to the south-west came to his ears, and he realized with a sickening sinking of the heart what it means to be up against one of these Indian Army strategists, trained from early youth to do the dirty on the lawless tribes of the North-Western Frontier. With consummate military skill, Captain Bradbury, his advance checked at the front door, was trying to outflank him by oozing in through the sitting-room window.

However, most fortunately it happened that whoever washed and brushed up this house had left a mop in the hall. It was a good outsize mop, and Freddie whisked it up in his stride and shot into the sitting-room. He arrived just in time to see a leg coming over the sill. Then a face came into view, and Freddie tells me that the eyes into which he found himself gazing have kept him awake at night ever since.

For an instant, they froze him stiff, like a snake's. Then reason returned to her throne and, recovering himself with a strong effort, he rammed the mop home, sending his adversary base over apex into a bed of nasturtiums. This done, he shut the window and bolted it.

You might have thought that with a pane of glass in between them Captain Bradbury's glare would have lost in volume. This, Freddie tells me, was not the case. As he had now recognized his assailant, it had become considerably more above proof. It scorched Freddie like a death ray.

But the interchange of glances did not last long. These Indian Army men do not look, they act. And it has been well said of them that, while you may sometimes lay them a temporary stymie, you cannot baffle them permanently. The Captain suddenly turned and began to gallop round the corner of the house. It was plainly his intention to resume the attack from another and a less well-guarded quarter. This, I believe, is a common manœuvre on the North-West Frontier. You get your

Afghan shading his eyes and looking out over the *maidan*, and then you sneak up the *pahar* behind him and catch him bending.

This decided Freddie. He simply couldn't go on indefinitely, leaping from spot to spot, endeavouring with a mere mop to stem the advance of a foe as resolute as this Bradbury. The time had come for a strategic retreat. Not ten seconds, accordingly, after the other had disappeared, he was wrenching the front door open.

He was taking a risk, of course. There was the possibility that he might be walking into an ambush. But all seemed well. The Captain had apparently genuinely gone round to the back, and Freddie reached the gate with the comfortable feeling that in another couple of seconds he would be out in the open and in a position to leg it away from the danger zone.

All's well that ends well, felt Freddie.

It was at this juncture that he found that he had no trousers on.

I need scarcely enlarge upon the agony of spirit which this discovery caused poor old Freddie. Apart from being the soul of modesty, he is a chap who prides himself on always being well and suitably dressed for both town and country. In a costume which would have excited remark at the Four Arts Ball in Paris, he writhed with shame and embarrassment. And he was just saying: 'This is the end!' when what should he see before him but a two-seater car, which he recognized as the property of his late host.

And in the car was a large rug.

It altered the whole aspect of affairs. From neck to waist, you will recall, Freddie was adequately, if not neatly, clad. The garments which he had borrowed from Captain Bradbury were a good deal too large, but at least they covered the person. In a car with that rug over his lap his outward appearance would be virtually that of the Well-Dressed Man.

He did not hesitate. He had never pinched a car before, but he did it now with all the smoothness of a seasoned professional. Springing into the driving-seat, he tucked the rug about his knees, trod on the self-starter, and was off.

His plans were all neatly shaped. It was his intention to make straight for the Blue Lion. Arrived there, a swift dash would take him through the lobby and up the stairs to his room, where no fewer than seven pairs of trousers awaited his choice. And as the lobby was usually deserted except for the growing boy who cleaned the knives and boots, a lad who could be relied on merely to give a cheery guffaw and then dismiss the matter from his mind, he anticipated no further trouble.

But you never know. You form your schemes and run them over in your mind and you can't see a flaw in them, and then something happens out of a blue sky which dishes them completely. Scarcely had Freddie got half a mile down the road when a girlish figure leaped out of some bushes at the side, waving its arms, and he saw that it was April Carroway.

If you had told Freddie only a few hours before that a time would come when he would not be pleased to see April Carroway, he would have laughed derisively. But it was without pleasure that he looked upon her now. Nor, as he stopped the car and was enabled to make a closer inspection of the girl, did it seem as if she were pleased to see him. Why this should be so he could not imagine, but beyond a question she was not looking chummy. Her face was set, and there was an odd, stony expression in her eyes.

'Oh, hullo!' said Freddie. 'So you got away from your lunch party all right.'

'Yes.'

Freddie braced himself to break the bad news. The whole subject of the kid Prudence and her mysterious disappearance was one on which he would have preferred not to touch, but obviously it had to be done. I mean, you can't go about the place mislaying girls' sisters and just not mention it. He coughed.

'I say,' he said, 'a rather rummy thing has occurred. Odd, you might call it. With the best intentions in the world, I seem to have lost your sister Prudence.'

'So I gathered. Well, I've found her.'

'Eh?'

At this moment, a disembodied voice suddenly came from inside one of the bushes, causing Freddie to shoot a full two inches out of his seat. He tells me he remembered a similar experience having happened to Moses in the Wilderness, and he wondered if the prophet had taken it as big as he had done.

'I'm in here!'

Freddie gaped. 'Was that Prudence?' he gurgled.

'That was Prudence,' said April coldly.

'But what's she doing there?'

'She is obliged to remain in those bushes, because she has nothing on.'

'Nothing on? No particular engagements, you mean?'

'I mean no clothes. The horse kicked hers into the river.'

Freddie blinked. He could make nothing of this.

'A horse kicked the clothes off her?'

'It didn't kick them off me,' said the voice. 'They were lying on the bank in a neat bundle. Miss Maitland always taught us to be neat with our clothes. You see, I was playing Lady Godiva, as you advised me to.'

Freddie clutched at his brow. He might have known, he told himself, that the moment he dropped off for a few minutes refreshing sleep this ghastly kid would be up to something frightful. And he might also have known, he reflected, that she would put the blame on him. He had studied Woman, and he knew that when Woman gets into a tight place her first act is to shovel the blame off on to the nearest male.

'When did I ever advise you to play Lady Godiva?'

'You told me I couldn't go wrong in imitating any of Tennyson's heroines.'

'You appear to have encouraged her and excited her imagination,' said April, giving him a look which, while it was of a different calibre from Captain Bradbury's, was almost as unpleasant to run up against. 'I can't blame the poor child for being carried away.'

Freddie did another spot of brow-clutching. No wooer, he knew, makes any real progress with the girl he loves by encouraging her young sister to ride horses about the countryside in the nude.

'But, dash it . . .'

'Well, we need not go into that now. The point is that she is in those bushes with only a small piece of sacking over her, and is likely to catch cold. Perhaps you will be kind enough to drive her home?'

'Oh, rather. Of course. Certainly.'

'And put that rug over her,' said April Carroway. 'It may save her from a bad chill.'

The world reeled about Freddie. The voice of a donkey

braying in a neighbouring meadow seemed like the mocking laughter of demons. The summer breeze was still murmuring through the tree-tops and birds still twittered in the hedgerows, but he did not hear them.

He swallowed a couple of times.

'I'm sorry...'

April Carroway was staring at him incredulously. It was as if she could not believe her ears.

'You don't mean to say that you refuse to give up your rug to a child who is sneezing already?'

'I'm sorry...'

'Do you realize...'

'I'm sorry...Cannot relinquish rug...Rheumatism...Bad ...In the knee-joints...Doctor's orders...'

'Mr Widgeon,' said April Carroway imperiously, 'give me that rug immediately!'

An infinite sadness came into Frederick Widgeon's eyes. He gave the girl one long, sorrowful look – a look in which remorse, apology, and a lifelong devotion were nicely blended. Then, without a word, he put the clutch in and drove on, out into the sunset.

Somewhere on the outskirts of Wibbleton-in-the-Vale, when the dusk was falling and the air was fragrant with the evening dew, he managed to sneak a pair of trousers from a scarecrow in a field. Clad in these, he drove to London. He is now living down in the suburbs somewhere, trying to grow a beard in order to foil possible pursuit from Captain Bradbury.

And what he told me to say was that, if anybody cares to have an only slightly soiled copy of the works of Alfred, Lord Tennyson, at a sacrifice price, he is in the market. Not only has he taken an odd dislike to this particular poet, but he had a letter from April Carroway this morning, the contents of which have solidified his conviction that the volume to which I allude is of no further use to owner.

A BEAN was in a nursing-home with a broken leg as the result of trying to drive his sports-model Poppenheim through the Marble Arch instead of round it, and a kindly Crumpet had looked in to give him the gossip of the town. He found him playing halma with the nurse, and he sat down on the bed and took a grape, and the Bean asked what was going on in the great world.

'Well,' said the Crumpet, taking another grape, 'the finest minds in the Drones are still wrestling with the great Hat mystery.'

'What's that?'

'You don't mean you haven't heard about it?'

'Not a word.'

The Crumpet was astounded. He swallowed two grapes at once in his surprise.

'Why, London's seething with it. The general consensus of opinion is that it has something to do with the Fourth Dimension. You know how things go. I mean to say, something rummy occurs and you consult some big-brained bird and he wags his head and says "Ah! The Fourth Dimension!" Extraordinary nobody's told you about the great Hat mystery.'

'You're the first visitor I've had. What is it, anyway? What hat?'

'Well, there were two hats. Reading from left to right, Percy Wimbolt's and Nelson Cork's.'

The Bean nodded intelligently.

'I see what you mean. Percy had one, and Nelson had the other.'

'Exactly. Two hats in all. Top hats.'

'What was mysterious about them?'

'Why, Elizabeth Bottsworth and Diana Punter said they didn't fit.'

'Well, hats don't sometimes.'

'But these came from Bodmin's.'

The Bean shot up in bed. 'What?'

'You mustn't excite the patient,' said the nurse, who up to this point had taken no part in the conversation.

'But, dash it, nurse,' cried the Bean, 'you can't have caught what he said. If we are to give credence to his story, Percy Wimbolt and Nelson Cork bought a couple of hats at Bodmin's – at *Bodmin's*, I'll trouble you – and they didn't fit. It isn't possible.'

He spoke with strong emotion, and the Crumpet nodded understandingly. People can say what they please about the modern young man believing in nothing nowadays, but there is one thing every right-minded young man believes in, and that is the infallibility of Bodmin's hats. It is one of the eternal verities. Once admit that it is possible for a Bodmin hat not to fit, and you leave the door open for Doubt, Schism, and Chaos generally.

'That's exactly how Percy and Nelson felt, and it was for that reason that they were compelled to take the strong line they did with E. Bottsworth and D. Punter.'

'They took a strong line, did they?'

'A very strong line.'

'Won't you tell us the whole story from the beginning?' said the nurse.

'Right ho,' said the Crumpet, taking a grape. 'It'll make your head swim.'

'So mysterious?'

'So absolutely dashed uncanny from start to finish.'

You must know, to begin with, my dear old nurse (said the Crumpet), that these two blokes, Percy Wimbolt and Nelson Cork, are fellows who have to exercise the most watchful care about their lids, because they are so situated that in their case there can be none of that business of just charging into any old hattery and grabbing the first thing in sight. Percy is one of those large, stout, outsize chaps with a head like a water-melon, while Nelson is built more on the lines of a minor jockey and has a head like a peanut.

You will readily appreciate, therefore, that it requires an artist hand to fit them properly and that is why they have always gone to Bodmin. I have heard Percy say that his trust in Bodmin is like the unspotted faith of a young curate in his Bishop and I have no doubt that Nelson would have said the same, if he had thought of it.

It was at Bodmin's door that they ran into each other on the morning when my story begins.

'Hullo,' said Percy. 'You come to buy a hat?'

'Yes,' said Nelson. 'You come to buy a hat?'

'Yes.' Percy glanced cautiously about him, saw that he was alone (except for Nelson, of course) and unobserved, and drew closer and lowered his voice. 'There's a reason!'

'That's rummy,' said Nelson. He, also, spoke in a hushed tone. 'I have a special reason, too.'

Percy looked warily about, and lowered his voice another notch.

'Nelson,' he said, 'you know Elizabeth Bottsworth?'

'Intimately,' said Nelson.

'Rather a sound young potato, what?'

'Very much so.'

'Pretty.'

'I've often noticed it.'

'Me, too. She is so small, so sweet, so dainty, so lively, so viv—what's-the-word? – that a fellow wouldn't be far out in calling her an angel in human shape.'

'Aren't all angels in human shape?'

'Are they?' said Percy, who was a bit foggy on angels. 'Well, be that as it may,' he went on, his cheeks suffused to a certain extent, 'I love that girl, Nelson, and she's coming with me to the first day of Ascot, and I'm relying on this new hat of mine to do just that extra bit that's needed in the way of making her reciprocate my passion. Having only met her so far at country-houses, I've never yet flashed upon her in a topper.'

Nelson Cork was staring.

'Well, if that isn't the most remarkable coincidence I ever came across in my puff!' he exclaimed, amazed. 'I'm buying my new hat for exactly the same reason.'

A convulsive start shook Percy's massive frame. His eyes bulged.

'To fascinate Elizabeth Bottsworth?' he cried, beginning to writhe.

'No, no,' said Nelson, soothingly. 'Of course not. Elizabeth and I have always been great friends, but nothing more. What I meant was that I, like you, am counting on this forthcoming topper of mine to put me across with the girl I love.'

Percy stopped writhing.

'Who is she?' he asked, interested.

'Diana Punter, the niece of my godmother, old Ma Punter. It's an odd thing, I've known her all my life – brought up as kids together and so forth – but it's only recently that passion has burgeoned. I now worship that girl, Percy, from the top of her head to the soles of her divine feet.'

Percy looked dubious.

'That's a pretty longish distance, isn't it? Diana Punter is one of my closest friends, and a charming girl in every respect, but isn't she a bit tall for you, old man?'

'My dear chap, that's just what I admire so much about her, her superb statuesqueness. More like a Greek goddess than anything I've struck for years. Besides, she isn't any taller for me than you are for Elizabeth Bottsworth.'

'True,' admitted Percy.

'And, anyway, I love her, blast it, and I don't propose to argue the point. I love her, I love her, I love her, and we are lunching together the first day of Ascot.'

'At Ascot?'

'No. She isn't keen on racing, so I shall have to give Ascot a miss.'

'That's Love,' said Percy, awed.

'The binge will take place at my godmother's house in Berkeley Square, and it won't be long after that, I feel, before you see an interesting announcement in the *Morning Post*.'

Percy extended his hand. Nelson grasped it warmly.

'These new hats are pretty well bound to do the trick, I should say, wouldn't you?'

'Infallibly. Where girls are concerned, there is nothing that brings home the gravy like a well-fitting topper.'

'Bodmin must extend himself as never before,' said Percy.

'He certainly must,' said Nelson.

They entered the shop. And Bodmin, having measured them with his own hands, promised that two of his very finest efforts should be at their respective addresses in the course of the next few days.

Now, Percy Wimbolt isn't a chap you would suspect of having nerves, but there is no doubt that in the interval which elapsed before Bodmin was scheduled to deliver he got pretty twittery. He kept having awful visions of some great disaster happening to his new hat: and, as things turned out, these visions came jolly near being fulfilled. It has made Percy feel that he is psychic.

What occurred was this. Owing to these jitters of his, he hadn't been sleeping any too well, and on the morning before Ascot he was up as early as ten-thirty, and he went to his sitting-room window to see what sort of a day it was, and the sight he beheld from that window absolutely froze the blood in his veins.

For there below him, strutting up and down the pavement, were a uniformed little blighter whom he recognized as Bodmin's errand-boy and an equally foul kid in mufti. And balanced on each child's loathsome head was a top hat. Against the railings were leaning a couple of cardboard hat-boxes.

Now, considering that Percy had only just woken from a dream in which he had been standing outside the Guildhall in his new hat, receiving the Freedom of the City from the Lord Mayor, and the Lord Mayor had suddenly taken a terrific swipe at the hat with his mace, knocking it into hash, you might have supposed that he would have been hardened to anything. But he wasn't. His reaction was terrific. There was a moment of sort of paralysis, during which he was telling himself that he had always suspected this beastly little boy of Bodmin's of having a low and frivolous outlook and being temperamentally unfitted for his high office: and then he came alive with a jerk and let out probably the juiciest yell the neighbourhood had heard for years.

It stopped the striplings like a high-powered shell. One moment, they had been swanking up and down in a mincing and affected sort of way: the next, the second kid had legged it like a streak and Bodmin's boy was shoving the hats back in the boxes and trying to do it quickly enough to enable him to be elsewhere when Percy should arrive.

And in this he was successful. By the time Percy had got to the front door and opened it, there was nothing to be seen but a hat-box standing on the steps. He took it up to his flat and removed the contents with a gingerly and reverent hand, holding his breath for fear the nap should have got rubbed the wrong way or a dent of any nature been made in the gleaming surface; but apparently all was well. Bodmin's boy might sink to taking hats out of their boxes and fooling about with them, but at least he hadn't gone to the last awful extreme of dropping them.

The lid was O.K. absolutely: and on the following morning Percy, having spent the interval polishing it with stout, assembled the boots, the spats, the trousers, the coat, the flowered waistcoat, the collar, the shirt, the quiet grey tie, and the good old gardenia, and set off in a taxi for the house where Elizabeth was staying. And presently he was ringing the bell and being told she would be down in a minute, and eventually down she came, looking perfectly marvellous.

'What ho, what ho!' said Percy.

'Hullo, Percy,' said Elizabeth.

Now, naturally, up to this moment Percy had been standing with bared head. At this point, he put the hat on. He wanted her to get the full effect suddenly in a good light. And very strategic, too. I mean to say, it would have been the act of a juggins to have waited till they were in the taxi, because in a taxi all toppers look much alike.

So Percy popped the hat on his head with a meaning glance and stood waiting for the uncontrollable round of applause.

And instead of clapping her little hands in girlish ecstasy and doing Spring dances round him, this young Bottsworth gave a sort of gurgling scream not unlike a coloratura soprano choking on a fish-bone.

Then she blinked and became calmer.

'It's all right,' she said. 'The momentary weakness has passed. Tell me, Percy, when do you open?'

'Open?' said Percy, not having the remotest.

'On the Halls. Aren't you going to sing comic songs on the Music Halls?'

Percy's perplexity deepened.

'Me? No. How? Why? What do you mean?'

'I thought that hat must be part of the make-up and that you were trying it on the dog. I couldn't think of any other reason why you should wear one six sizes too small.'

Percy gasped. 'You aren't suggesting this hat doesn't fit me?'

'It doesn't fit you by a mile.'

'But it's a Bodmin.'

'Call it that if you like. I call it a public outrage.'

Percy was appalled. I mean, naturally. A nice thing for a chap to give his heart to a girl and then find her talking in this hideous, flippant way of sacred subjects.

Then it occurred to him that, living all the time in the country, she might not have learned to appreciate the holy significance of the name Bodmin.

'Listen,' he said gently. 'Let me explain. This hat was made by Bodmin, the world-famous hatter of Vigo Street. He measured me in person and guaranteed a fit.'

'And I nearly had one.'

'And if Bodmin guarantees that a hat shall fit,' proceeded Percy, trying to fight against a sickening sort of feeling that he had been all wrong about this girl, 'it fits. I mean, saying a Bodmin hat doesn't fit is like saying...well, I can't think of anything awful enough.'

'That hat's awful enough. It's like something out of a two-reel comedy. Pure Chas. Chaplin. I know a joke's a joke, Percy, and I'm as fond of a laugh as anyone, but there is such a thing as cruelty to animals. Imagine the feelings of the horses at Ascot when they see that hat.'

Poets and other literary blokes talk a lot about falling in love at first sight, but it's equally possible to fall out of love just as quickly. One moment, this girl was the be-all and the end-all, as you might say, of Percy Wimbolt's life. The next, she was just a regrettable young blister with whom he wished to hold no further communication. He could stand a good deal from the sex. Insults directed at himself left him unmoved. But he was not prepared to countenance destructive criticism of a Bodmin hat.

'Possibly,' he said, coldly, 'you would prefer to go to this bally race-meeting alone?'

'You bet I'm going alone. You don't suppose I mean to be seen in broad daylight in the paddock at Ascot with a hat like that?'

Percy stepped back and bowed formally.

'Drive on, driver,' he said to the driver, and the driver drove on.

Now, you would say that that was rummy enough. A full-sized mystery in itself, you might call it. But wait. Mark the sequel. You haven't heard anything yet.

*

We now turn to Nelson Cork. Shortly before one-thirty, Nelson had shoved over to Berkeley Square and had lunch with his godmother and Diana Punter, and Diana's manner and deportment had been absolutely all that could have been desired. In fact, so chummy had she been over the cutlets and fruit salad that it seemed to Nelson that, if she was like this now, imagination boggled at the thought of how utterly all over him she would be when he sprang his new hat on her.

So when the meal was concluded and coffee had been drunk and old Lady Punter had gone up to her boudoir with a digestive tablet and a sex-novel, he thought it would be a sound move to invite her to come for a stroll along Bond Street. There was the chance, of course, that she would fall into his arms right in the middle of the pavement: but if that happened, he told himself, they could always get into a cab. So he mooted the saunter, and she checked up, and presently they started off.

And you will scarcely believe this, but they hadn't gone more than half-way along Bruton Street when she suddenly stopped and looked at him in an odd manner.

'I don't want to be personal, Nelson,' she said, 'but really I do think you ought to take the trouble to get measured for your hats.'

If a gas main had exploded beneath Nelson's feet, he could hardly have been more taken aback.

'M-m-m-m . . .' he gasped. He could scarcely believe that he had heard aright.

'It's the only way with a head like yours. I know it's a temptation for a lazy man to go into a shop and take just whatever is offered him, but the result is so sloppy. That thing you're wearing now looks like an extinguisher.'

Nelson was telling himself that he must be strong.

'Are you endeavouring to intimate that this hat does not fit?'

'Can't you feel that it doesn't fit?'

'But it's a Bodmin.'

'I don't know what you mean. It's just an ordinary silk hat.'

'Not at all. It's a Bodmin.'

'I don't know what you are talking about.'

'The point I am trying to drive home,' said Nelson, stiffly, 'is that this hat was constructed under the personal auspices of Jno. Bodmin of Vigo Street.'

'Well, it's too big.'

'It is not too big.'

'I say it is too big.'

'And I say a Bodmin hat cannot be too big.'

'Well, I've got eyes, and I say it is.'

Nelson controlled himself with an effort.

'I would be the last person,' he said, 'to criticize your eyesight, but on the present occasion you will permit me to say that it has let you down with a considerable bump. Myopia is indicated. Allow me,' said Nelson, hot under the collar, but still dignified, 'to tell you something about Jno. Bodmin, as the name appears new to you. Jno. is the last of a long line of Bodmins, all of whom have made hats assiduously for the nobility and gentry all their lives. Hats are in Jno. Bodmin's blood.'

'I don't ...'

Nelson held up a restraining hand.

'Over the door of his emporium in Vigo Street the passers-by may read a significant legend. It runs: "Bespoke Hatter To The Royal Family". That means, in simple language adapted to the lay intelligence, that if the King wants a new topper he simply ankles round to Bodmin's and says: "Good morning, Bodmin, we want a topper." He does not ask if it will fit. He takes it for granted that it will fit. He has bespoken Jno. Bodmin, and he trusts him blindly. You don't suppose His Gracious Majesty would bespeak a hatter whose hats did not fit. The whole essence of being a hatter is to make hats that fit, and it is to this end that Jno. Bodmin has strained every nerve for years. And that is why I say again – simply and without heat – This hat is a Bodmin.'

Diana was beginning to get a bit peeved. The blood of the Punters is hot, and very little is required to steam it up. She tapped Bruton Street with a testy foot.

'You always were an obstinate, pig-headed little fiend, Nelson, even as a child. I tell you once more, for the last time, that that hat is too big. If it were not for the fact that I can see a pair of boots and part of a pair of trousers, I should not know that there was a human being under it. I don't care how much you argue, I still think you ought to be ashamed of yourself for coming out in the thing. Even if you didn't mind for your own sake, you might have considered the feelings of the pedestrians and traffic.'

Nelson quivered.

'You do, do you?'

'Yes, I do.'

'Oh, you do?'

'I said I did. Didn't you hear me? No, I suppose you could hardly be expected to, with an enormous great hat coming down over your ears.'

'You say this hat comes down over my ears?'

'Right over your ears. It's a mystery to me why you think it worth while to deny it.'

I fear that what follows does not show Nelson Cork in the role of a parfait gentil knight, but in extenuation of his behaviour

I must remind you that he and Diana Punter had been brought up as children together, and a dispute between a couple who have shared the same nursery is always liable to degenerate into an exchange of personalities and innuendos. What starts as an academic discussion on hats turns only too swiftly into a raking-up of old sores and a grand parade of family skeletons.

It was so in this case. At the word 'mystery,' Nelson uttered a nasty laugh.

'A mystery, eh? As much a mystery, I suppose, as why your uncle George suddenly left England in the year 1920 without stopping to pack up?'

Diana's eyes flashed. Her foot struck the pavement another shrewd wallop.

'Uncle George,' she said haughtily, 'went abroad for his health.'

'You bet he did,' retorted Nelson. 'He knew what was good for him.'

'Anyway, he wouldn't have worn a hat like that.'

'Where they would have put him if he hadn't been off like a scalded kitten, he wouldn't have worn a hat at all.'

A small groove was now beginning to appear in the paving-stone on which Diana Punter stood.

'Well, Uncle George escaped one thing by going abroad, at any rate,' she said. 'He missed the big scandal about your aunt Clarissa in 1922.'

Nelson clenched his fists. 'The jury gave Aunt Clarissa the benefit of the doubt,' he said hoarsely.

'Well, we all know what that means. It was accompanied, if you recollect, by some very strong remarks from the Bench.'

There was a pause.

'I may be wrong,' said Nelson, 'but I should have thought it ill beseemed a girl whose brother Cyril was warned off the Turf in 1924 to haul up her slacks about other people's Aunt Clarissas.'

'Passing lightly over my brother Cyril in 1924,' rejoined Diana, 'what price your cousin Fred in 1927?'

They glared at one another in silence for a space, each realizing with a pang that the supply of erring relatives had now given out. Diana was still pawing the paving-stone, and Nelson was wondering what on earth he could ever have seen in a girl who, in addition to talking subversive drivel about hats, was eight feet tall and ungainly, to boot.

'While as for your brother-in-law's niece's sister-in-law Muriel...' began Diana, suddenly brightening.

Nelson checked her with a gesture.

'I prefer not to continue this discussion,' he said, frigidly.

'It is no pleasure to me,' replied Diana, with equal coldness, 'to have to listen to your vapid gibberings. That's the worst of a man who wears his hat over his mouth – he will talk through it.'

'I bid you a very hearty good afternoon, Miss Punter,' said Nelson.

He strode off without a backward glance.

Now, one advantage of having a row with a girl in Bruton Street is that the Drones is only just round the corner, so that you can pop in and restore the old nervous system with the minimum of trouble. Nelson was round there in what practically amounted to a trice, and the first person he saw was Percy, hunched up over a double and splash.

'Hullo,' said Percy.

'Hullo,' said Nelson.

There was a silence, broken only by the sound of Nelson ordering a mixed vermouth. Percy continued to stare before him like a man who has drained the wine-cup of life to its lees, only to discover a dead mouse at the bottom.

'Nelson,' he said at length, 'what are your views on the Modern Girl?'

'I think she's a mess.'

'I thoroughly agree with you,' said Percy. 'Of course, Diana Punter is a rare exception, but, apart from Diana, I wouldn't give you twopence for the modern girl. She lacks depth and reverence and has no sense of what is fitting. Hats, for example.'

'Exactly. But what do you mean Diana Punter is an exception? She's one of the ringleaders – the spearhead of the movement, if you like to put it that way. Think,' said Nelson, sipping his vermouth, 'of all the unpleasant qualities of the Modern Girl, add them up, double them, and what have you got? Diana Punter. Let me tell you what took place between me and this Punter only a few minutes ago.'

'No,' said Percy. 'Let me tell you what transpired between me and Elizabeth Bottsworth this morning. Nelson, old man, she said my hat – my Bodmin hat – was too small.'

'You don't mean that?'

'Those were her very words.'

'Well, I'm dashed. Listen. Diana Punter told me my equally Bodmin hat was too large.'

They stared at one another.

'It's the Spirit of something,' said Nelson. 'I don't know what, quite, but of something. You see it on all sides. Something very serious has gone wrong with girls nowadays. There is lawlessness and licence abroad.'

'And here in England, too.'

'Well, naturally, you silly ass,' said Nelson, with some asperity. 'When I said abroad, I didn't mean abroad, I meant abroad.'

He mused for a moment.

'I must say, though,' he continued, 'I am surprised at what you tell me about Elizabeth Bottsworth, and am inclined to think there must have been some mistake. I have always been a warm admirer of Elizabeth.'

'And I have always thought Diana one of the best, and I find it hard to believe that she should have shown up in such a dubious light as you suggest. Probably there was a misunderstanding of some kind.'

'Well, I ticked her off properly, anyway.'

Percy Wimbolt shook his head.

'You shouldn't have done that, Nelson. You may have wounded her feelings. In my case, of course, I had no alternative but to be pretty crisp with Elizabeth.'

Nelson Cork clicked his tongue.

'A pity,' he said. 'Elizabeth is sensitive.'

'So is Diana.'

'Not so sensitive as Elizabeth.'

'I should say, at a venture, about five times as sensitive as Elizabeth. However, we must not quarrel about a point like that, old man. The fact that emerges is that we seem both to have been dashed badly treated. I think I shall toddle home and take an aspirin.'

'Me, too.'

They went off to the cloak-room, where their hats were, and Percy put his on.

'Surely,' he said, 'nobody but a half-witted little pipsqueak who can't see straight would say this was too small?'

'It isn't a bit too small,' said Nelson. 'And take a look at this one. Am I not right in supposing that only a female giantess with straws in her hair and astigmatism in both eyes could say it was too large?'

'It's a lovely fit.'

And the cloak-room waiter, a knowledgeable chap of the name of Robinson, said the same.

'So there you are,' said Nelson.

'Ah, well,' said Percy.

They left the club, and parted at the top of Dover Street.

Now, though he had not said so in so many words, Nelson Cork's heart had bled for Percy Wimbolt. He knew the other's fine sensibilities and he could guess how deeply they must have been gashed by this unfortunate breaking-off of diplomatic relations with the girl he loved. For, whatever might have happened, however sorely he might have been wounded, the way Nelson Cork looked at it was that Percy loved Elizabeth Bottsworth in spite of everything. What was required here, felt Nelson, was a tactful mediator – a kindly, sensible friend of both parties who would hitch up his socks and plunge in and heal the breach.

So the moment he had got rid of Percy outside the club he hared round to the house where Elizabeth was staying and was lucky enough to catch her on the front door steps. For, naturally, Elizabeth hadn't gone off to Ascot by herself. Directly Percy was out of sight, she had told the taxi-man to drive her home, and she had been occupying the interval since the painful scene in thinking of things she wished she had said to him and taking her hostess's dog for a run – a Pekingese called Clarkson.

She seemed very pleased to see Nelson, and started to prattle of this and that, her whole demeanour that of a girl who, after having been compelled to associate for a while with the Under-world, has at last found a kindred soul. And the more he listened, the more he wanted to go on listening. And the more he looked at her, the more he felt that a lifetime spent in gazing at Elizabeth Bottsworth would be a lifetime dashed well spent.

There was something about the girl's exquisite petiteness and fragility that appealed to Nelson Cork's depths. After having wasted so much time looking at a female Carnera like Diana Punter, it was a genuine treat to him to be privileged to feast the eyes on one so small and dainty. And, what with one thing and another, he found the most extraordinary difficulty in lugging Percy into the conversation.

They strolled along, chatting. And, mark you, Elizabeth Bottsworth was a girl a fellow could chat with without getting a crick in the neck from goggling up at her, the way you had to do when you took the air with Diana Punter. Nelson realized now that talking to Diana Punter had been like trying to exchange thoughts with a flag-pole sitter. He was surprised that this had never occurred to him before.

'You know, you're looking perfectly ripping, Elizabeth,' he said.

'How funny!' said the girl. 'I was just going to say the same thing about you.'

'Not really?'

'Yes, I was. After some of the gargoyles I've seen today – Percy Wimbolt is an example that springs to the mind – it's such a relief to be with a man who really knows how to turn himself out.'

Now that the Percy *motif* had been introduced, it should have been a simple task for Nelson to turn the talk to the subject of his absent friend. But somehow he didn't. Instead, he just simpered a bit and said: 'Oh no, I say, really, do you mean that?'

'I do, indeed,' said Elizabeth earnestly. 'It's your hat, principally, I think. I don't know why it is, but ever since a child I have been intensely sensitive to hats, and it has always been a pleasure to me to remember that at the age of five I dropped a pot of jam out of the nursery window on to my Uncle Alexander when he came to visit us in a deer-stalker cap with ear-flaps, as worn by Sherlock Holmes. I consider the hat the final test of a man. Now, yours is perfect. I never saw such a beautiful fit. I can't tell you how much I admire that hat. It gives you quite an ambassadorial look.'

Nelson Cork drew a deep breath. He was tingling from head to foot. It was as if the scales had fallen from his eyes and a new life begun for him.

'I say,' he said, trembling with emotion, 'I wonder if you would mind if I pressed your little hand?'

'Do,' said Elizabeth cordially.

'I will,' said Nelson, and did so. 'And now,' he went on, clinging to the fin like glue and hiccoughing a bit, 'how about buzzing off somewhere for a quiet cup of tea? I have a feeling that we have much to say to one another.'

It is odd how often it happens in this world that when there are two chaps and one chap's heart is bleeding for the other chap you find that all the while the second chap's heart is bleeding just as much for the first chap. Both bleeding, I mean to say, not only one. It was so in the case of Nelson Cork and Percy Wimbolt. The moment he had left Nelson, Percy charged straight off in search of Diana Punter with the intention of putting everything right with a few well-chosen words.

Because what he felt was that, though at the actual moment of going to press pique might be putting Nelson off Diana, this would pass off and love come into its own again. All that was required, he considered, was a suave go-between, a genial mutual pal who would pour oil on the troubled w.'s and generally fix things up.

He found Diana walking round and round Berkeley Square with her chin up, breathing tensely through the nostrils. He drew up alongside and what-hoed, and as she beheld him the cold, hard gleam in her eyes changed to a light of cordiality. She appeared charmed to see him and at once embarked on an animated conversation. And with every word she spoke his conviction deepened that of all the ways of passing a summer afternoon there was none fruitier than having a friendly hike with Diana Punter.

And it was not only her talk that enchanted him. He was equally fascinated by that wonderful physique of hers. When he considered that he had actually wasted several valuable minutes that day conversing with a young shrimp like Elizabeth Bottsworth, he could have kicked himself.

Here, he reflected, as they walked round the square, was a girl whose ear was more or less on a level with a fellow's mouth, so that such observations as he might make were enabled to get from point to point with the least possible delay. Talking to Elizabeth Bottsworth had always been like bellowing down a well in the hope of attracting the attention of one of the smaller infusoria at the bottom. It surprised him that he had been so long in coming to this conclusion.

He was awakened from this reverie by hearing his companion utter the name of Nelson Cork.

'I beg your pardon?' he said.

'I was saying,' said Diana, 'that Nelson Cork is a wretched little undersized blob who, if he were not too lazy to work, would long since have signed up with some good troupe of midgets.'

'Oh, would you say that?'

'I would say more than that,' said Diana firmly. 'I tell you, Percy, that what makes life so ghastly for girls, what causes girls to get grey hair and go into convents, is the fact that it is not always possible for them to avoid being seen in public with men like Nelson Cork. I trust I am not uncharitable. I try to view these things in a broad-minded way, saying to myself that if a man looks like something that has come out from under a flat stone it is his misfortune rather than his fault and that he is more to be pitied than censured. But on one thing I do insist, that such a man does not wantonly aggravate the natural unpleasantness of his appearance by prancing about London in a hat that reaches down to his ankles. I cannot and will not endure being escorted along Bruton Street by a sort of human bacillus the brim of whose hat bumps on the pavement with every step he takes. What I have always said and what I shall always say is that the hat is the acid test. A man who cannot buy the right-sized hat is a man one could never like or trust. Your hat, now, Percy, is exactly right. I have seen a good many hats in my time, but I really do not think that I have ever come across a more perfect specimen of all that a hat should be. Not too large, not too small, fitting snugly to the head like the skin on a sausage. And you have just the kind of head that a silk hat shows off. It gives you a sort of look ... how shall I describe it? ... it conveys the idea of a master of men. Leonine is the word I want. There is something about the way it rests on the brow and the almost imperceptible tilt towards the south-east ...'

Percy Wimbolt was quivering like an Oriental muscle-dancer. Soft music seemed to be playing from the direction of

Hay Hill, and Berkeley Square had begun to skip round him on one foot.

He drew a deep breath.

'I say,' he said, 'stop me if you've heard this before, but what I feel we ought to do at this juncture is to dash off somewhere where it's quiet and there aren't so many houses dancing the "Blue Danube" and shove some tea into ourselves. And over the pot and muffins I shall have something very important to say to you.'

'So that,' concluded the Crumpet, taking a grape, 'is how the thing stands; and, in a sense, of course, you could say that it is a satisfactory ending.

'The announcement of Elizabeth's engagement to Nelson Cork appeared in the Press on the same day as that of Diana's projected hitching-up with Percy Wimbolt: and it is pleasant that the happy couples should be so well matched as regards size.

'I mean to say, there will be none of that business of a six-foot girl tripping down the aisle with a five-foot-four man, or a six-foot-two man trying to keep step along the sacred edifice with a four-foot-three girl. This is always good for a laugh from the ringside pews, but it does not make for wedded bliss.

'No, as far as the principals are concerned, we may say that all has ended well. But that doesn't seem to me the important point. What seems to me the important point is this extraordinary, baffling mystery of those hats.'

'Absolutely,' said the Bean.

'I mean to say, if Percy's hat really didn't fit, as Elizabeth Bottsworth contended, why should it have registered as a winner with Diana Punter?'

'Absolutely,' said the Bean.

'And, conversely, if Nelson's hat was the total loss which Diana Punter considered it, why, only a brief while later, was it going like a breeze with Elizabeth Bottsworth?'

'Absolutely,' said the Bean.

'The whole thing is utterly inscrutable.'

It was at this point that the nurse gave signs of wishing to catch the Speaker's eye.

'Shall I tell you what I think?'

'Say on, my dear young pillow-smoother.'

'I believe Bodmin's boy must have got those hats mixed. When he was putting them back in the boxes, I mean.'

The Crumpet shook his head, and took a grape.

'And then at the club they got the right ones again.'

The Crumpet smiled indulgently.

'Ingenious,' he said, taking a grape. 'Quite ingenious. But a little far-fetched. No, I prefer to think the whole thing, as I say, has something to do with the Fourth Dimension. I am convinced that that is the true explanation, if our minds could only grasp it.'

'Absolutely,' said the Bean.

As the club kitten sauntered into the smoking-room of the Drones Club and greeted those present with a friendly miauw, Freddie Widgeon, who had been sitting in a corner with his head between his hands, rose stiffly.

'I had supposed,' he said, in a cold, level voice, 'that this was a quiet retreat for gentlemen. As I perceive that it is a blasted Zoo, I will withdraw.'

And he left the room in a marked manner.

There was a good deal of surprise, mixed with consternation.

'What's the trouble?' asked an Egg, concerned. Such exhibitions of the naked emotions are rare at the Drones. 'Have they had a row?'

A Crumpet, always well-informed, shook his head.

'Freddie has had no personal breach with this particular kitten,' he said. 'It is simply that since that week-end at Matcham Scratchings he can't stand the sight of a cat.'

'Matcham what?'

'Scratchings. The ancestral home of Dahlia Prenderby in Oxfordshire.'

'I met Dahlia Prenderby once,' said the Egg. 'I thought she seemed a nice girl.'

'Freddie thought so, too. He loved her madly.'

'And lost her, of course?'

'Absolutely.'

'Do you know,' said a thoughtful Bean, 'I'll bet that if all the girls Freddie Widgeon has loved and lost were placed end to end – not that I suppose one could do it – they would reach half-way down Piccadilly.'

'Further than that,' said the Egg. 'Some of them were pretty tall. What beats me is why he ever bothers to love them. They always turn him down in the end. He might just as well never begin. Better, in fact, because in the time saved he could be reading some good book.'

'I think the trouble with Freddie,' said the Crumpet, 'is that he always gets off to a flying start. He's a good-looking sort of chap who dances well and can wiggle his ears, and the girl is dazzled for the moment, and this encourages him. From what he tells me, he appears to have gone very big with this Prenderby girl at the outset. So much so, indeed, that when she invited him down to Matcham Scratchings he had already bought his copy of *What Every Young Bridegroom Ought To Know*.'

'Rummy, these old country-house names,' mused the Bean. 'Why Scratchings, I wonder?'

'Freddie wondered, too, till he got to the place. Then he tells me he felt it was absolutely the *mot juste*. This girl Dahlia's family, you see, was one of those animal-loving families, and the house, he tells me, was just a frothing maelstrom of dumb chums. As far as the eye could reach, there were dogs scratching themselves and cats scratching the furniture. I believe, though he never met it socially, there was even a tame chimpanzee somewhere on the premises, no doubt scratching away as assiduously as the rest of them. You get these conditions here and there in the depths of the country, and this Matcham place was well away from the centre of things, being about six miles from the nearest station.

'It was at this station that Dahlia Prenderby met Freddie in her two-seater, and on the way to the house there occurred a conversation which I consider significant – showing, as it does, the cordial relations existing between the young couple at that point in the proceedings. I mean, it was only later that the bitter awakening and all that sort of thing popped up.'

'I do want you to be a success, Freddie,' said the girl, after talking a while of this and that. 'Some of the men I've asked down here have been such awful flops. The great thing is to make a good impression on Father.'

'I will,' said Freddie.

'He can be a little difficult at times.'

'Lead me to him,' said Freddie. 'That's all I ask. Lead me to him.'

'The trouble is, he doesn't much like young men.'

'He'll like me.'

'He will, will he?'

'Rather!'

'What makes you think that?'

'I'm a dashed fascinating chap.'

'Oh, you are?'

'Yes, I am.'

'You are, are you?'

'Rather!'

Upon which, she gave him a sort of push and he gave her a sort of push, and she giggled and he laughed like a paper bag bursting, and she gave him a kind of shove and he gave her a kind of shove, and she said, 'You *are* a silly ass!' and he said, 'What ho!'

All of which shows you, I mean to say, the stage they had got to by this time. Nothing definitely settled, of course, but Love obviously beginning to burgeon in the girl's heart.

Well, naturally, Freddie gave a good deal of thought during the drive to this father of whom the girl had spoken so feelingly, and he resolved that he would not fail her. The way he would suck up to the old dad would be nobody's business. He proposed to exert upon him the full force of his magnetic personality, and looked forward to registering a very substantial hit.

Which being so, I need scarcely tell you, knowing Freddie as you do, that his first act on entering Sir Mortimer Prenderby's orbit was to make the scaliest kind of floater, hitting him on the back of the neck with a tortoiseshell cat not ten minutes after his arrival.

His train having been a bit late, there was no time on reaching the house for any stately receptions or any of that 'Welcome to Meadowsweet Hall' stuff. The girl simply shot him up to his room and told him to dress like a streak, because dinner was in a quarter of an hour, and then buzzed off to don the soup and fish herself. And Freddie was just going well when, looking round for his shirt, which he had left on the bed, he saw a large tortoiseshell cat standing on it, kneading it with its paws.

Well, you know how a fellow feels about his shirt-front. For an instant, Freddie stood spellbound. Then with a hoarse cry he bounded forward, scooped up the animal, and, carrying it out on to the balcony, flung it into the void. And an elderly gentleman, coming round the corner at this moment, received a direct hit on the back of his neck.

'Hell!' cried the elderly gentleman.

A head popped out of a window.

'Whatever is the matter, Mortimer?'

'It's raining cats.'

'Nonsense. It's a lovely evening,' said the head, and disappeared.

Freddie thought an apology would be in order.

'I say,' he said.

The old gentleman looked in every direction of the compass, and finally located Freddie on his balcony.

'I say,' said Freddie, 'I'm awfully sorry you got that nasty buffet. It was me.'

'It was not you. It was a cat.'

'I know. I threw the cat.'

'Why?'

'Well . . .'

'Dam' fool.'

'I'm sorry,' said Freddie.

'Go to blazes,' said the old gentleman.

Freddie backed into the room, and the incident closed.

Freddie is a pretty slippy dresser, as a rule, but this episode had shaken him, and he not only lost a collar-stud but made a mess of the first two ties. The result was that the gong went while he was still in his shirt-sleeves: and on emerging from his boudoir he was informed by a footman that the gang were already nuzzling their *bouillon* in the dining-room. He pushed straight on there, accordingly, and sank into a chair beside his hostess just in time to dead-heat with the final spoonful.

Awkward, of course, but he was feeling in pretty good form owing to the pleasantness of the thought that he was shoving his knees under the same board as the girl Dahlia: so, having nodded to his host, who was glaring at him from the head of the table, as much as to say that all would be explained in God's good time, he shot his cuffs and started to make sparkling conversation to Lady Prenderby.

'Charming place you have here, what?'

Lady Prenderby said that the local scenery was generally admired. She was one of those tall, rangy, Queen Elizabeth sort of women, with tight lips and cold, blanc-mange-y eyes. Freddie didn't like her looks much, but he was feeling, as I say, fairly fizzy, so he carried on with a bright zip.

'Pretty good hunting country, I should think?'

'I believe there is a good deal of hunting near here, yes.'

'I thought as much,' said Freddie. 'Ah, that's the stuff, is it not? A cracking gallop across good country with a jolly fine kill at the end of it, what, what? Hark for'ard, yoicks, tally-ho, I mean to say, and all that sort of thing.'

Lady Prenderby shivered austerely.

'I fear I cannot share your enthusiasm,' she said. 'I have the strongest possible objection to hunting. I have always set my face against it, as against all similar brutalizing blood-sports.'

This was a nasty jar for poor old Freddie, who had been relying on the topic to carry him nicely through at least a couple of courses. It silenced him for the nonce. And as he paused to collect his faculties, his host, who had now been glowering for six and a half minutes practically without cessation, put a hand in front of his mouth and addressed the girl Dahlia across the table. Freddie thinks he was under the impression that he was speaking in a guarded whisper, but, as a matter of fact, the words boomed through the air as if he had been a costermonger calling attention to his Brussels sprouts.

'Dahlia!'

'Yes, Father?'

'Who's that ugly feller?'

'Hush!'

'What do you mean, hush? Who is he?'

'Mr Widgeon.'

'Mr Who?'

'Widgeon.'

'I wish you would articulate clearly and not mumble,' said Sir Mortimer fretfully. 'It sounds to me just like "Widgeon". Who asked him here?'

'I did.'

'Why?'

'He's a friend of mine.'

'Well, he looks a pretty frightful young slab of damnation to me. What I'd call a criminal face.'

'Hush!'

'Why do you keep saying "Hush"? Must be a lunatic, too. Throws cats at people.'

'Please, Father!'

'Don't say "Please, Father!" No sense in it. I tell you he does throw cats at people. He threw one at me. Half-witted, I'd call him – if that. Besides being the most offensive-looking young toad I've ever seen on the premises. How long's he staying?'

'Till Monday.'

'My God! And today's only Friday!' bellowed Sir Mortimer Prenderby.

It was an unpleasant situation for Freddie, of course, and I'm bound to admit he didn't carry it off particularly well. What he ought to have done, obviously, was to have plunged into an easy flow of small-talk: but all he could think of was to ask Lady Prenderby if she was fond of shooting. Lady Prenderby having replied that, owing to being deficient in the savage instincts and wanton blood-lust that went to make up a callous and cold-hearted murderess, she was not, he relapsed into silence with his lower jaw hanging down.

All in all, he wasn't so dashed sorry when dinner came to an end.

As he and Sir Mortimer were the only men at the table, most of the seats having been filled by a covey of mildewed females whom he had classified under the general heading of Aunts, it seemed to Freddie that the moment had now arrived when they would be able to get together once more, under happier conditions than those of their last meeting, and start to learn to appreciate one another's true worth. He looked forward to a cosy *tête-à-tête* over the port, in the course of which he would smooth over that cat incident and generally do all that lay within his power to revise the unfavourable opinion of him which the other must have formed.

But apparently Sir Mortimer had his own idea of the duties and obligations of a host. Instead of clustering round Freddie with decanters, he simply gave him a long, lingering look of distaste and shot out of the french window into the garden. A moment later, his head reappeared and he uttered the words: 'You and your dam' cats!' Then the night swallowed him again.

Freddie was a good deal perplexed. All this was new stuff to him. He had been in and out of a number of country-houses in his time, but this was the first occasion on which he had ever been left flat at the conclusion of the evening meal, and he wasn't quite sure how to handle the situation. He was still wondering, when Sir Mortimer's head came into view again and its owner, after giving him another of those long, lingering looks, said: 'Cats, forsooth!' and disappeared once more.

Freddie was now definitely piqued. It was all very well, he felt,

Dahlia Prenderby telling him to make himself solid with her father, but how can you make yourself solid with a fellow who doesn't stay put for a couple of consecutive seconds? If it was Sir Mortimer's intention to spend the remainder of the night flashing past like a merry-go-round, there seemed little hope of anything amounting to a genuine *rapprochement*. It was a relief to his feelings when there suddenly appeared from nowhere his old acquaintance the tortoiseshell cat. It seemed to offer to him a means of working off his spleen.

Taking from Lady Prenderby's plate, accordingly, the remains of a banana, he plugged the animal at a range of two yards. It yowled and withdrew. And a moment later, there was Sir Mortimer again.

'Did you kick that cat?' said Sir Mortimer.

Freddie had half a mind to ask this old disease if he thought he was a man or a jack-in-the-box, but the breeding of the Widgeons restrained him.

'No,' he said, 'I did not kick that cat.'

'You must have done something to it to make it come charging out at forty miles an hour.'

'I merely offered the animal a piece of fruit.'

'Do it again and see what happens to you.'

'Lovely evening,' said Freddie, changing the subject.

'No, it's not, you silly ass,' said Sir Mortimer. Freddie rose. His nerve, I fancy, was a little shaken.

'I shall join the ladies,' he said, with dignity.

'God help them!' replied Sir Mortimer Prenderby in a voice instinct with the deepest feeling, and vanished once more.

Freddie's mood, as he made for the drawing-room, was thoughtful. I don't say he has much sense, but he's got enough to know when he is and when he isn't going with a bang.

Tonight, he realized, he had been very far from going in such a manner. It was not, that is to say, as the Idol of Matcham Scratchings that he would enter the drawing-room, but rather as a young fellow who had made an unfortunate first impression and would have to do a lot of heavy ingratiating before he could regard himself as really popular in the home.

He must bustle about, he felt, and make up leeway. And, knowing that what counts with these old-style females who have lived in the country all their lives is the exhibition of those little politenesses and attentions which were all the go in Queen Victoria's time, his first action, on entering, was to make a dive for one of the aunts who seemed to be trying to find a place to put her coffee-cup.

'Permit me,' said Freddie, suave to the eyebrows.

And bounding forward with the feeling that this was the stuff to give them, he barged right into a cat.

'Oh, sorry,' he said, backing and bringing down his heel on another cat.

'I say, most frightfully sorry,' he said.

And, tottering to a chair, he sank heavily on to a third cat.

Well, he was up and about again in a jiffy, of course, but it was too late. There was the usual not-at-all-ing and don't-mention-it-ing, but he could read between the lines. Lady Prenderby's eyes had rested on his for only a brief instant, but it had been enough. His standing with her, he perceived, was now approximately what King Herod's would have been at an Israelite Mothers Social Saturday Afternoon.

The girl Dahlia during these exchanges had been sitting on a sofa at the end of the room, turning the pages of a weekly paper, and the sight of her drew Freddie like a magnet. Her womanly sympathy was just what he felt he could do with at this juncture.

Treading with infinite caution, he crossed to where she sat: and, having scanned the terrain narrowly for cats, sank down on the sofa at her side. And conceive his agony of spirit when he discovered that womanly sympathy had been turned off at the main. The girl was like a chunk of ice-cream with spikes all over it.

'Please do not trouble to explain,' she said coldly, in answer to his opening words. 'I quite understand that there are people who have this odd dislike of animals.'

'But, dash it . . .' cried Freddie, waving his arm in a frenzied sort of way. 'Oh, I say, sorry,' he added, as his fist sloshed another of the menagerie in the short ribs.

Dahlia caught the animal as it flew through the air.

'I think perhaps you had better take Augustus, Mother,' she said. 'He seems to be annoying Mr Widgeon.'

'Quite,' said Lady Prenderby. 'He will be safer with me.'

'But, dash it . . .' bleated Freddie.

Dahlia Prenderby drew in her breath sharply.

'How true it is,' she said, 'that one never really knows a man till after one has seen him in one's own home.'

'What do you mean by that?'

'Oh, nothing,' said Dahlia Prenderby.

She rose and moved to the piano, where she proceeded to sing old Breton folk-songs in a distant manner, leaving Freddie to make out as best he could with a family album containing faded photographs with 'Aunt Emily bathing at Llandudno, 1893', and 'This is Cousin George at the fancy-dress ball' written under them.

And so the long, quiet, peaceful home evening wore on, till eventually Lady Prenderby mercifully blew the whistle and he was at liberty to sneak off to his bedroom.

*

You might have supposed that Freddie's thoughts, as he toddled upstairs with his candle, would have dwelt exclusively on the girl Dahlia. This, however, was not so. He did give her obvious shirtiness a certain measure of attention, of course, but what really filled his mind was the soothing reflection that at long last his path and that of the animal kingdom of Matcham Scratchings had now divided. He, so to speak, was taking the high road while they, as it were, would take the low road. For whatever might be the conditions prevailing in the dining-room, the drawing-room, and the rest of the house, his bedroom, he felt, must surely be a haven totally free from cats of all descriptions.

Remembering, however, that unfortunate episode before dinner, he went down on all fours and subjected the various nooks and crannies to a close examination. His eye could detect no cats. Relieved, he rose to his feet with a gay song on his lips: and he hadn't got much beyond the first couple of bars when a voice behind him suddenly started taking the bass: and, turning, he perceived on the bed a fine Alsatian dog.

Freddie looked at the dog. The dog looked at Freddie. The situation was one fraught with embarrassment. A glance at the animal was enough to convince him that it had got an entirely wrong angle on the position of affairs and was regarding him purely in the light of an intrusive stranger who had muscled in on its private sleeping quarters. Its manner was plainly resentful. It fixed Freddie with a cold, yellow eye and curled its upper lip slightly, the better to display a long, white tooth. It also twitched its nose and gave a *sotto-voce* imitation of distant thunder.

Freddie did not know quite what avenue to explore. It was impossible to climb between the sheets with a thing like that on the counterpane. To spend the night in a chair, on the other hand, would have been foreign to his policy. He did what I consider the most statesmanlike thing by sidling out on to the balcony and squinting along the wall of the house to see if there wasn't a lighted window hard by, behind which might lurk somebody who would rally round with aid and comfort.

There was a lighted window only a short distance away, so he shoved his head out as far as it would stretch and said:

'I say!'

There being no response, he repeated:

'I say!'

And, finally, to drive his point home, he added:

'I say! I say! I say!'

This time he got results. The head of Lady Prenderby suddenly protruded from the window.

'Who,' she enquired, 'is making that abominable noise?'

It was not precisely the attitude Freddie had hoped for, but he could take the rough with the smooth.

'It's me. Widgeon, Frederick.'

'Must you sing on your balcony, Mr Widgeon?'

'I wasn't singing. I was saying "I say".'

'What were you saying?'

'"I say".'

'You say what?'

'I say I was saying "I say". Kind of a heart-cry, if you know what I mean. The fact is, there's a dog in my room.'

'What sort of dog?'

'A whacking great Alsatian.'

'Ah, that would be Wilhelm. Good night, Mr Widgeon.'

The window closed. Freddie let out a heart-stricken yip.

'But I say!'

The window reopened. 'Really, Mr Widgeon!'

'But what am I to do?'

'Do?'

'About this whacking great Alsatian!'

Lady Prenderby seemed to consider.

'No sweet biscuits,' she said. 'And when the maid brings you your tea in the morning please do not give him sugar. Simply a little milk in the saucer. He is on a diet. Good night, Mr Widgeon.'

Freddie was now pretty well nonplussed. No matter what his hostess might say about this beastly dog being on a diet, he was convinced from its manner that its medical adviser had not forbidden it Widgeons, and once more he bent his brain to the task of ascertaining what to do next.

There were several possible methods of procedure. His balcony being not so very far from the ground, he could, if he pleased, jump down and pass a health-giving night in the nasturtium bed. Or he might curl up on the floor. Or he might get out of the room and doss downstairs somewhere.

This last scheme seemed about the best. The only obstacle in the way of its fulfilment was the fact that, when he started for the door, his room-mate would probably think he was a burglar about to loot silver of lonely country-house and pin him. Still, it had to be risked, and a moment later he might have been observed tiptoeing across the carpet, with all the caution of a slack-wire artist who isn't any too sure he remembers the correct steps.

Well, it was a near thing. At the instant when he started, the dog seemed occupied with something that looked like a cushion on the bed. It was licking this object in a thoughtful way, and paid no attention to Freddie till he was half-way across No

Man's Land. Then it suddenly did a sort of sitting high-jump in his direction, and two seconds later Freddie, with a draughty feeling about the seat of his trouserings, was on top of a wardrobe, with the dog underneath looking up. He tells me that if he ever moved quicker in his life it was only on the occasion when, a lad of fourteen, he was discovered by his uncle, Lord Blicester, smoking one of the latter's cigars in the library: and he rather thinks he must have clipped at least a fifth of a second off the record then set up.

It looked to him now as if his sleeping arrangements for the night had been settled for him. And the thought of having to roost on top of a wardrobe at the whim of a dog was pretty dashed offensive to his proud spirit, as you may well imagine. However, as you cannot reason with Alsatians, it seemed the only thing to be done: and he was trying to make himself as comfortable as a sharp piece of wood sticking into the fleshy part of his leg would permit, when there was a snuffling noise in the passage and through the door came an object which in the dim light he was at first not able to identify. It looked something like a pen-wiper and something like a piece of a hearth-rug. A second and keener inspection revealed it as a Pekingese puppy.

The uncertainty which Freddie had felt as to the newcomer's status was shared, it appeared, by the Alsatian: for after raising its eyebrows in a puzzled manner it rose and advanced enquiringly. In a tentative way it put out a paw and rolled the intruder over. Then, advancing again, it lowered its nose and sniffed.

It was a course of action against which its best friends would have advised it. These Pekes are tough eggs, especially when, as in this case, female. They look the world in the eye, and are swift to resent familiarity. There was a sort of explosion, and the next moment the Alsatian was shooting out of the room with its tail between its legs, hotly pursued. Freddie could hear the noise of battle rolling away along the passage, and it was music to his ears. Something on these lines was precisely what that Alsatian had been asking for, and now it had got it.

Presently, the Peke returned, dashing the beads of perspiration from its forehead, and came and sat down under the wardrobe, wagging a stumpy tail. And Freddie, feeling that the All Clear had been blown and that he was now at liberty to descend, did so.

His first move was to shut the door, his second to fraternize with his preserver. Freddie is a chap who believes in giving credit where credit is due, and it seemed to him that this Peke had shown itself an ornament of its species. He spared no effort, accordingly, to entertain it. He lay down on the floor and let it lick his face two hundred and thirty-three times. He tickled it under the left ear, the right ear, and at the base of the tail, in the order named. He also scratched its stomach.

All these attentions the animal received with cordiality and marked gratification: and as it seemed still in pleasure-seeking mood and had come to look upon him as the official Master of the Revels, Freddie, feeling that he could not disappoint it but must play the host no matter what the cost to himself, took off his tie and handed it over. He would not have done it for everybody, he says, but where this life-saving Peke was concerned the sky was the limit.

Well, the tie went like a breeze. It was a success from the start. The Peke chewed it and chased it and got entangled in it and dragged it about the room, and was just starting to shake it from side to side when an unfortunate thing happened. Misjudging its distance, it banged its head a nasty wallop against the leg of the bed.

There is nothing of the Red Indian at the stake about a puppy in circumstances like this. A moment later, Freddie's blood was chilled by a series of fearful shrieks that seemed to ring through the night like the dying cries of the party of the second part to a first-class murder. It amazed him that a mere Peke, and a juvenile Peke at that, should have been capable of producing such an uproar. He says that a Baronet, stabbed in the back with a paper-knife in his library, could not have made half such a row.

Eventually, the agony seemed to abate. Quite suddenly, as if nothing had happened, the Peke stopped yelling and with an amused smile started to play with the tie again. And at the same moment there was a sound of whispering outside, and then a knock at the door.

'Hullo?' said Freddie.

'It is I, sir. Biggleswade.'

'Who's Biggleswade?'

'The butler, sir.'

'What do you want?'

'Her ladyship wishes me to remove the dog which you are torturing.'

There was more whispering.

'Her ladyship also desires me to say that she will be reporting the affair in the morning to the Society for the Prevention of Cruelty to Animals.'

There was another spot of whispering.

'Her ladyship further instructs me to add that, should you prove recalcitrant, I am to strike you over the head with the poker.'

Well, you can't say this was pleasant for poor old Freddie, and he didn't think so himself. He opened the door, to perceive, without, a group consisting of Lady Prenderby, her daughter

Dahlia, a few assorted aunts, and the butler, with poker. And he says he met Dahlia's eyes and they went through him like a knife.

'Let me explain...' he began.

'Spare us the details,' said Lady Prenderby with a shiver. She scooped up the Peke and felt it for broken bones.

'But listen...'

'Good night, Mr Widgeon.'

The aunts said good night, too, and so did the butler. The girl Dahlia preserved a revolted silence.

'But, honestly, it was nothing, really. It banged its head against the bed...'

'What did he say?' asked one of the aunts, who was a little hard of hearing.

'He says he banged the poor creature's head against the bed,' said Lady Prenderby.

'Dreadful!' said the aunt.

'Hideous!' said a second aunt.

A third aunt opened up another line of thought. She said that with men like Freddie in the house, was anyone safe? She mooted the possibility of them all being murdered in their beds. And though Freddie offered to give her a written guarantee that he hadn't the slightest intention of going anywhere near her bed, the idea seemed to make a deep impression.

'Biggleswade,' said Lady Prenderby.

'M'lady?'

'You will remain in this passage for the remainder of the night with your poker.'

'Very good, m'lady.'

'Should this man attempt to leave his room, you will strike him smartly over the head.'

'Just so, m'lady.'

'But, listen . . .' said Freddie.

'Good night, Mr Widgeon.'

The mob scene broke up. Soon the passage was empty save for Biggleswade the butler, who had begun to pace up and down, halting every now and then to flick the air with his poker as if testing the lissomness of his wrist-muscles and satisfying himself that they were in a condition to ensure the right amount of follow-through.

The spectacle he presented was so unpleasant that Freddie withdrew into his room and shut the door. His bosom, as you may imagine, was surging with distressing emotions. That look which Dahlia Prenderby had given him had churned him up to no little extent. He realized that he had a lot of tense thinking to do, and to assist thought he sat down on the bed.

Or, rather, to be accurate, on the dead cat which was lying on the bed. It was this cat which the Alsatian had been licking just before the final breach in his relations with Freddie – the object, if you remember, which the latter had supposed to be a cushion.

He leaped up as if the corpse, instead of being cold, had been piping hot. He stared down, hoping against hope that the animal was merely in some sort of coma. But a glance told him that it had made the great change. He had never seen a deader cat. After life's fitful fever it slept well.

You wouldn't be far out in saying that poor old Freddie was now appalled. Already his reputation in this house was at zero, his name mud. On all sides he was looked upon as Widgeon the Amateur Vivisectionist. This final disaster could not but put the tin hat on it. Before, he had had a faint hope that in the morning, when calmer moods would prevail, he might be able to explain that matter of the Peke. But who was going to listen to him if he were discovered with a dead cat on his person?

And then the thought came to him that it might be possible not to be discovered with it on his person. He had only to nip downstairs and deposit the remains in the drawing-room or somewhere and suspicion might not fall upon him. After all, in a super-catted house like this, cats must always be dying like flies all over the place. A housemaid would find the animal in the morning and report to G.H.Q. that the cat-strength of the establishment had been reduced by one, and there would be a bit of tut-tutting and perhaps a silent tear or two, and then the thing would be forgotten.

The thought gave him new life. All briskness and efficiency, he picked up the body by the tail and was just about to dash out of the room when, with a silent groan, he remembered Biggleswade.

He peeped out. It might be that the butler, once the eye of authority had been removed, had departed to get the remainder of his beauty-sleep. But no. Service and Fidelity were evidently the watchwords at Matcham Scratchings. There the fellow was, still practising half-arm shots with the poker. Freddie closed the door.

And, as he did so, he suddenly thought of the window. There lay the solution. Here he had been, fooling about with doors and thinking in terms of drawing-rooms, and all the while there was the balcony staring him in the face. All he had to do was to shoot the body out into the silent night, and let gardeners, not house-maids, discover it.

He hurried out. It was a moment for swift action. He raised his burden. He swung it to and fro, working up steam. Then he let it go, and from the dark garden there came suddenly the cry of a strong man in his anger.

'Who threw that cat?'

It was the voice of his host, Sir Mortimer Prenderby.

'Show me the man who threw that cat!' he thundered.

Windows flew up. Heads came out. Freddie sank to the floor of the balcony and rolled against the wall.

'Whatever is the matter, Mortimer?'

'Let me get at the man who hit me in the eye with a cat.'

'A cat?' Lady Prenderby's voice sounded perplexed. 'Are you sure?'

'Sure? What do you mean sure? Of course I'm sure. I was just dropping off to sleep in my hammock, when suddenly a great beastly cat came whizzing through the air and caught me properly in the eyeball. It's a nice thing. A man can't sleep in hammocks in his own garden without people pelting him with cats. I insist on the blood of the man who threw that cat.'

'Where did it come from?'

'Must have come from that balcony there.'

'Mr Widgeon's balcony,' said Lady Prenderby in an acid voice. 'As I might have guessed.'

Sir Mortimer uttered a cry.

'So might I have guessed! Widgeon, of course! That ugly feller. He's been throwing cats all the evening. I've got a nasty sore place on the back of my neck where he hit me with one before dinner. Somebody come and open the front door. I want my heavy cane, the one with the carved ivory handle. Or a horsewhip will do.'

'Wait, Mortimer,' said Lady Prenderby. 'Do nothing rash. The man is evidently a very dangerous lunatic. I will send Biggleswade to overpower him. He has the kitchen poker.'

Little (said the Crumpet) remains to be told. At two-fifteen that morning a sombre figure in dress clothes without a tie limped into the little railway station of Lower-Smattering-on-the-Wissel, some six miles from Matcham Scratchings. At three-forty-seven it departed Londonwards on the up milk-train. It was Frederick Widgeon. He had a broken heart and blisters on both heels. And in that broken heart was that loathing for all cats of which you recently saw so signal a manifestation. I am revealing no secrets when I tell you that Freddie Widgeon is permanently through with cats. From now on, they cross his path at their peril.

T H E bar of the Drones Club was packed to bursting point. The word had gone round that Pongo Twistleton was standing free drinks, and a man who does that at the Drones can always rely on a full house and the sympathy of the audience. Eggs jostled Crumpets, Crumpets elbowed Beans, and the air was vibrant with the agonized cries of strong men who see their cocktails in danger of being upset.

A couple of Eggs, their thirst slaked, detached themselves from the crowd and made for the deserted smoking-room. They were both morning-coated, spatted and gardeniaed, for like most of those present they had just come from the Stiffham-Spettisbury wedding reception.

For a while they sat in thoughtful silence. In addition to their more recent potations, they had tucked fairly freely into the nuptial champagne provided by the bride's father, the Earl of Wivelscombe. At length the first Egg spoke.

'Oofy Prosser's as sore as a gumboil,' he said.

'Who is?' asked the second Egg, opening his eyes.

'Oofy Prosser.'

'As sore as a what?'

'A gumboil. It's his money that young Pongo is spending out there. Oofy gave him a hundred to eight that Adolphus Stiffham would never marry Geraldine Spettisbury, and Pongo collected the cash the moment the parson had said, "Wilt thou, Adolphus?" and the All Right flag had gone up.'

'And Oofy's sore about losing?'

'Naturally. He thought he had the event sewn up. At the time when he made the bet, it looked as if Stiffy hadn't an earthly. Consider the facts. Except for about a couple of hundred a year, the only money Stiffy had in the world was his salary as secretary to old Wivelscombe. And then he lost even that meagre pittance. One morning, happening to stroll into the yew alley at the ancestral seat and finding the young couple locked in a close embrace, the aged parent unlimbered his right leg and kicked Stiffy eleven feet, two inches – a record for the Midland counties. He then lugged Geraldine back to the house, shut her up in her room, handed Stiffy a cheque in lieu of a month's notice, and told him that if he was within a mile of the premises at the expiration of ten minutes dogs would be set upon him. You can't say the outlook was promising for Stiffy, and I am not surprised that Oofy regarded the bet as money for jam.'

'How did it come unstuck?'

'Nobody knows.'

'Yes, they do,' said a fresh young voice. It was a Crumpet who, unperceived, had left the throng about the human drinking-fountain and joined them in their solitude. 'I do, for one. I had it straight from Stiffy's own lips, and it has proved to me that what a fellow needs in this world is luck. Without luck, Stiffy would never have made a large fortune in New York.'

'He didn't,' said the first Egg.

'He did.'

'He couldn't have. How could Stiffy have been in New York? He once went to Le Touquet for Whitsun and was so seasick that he swore he would never set foot on a boat again. And you can't get to New York, I happen to know, without taking a boat. So your story breaks down.'

'My story jolly well does not break down,' said the Crumpet warmly, 'because Stiffy beyond question did go to New York not a week after the painful episode in the yew alley.

'It was love that nerved him to the ordeal. Geraldine got him on the phone at the club and told him that the only thing for him to do was to go to America and make his fortune, and Stiffy went. And after he had been there about a fortnight he made the acquaintance of a very decent sort of chap with eyes a bit close together and a rather rummy way of talking out of the south-west corner of his mouth, and this bird took him off to a place where a lot of similar blokes were playing a local game they have over there called craps.'

You conduct this pastime, apparently, with dice, though what you aim to do with them remained a mystery to Stiffy from start to finish. However, when one of the blokes was preparing to heave the dice and another bloke offered to bet anybody ten that he wouldn't make it, he felt the old Stiffham sporting blood stir in his veins. After all, he reasoned, ten dollars wasn't so much to lose, and a little flutter helped to pass the time and make the evening interesting. So he booked the bet – to discover a moment later that what the chap had really meant was ten thousand.

Stiffy freely confesses that this was a nasty moment. It was too late to back out now, and he watched the proceedings with a bulging eye, fully cognizant of the fact that all that stood between him and a very sticky finish was the luck of the Stiffhams.

It held, of course. Half a minute later, the chap was paying up like a gentleman, and with ten thousand dollars in his pocket Stiffy decided that this was a good thing and should be pushed along. And the upshot of the whole affair was that about an hour afterwards he found himself in the open spaces in possession of a sum amounting to around thirty thousand quid.

He was a good deal bucked, of course, and I don't blame him. There he was, you see, set up for life and in a position to return to old Wivelscombe riding on a camel laden with gold and precious stones and demand the hand of his daughter. Pretty soft it all looked to old Stiffy at this juncture.

Next day, he bunged the stuff into a bank, and at nightfall left his hotel and started out to celebrate.

Now, as I have no doubt you know, when Stiffy celebrates, he celebrates. Exactly how and where he did it on this occasion, I couldn't tell you. He is a bit vague about it himself. He seems to have collected a gang of sorts, for he can distinctly recall, he tells me, that from the very inception of the affair he did not lack for friends: and they apparently roamed hither and thither, getting matier all the time, and the next thing he remembers is waking up in the back premises of some sort of pub or hostelry with nothing on his person except a five-cent stamp, two balloons, three champagne corks, and a rattle.

This evidence of a well-spent evening pleased him a good deal. He popped the balloons, rattled the rattle for a while, and then, feeling that he had better collect a little loose cash for the day's expenses, toddled off to his bank to draw a cheque.

And conceive his emotion when, arriving there, he found that the bank had closed its doors. There they were, both of them, shut as tight as oysters. Too late, he remembered now having read in the papers that this sort of thing was happening all the time in New York.

For some minutes he stood staring, while everything seemed to go black. Then he tottered back to his hotel and sank into a chair in the lobby, to think things over.

Bim, obviously, had gone his chance of ever marrying the daughter of the haughty Earl of Wivelscombe. That project could be washed right out. And for some time he remained mourning over this fact.

It was only quite a while later that there came into his mind a sudden thought, and for the first time since this hideous disaster had occurred he felt a little better.

With his last hope of wedding Geraldine gone, he told himself, there was nothing now to prevent him writing that strong letter to her father.

For weeks and weeks, you see, Stiffy had been yearning to write an absolute stinker to old Wivelscombe, telling him exactly what he thought of him. And naturally as long as there had been any chance of the other relenting and allowing the marriage to come off such a stinker did not fall within the sphere of practical politics. But now he had nothing to lose he could go ahead and give of his best. He felt in his pocket to see if the five-cent stamp was still there. Then he raced to the writing-table and seized pen and paper.

I don't know if you have ever had dealings with Stiffy in his capacity of a writer of stinkers. I have. I was with him once when he composed a four-page effort to Oofy Prosser in reply to Oofy's communication declining to lend him a tenner. It was real, ripe stuff, without a dull line, and I was proud to call the author my friend.

Well, on this occasion, he tells me, he absolutely surpassed himself. It was as if he was inspired. Sheet after sheet he covered, each sheet filled with burning thoughts. He left no aspect of Lord Wivelscombe untouched. He stated in the most precise detail exactly what he felt about the old blighter's habits, manners, face, ties, trousers, morals, method of drinking soup, ditto of chewing moustache, and a hundred more such matters. To a single pimple on the other's nose, he tells me he devoted as much as six lines. Then, addressing the envelope, he attached the five-cent stamp and posted the letter personally in the box by the reception desk.

And, being by the reception desk and happening to note standing behind it the manager of the hotel, he thought that this was a good opportunity of putting him abreast of the position of affairs.

'I say,' said Stiffy.

'Sir?' said the manager.

'Tell me, my dear old hotel manager,' said Stiffy, 'you know that room of mine with bath?'

'I know it well,' said the manager.

'What do you get paid for it?'

'Six dollars a day.'

Stiffy broke the bad news gently.

'Not by me you don't,' he said. 'Because I haven't a penny in the world.'

'Eh?' said the manager, not looking any too chirpy.

'No,' said Stiffy. 'Not a penny. My bank's gone bust.'

'Which bank is that?'

'The Inter-State Superlative.'

The manager seemed surprised.

'It's the first I've heard of it. We bank there ourselves.'

'Meaning by "we" you and the wife and the tots?'

'Meaning this hotel.'

'I'm sorry,' said Stiffy, genuinely moved, for they had treated him with marked civility. 'But there it is. I was down there just now and the institution had closed its doors.'

'Didn't you expect it to on a Sunday?' asked the manager. Stiffy gaped.

'On a what?'

'On a Sunday.'

'Is today Sunday?'

'It is.'

'Then what became of Saturday?' asked Stiffy, amazed.

'We had it all right,' said the manager. 'Quite a nice Saturday.'

And Stiffy realized that, what with this and what with that, he must have slept right through Saturday. And he also realized – and, as he did so, he paled visibly – that he had just written the supreme stinker of all time to old Wivelscombe and that it had been posted beyond recall.

Yes, that was the position. He, Stiffy, had written him, Wivelscombe, a letter which would make him, Wivelscombe, reject him, Stiffy, as a suitor for his daughter's hand even if he, Stiffy, had all the money in the world and proposed to hand it over to him, Wivelscombe, as a personal present. Pretty rotten for him, Stiffy, you will admit.

It was a crisis that called for rapid thinking, and that was just what he gave it. For some little time he obtained no results. Then something clicked in his brain.

'Hotel manager,' he said.

'Sir?' said the manager.

'If you posted a letter to England, when would it get there?'

'Much,' said the manager, 'would depend on when you posted it.'

'I dropped it in the box just now.'

The manager consulted a list of sailings.

'It will go by the *Senator J. Freylinghusen Botts* on Tuesday.'

'So shall I,' said Stiffy.

He had seen the way out. He had been secretary to old Wivelscombe long enough to know the procedure as regarded the arrival of letters at the family seat. The postman shot them into the box at the front door, and Gascoigne, the butler, hoiked them out and placed them on the breakfast table in the morning-room, to be opened by the addressee when he or she came down to shove his or her nose in the trough.

It would be a simple task to get to the house, lurk in the shrubbery outside the morning-room and, when Gascoigne had completed his duties, to nip in through the french windows and snitch the fatal papers. It was simply a matter of buzzing over to England by the same boat on which the letter travelled.

On the Tuesday, accordingly, those assembled to give the *Senator J. Freylinghusen Botts* a send-off might have observed a young man with a set, resolute face striding up the gang-plank, and I daresay some of them did.

I don't suppose you want to hear all about Stiffy's trip across. The salient point is that he did get across. He landed at Liverpool in due season and hit London towards the evenfall, at an hour when the last train for Upton Snodsbury, which is the station for Wivelscombe Court, had left. It seemed to him that his best plan was to hire a car and put up at Worcester for the night. This he did, leaving orders that he was to be called at six sharp in the morning.

*

Well, you know what it's like when you've got anything on your mind similar to what Stiffy had on his. You sleep fitfully. You rise with dawn. It wasn't six-thirty when he started out for the Court, and it couldn't have been much more than seven when he found himself standing on the old familiar lawn. And, as there wasn't a chance of the postman blowing in before eight-fifteen at the earliest, he thought he might as well take a stroll to keep the circulation brisk.

I have never been up as early as seven myself, but Stiffy tells me it is quite a pleasant hour to be abroad. You get Nature in its pristine freshness and all that sort of thing. The dew was still on the grass, the sun was shining nicely, and there were a goodish few birds tootling away in the shrubberies. All dashed pleasant, no doubt, for those who like these things. Stiffy did. The general effect of it all, he says, was to make him feel not a little romantic. I mean to say, the old spot, the scene of his great love, and so on and so forth. At any rate, he tells me that his bosom swelled, and I see no reason to disbelieve him.

And little by little, as the dew glistened and the sun shone and the birds tootled, there crept over him a feeling that in the existing circs. there was only one thing for a red-blooded young lover to do, viz. trickle round underneath Geraldine's window and bung gravel at it. This would result in her popping her head out, and then he would blow a silent kiss and she would blow a silent kiss and he would tell her in the language of the eyes that his heart was still hers and what not. A very jolly method of passing the time of waiting, felt Stiffy, and he collected a fistful of mud and pebbles and let it go with a will.

Now, slinging gravel at windows is a tricky business. If you're in form, fine. But if you haven't done it for a goodish time your aim is likely to suffer. This is what happened to Stiffy.

He had drawn a bead on his loved one's window, but instead of landing there the entire consignment went several feet to the left and sloshed up against the next one – the room in which Ferdinand James Delamere, sixth Earl of Wivelscombe, was sleeping.

At least, he wasn't sleeping, because it so happened that on the previous night he had taken the chair at the annual dinner of the Loyal Sons of Worcestershire and, despite doctor's orders, had done himself so well that he had woken early with that strange, jumpy feeling which always came to him the morning after this particular banquet. He was in the sort of overwrought state when a fly treading a little too heavily on the carpet is enough to make a man think he's one of the extras in *All Quiet On The Western Front*.

The effect, therefore, of about a quarter of a pound of mixed solids on the windowpane was to bring him leaping out of bed as if a skewer had suddenly come through the mattress. He reached the window in two jumps, and was just in time to see his late employee, Adolphus Stiffham, disappearing into the bushes. For Stiffy, observing that he had nearly cracked the wrong window, and remembering whose that window was, had not loitered.

Now, I want you to follow me very closely here, while I explain why old Wivelscombe took the view of the matter which he did. You see, the way he looked at it, his visitor could not possibly be Adolphus Stiffham in the flesh. He had studied human nature pretty closely and he knew that a man who has been kicked eleven feet, two inches does not willingly return to the spot where the incident occurred. He was aware, moreover, that Stiffy had gone to America. Furthermore, he was, as I say, in a highly nervous condition as the upshot or aftermath of the banquet of the Society of the Loyal Sons of Worcestershire.

The result was that a moment later he was charging into Geraldine's room with consternation and concern written on every feature.

'Why, Father,' said Geraldine, sitting up in bed, 'what's the matter? You look as if you had seen a ghost.'

'I have seen a ghost.'

'The White Lady of Wivelscombe?'

'No, the Pink Secretary of Wivelscombe. I give you my word, Geraldine, that not two minutes ago I heard a sort of uncanny tapping on my window and I looked out and there was the wraith of that young fathead, Adolphus Stiffham.'

'What do you mean, that young fathead, Adolphus Stiffham?' demanded Geraldine with a womanly warmth which became her well. 'Where do you get that young fathead stuff? You are speaking of the man I love.'

'Well, you had better dashed well stop loving him,' rejoined her father with equal heat, 'because he has passed beyond the veil.'

'Are you sure it was his ghost?'

'Of course it was his ghost. Do you think I don't know a ghost when I see one? I've been psychic all my life. All my family have been psychic. My mother was a Ballindalloch of Portknockie and used to see her friends in winding-sheets. It got her disliked in the county. Besides, you told me Stiffham was in America. Obviously what has happened is that somewhere out in those great open spaces the unhappy half-wit has handed in his dinner-pail.'

Geraldine faced him with burning eyes.

'And whose fault was it that he went to America? Yours.'

'Eh? What do you mean, dash it? I never asked him to go to America.'

'He went there as the direct result of your hard-heartedness and inhumanity. And now, I suppose, he has been shot by gangsters, like everybody else in America. Was there a bullet-wound in his forehead?'

'I couldn't tell you. He got away too quick. Just smiled a hideous sort of smile and seemed to melt into the bushes. Phew!' said Lord Wivelscombe. 'I'm going down to get a bite of breakfast. I need coffee. Strong, hot coffee with a kick in it. Put on a dressing-gown and come along.'

'I shall do nothing of the kind,' said Geraldine coldly. 'Breakfast, forsooth! It would choke me. I shall remain up here and try to get Adolphus on the ouija-board.'

Stiffy, meanwhile, after removing some twigs from his hair and brushing a few of the local beetles off his face, had come cautiously out of the bushes and made his way snakily to the french windows of the morning-room. A glance at his watch had told him that at any moment now the postman would be arriving. And, sure enough, he had not been there more than about two minutes when the door of the morning-room opened and the butler came in and placed a bundle of correspondence beside Lord Wivelscombe's plate. He then withdrew, and Stiffy, abandoning the role of snake, gave a spirited impersonation of a pouncing leopard. He was in through the windows in a matter of one and three-fifth seconds. It took him perhaps another second to locate and pouch the letter. And he was just about to buzz off, which would have taken him possibly another second and a quarter, when he heard a footstep outside.

There was no time for the smooth getaway. Already the door was beginning to open. With considerable presence of mind

Stiffy revised his whole plan of campaign at a moment's notice and shot silently under the table.

And there for a while the matter rested.

As far as Stiffy could gather from the look of the legs moving about in his vicinity, it was the butler who had returned, presumably with coffee and foodstuffs. He could just see the lower section of a pair of striped trousers, as worn by butlers.

Then the door opened once more, this time to admit a pair of pyjamaed legs terminating in bedroom slippers, and reason told him that this must be old Wivelscombe. When the pyjamas passed from his view to appear again under the table within a couple of inches of his nose, their owner having sunk heavily into a chair, he knew that he had been right, and he is not ashamed to confess that he was conscious of a certain qualm. Seeing at such close range the foot which had once landed so forcefully on his trouser seat was, he tells me, an unnerving experience.

A bit of dialogue now unshipped itself in the upper regions. The butler started it.

'Good morning, m'lord. Shall I assist your lordship to a little eggs and bacon?'

The table shook as the aged peer shuddered strongly.

'Don't try to be funny, Gascoigne. There is a time to speak of eggs and a time not to speak of eggs. At the moment, I would prefer to try to forget that there are such things in the world. What you can bring me – and dashed quick, too – is a very hot, very strong cup of coffee, liberally laced with old brandy, and a very dry slice of toast.'

The butler coughed in rather an unpleasant and censorious manner.

'Did your lordship exceed last night?'

'Certainly not.'

'Did your lordship imbibe champagne?'

'The merest spot.'

'A bottle?'

'It may have been a bottle.'

'Two bottles?'

'Yes. Possibly two bottles.'

The butler coughed again.

'I shall inform Doctor Spelvin.'

'Don't be a cad, Gascoigne.'

'He has expressly forbidden your lordship champagne.'

'Tchah!'

'I need scarcely remind your lordship that champagne brings your lordship out in spots.'

Old Wivelscombe barked querulously.

'I wish to goodness you wouldn't stand there babbling about champagne. It is a word that I do not wish to have mentioned in my presence.'

'Very good, m'lord,' said the butler stiffly. 'Your coffee, m'lord. The dry toast is at your lordship's elbow.'

There was a pause. From the sloshing sound which broke out above him at this point, Stiffy deduced that old Wivelscombe was drinking the coffee. The theory was borne out by the fact that when he spoke again it was in a stronger voice.

'It's no good your looking like that, Gascoigne. After all, what's an occasional binge? It's a poor heart that never rejoices.'

'At your lordship's age, all binges are highly injudicious.'

'What do you mean, my age? A man is as old as he feels.'

'Very good, m'lord.'

'Where you go wrong, Gascoigne – where you make your bloomer is in assuming that I have a hangover this morning.

Nothing could be further from the truth. I feel like a two-year-old. Look at my hand. Steady as a rock.'

Apparently, at this point, old Wivelscombe ventured on a physical demonstration. A napkin came fluttering down on the floor.

'Very wobbly, m'lord.'

'Nothing of the kind,' said old Wivelscombe testily. 'I dropped that napkin on purpose, just to show you how easily I could pick it up. See, Gascoigne. I will now pick up the napkin.'

But he didn't. He stooped down and his fingers touched the thing, but as they did so he suddenly found himself looking into Stiffy's bulging eyes. There was an embarrassing pause for a moment: then his face shot up out of sight and Stiffy heard him gulp.

'Gascoigne!'

'M'lord?'

'Gascoigne, there's a ghost under the table.'

'Very good, m'lord.'

'What do you mean, "Very good, m'lord"? Don't stand there saying, "Very good, m'lord." Do something about it, man, do something about it.'

'I beg your lordship's pardon, but I cannot comprehend just what it is that your lordship desires me to do.'

'Why, shoo it out.'

'Really, m'lord!'

Old Wivelscombe's voice grew tense.

'Gascoigne, do you hear me telling you that the room is overrun with ghosts?'

'Yes, m'lord.'

'Don't you believe me?'

'No, m'lord.'

'Well, look for yourself. I tell you it's there. The dashed thing's been following me about all the morning. Lift the cloth, Gascoigne, and take a dekko.'

'Very good, m'lord, if your lordship insists. But I do not anticipate that I shall be able to observe the spectre to which your lordship alludes.'

He did, of course. The first thing that met his eye was young Stiffy. But by this time Stiffy, who, chump though he is, can act on occasion with a good deal of rugged sense, was holding the forefinger of his left hand to his lips and stretching out the other hand with a fiver in it.

The butler scooped the fiver and straightened himself.

'Well, Gascoigne?'

'The light under the table is a little uncertain, m'lord. I will take another look.'

He bent down once more, and Stiffy repeated the business with fiver.

'No, m'lord. There is nothing there.'

'No spectres, Gascoigne?'

'No spectres, m'lord.'

Old Wivelscombe groaned in a hollow sort of way, and there was the sound of a chair being pushed back.

'I shall go for a brisk walk, Gascoigne.'

'Very good, m'lord.'

'You're sure you saw nothing?'

'Quite sure, m'lord.'

'Not the late Adolphus Stiffham?'

'No, m'lord.'

The door closed behind old Wivelscombe, and Stiffy crawled out.

'Good morning, Gascoigne.'

'Good morning, sir.'

'I expect I gave you a start, Gascoigne?'

'I must confess to a momentary sensation of surprise, sir. I had supposed that you were in the United States of Northern America.'

'It's a long story,' said Stiffy, 'but the nub of it is that I must see Lady Geraldine immediately. Is she in her room?'

'I cannot speak from first-hand observation, sir, but I am inclined to fancy that her ladyship has not yet descended. Would you desire me to announce you, sir?'

'No, thanks. I'll find my way up.'

So up Stiffy buzzed, and presently he was sitting on Geraldine's bed, gazing into her eyes and holding her little hand in his. The exact words of their conversation Stiffy did not reveal to me, but no doubt he opened with a brief explanation of his presence and then they spoke of those things which young lovers do speak about when they get together for a chat after long separation. At any rate, he tells me that they were more or less absorbed when the door handle rattled. He had just time to make a leap for a convenient cupboard as old Wivelscombe came in. There was a moment when the eyes of the two men met. And then Stiffy was in the cupboard among Geraldine's summer frocks.

Old Wivelscombe was gulping a bit.

'Geraldine,' he said, 'you see before you a haunted man.'

'Do I, Father?'

'You certainly do. When I went down to breakfast, guess what? There beneath the table was the phantasm of that fat-...of that excellent young fellow, Adolphus Stiffham, whom I always liked though he may have drawn wrong conclusions from my surface manner,' said old Wivelscombe, raising his voice slightly. 'He was staring at me with just that same idiot ...with precisely that same frank, winning expression on his face that I remember so well.'

'What did you do?'

'I requested Gascoigne to check up my facts. So Gascoigne took a look. But the apparition was invisible to him.'

'Was it?'

'It was. I gather that it is also invisible to you. For I assure you, on the word of a Worcestershire Wivelscombe, that as I entered this room I distinctly observed the spectre nip into that cupboard over there.'

'Nonsense.'

'It isn't nonsense.'

'That cupboard there?'

'That very cupboard.'

'I'll go and look.'

'Take care it doesn't bite you,' said Lord Wivelscombe anxiously.

The cupboard door opened, and Geraldine peeped in.

'No,' she said. 'There's nothing there.'

Old Wivelscombe unleashed another of those hollow groans of his.

'Of course you wouldn't see it. It's meant for me. A nice thing this is going to be, trying to run an estate with a beastly great ghost popping in and out all the time. Concentration will become impossible.'

Geraldine laid a soothing hand on his quivering shoulder.

'I don't think it is going to be as bad as that, Father. I think I see what has happened. In my opinion, this thing has been sent to you as a warning.'

'A warning?'

'Yes. I have read of such cases. It sometimes happens that the apparition of an entity . . . let us call him A. or B. . . .'

'Whichever you prefer.'

'The apparition of an entity, A. or B., will occasionally appear not after but before the entity has crossed the great divide. The object of this is to impress on the mind of the individual observing the phenomenon . . . shall we call him C. . . . ?'

'By all means.'

'. . . to impress on the mind of the individual, C., that, unless steps are taken promptly through the proper channels, the entity will pass over. It is, as it were, a cautionary projection of a distant personality.'

Lord Wivelscombe raised his head from his hands.

'You mean, then, that you think that that blasted . . . that that delightful lad, Adolphus Stiffham, on whom I have always looked more as a son than anything, is still alive?'

'For the moment, yes.'

'Tell me,' said Lord Wivelscombe, 'how do we keep him that way?'

Geraldine reflected.

'I think the best plan is for me to cable him today to return at once, as you are now prepared to give your full consent to our marriage.'

Lord Wivelscombe sat for a moment in thought.

'You consider that the best plan?'

'I do.'

'What's the next best?'

'There is no other.'

'You mean that, unless I want to be haunted for the rest of my life, I've got to have that – er – him for a son-in-law?'

'I do.'

Lord Wivelscombe looked once more at the cupboard. Then he spoke with what a close observer might have thought a slightly exaggerated heartiness.

'Charmed!' he said. 'Delighted. Capital. Splendid. Only too pleased.'

And that (concluded the Crumpet) is the inner history of the Stiffham-Spettisbury wedding which we have just seen solemnized at St George's, Hanover Square. And you can understand now what I meant when I said that what a man needs in this world is not virtue, character, steadiness, and nobility of mind – or I should have done better myself – but luck. It was his faith in the Luck of the Stiffhams that led young Pongo Twistleton-Twistleton to take the short end from Oofy Prosser against all the ruling of the form-book, and I honour him for it and am delighted that he has cleaned up.

On the usually unruffled brow of the Bean who had just entered the smoking-room of the Drones Club there was a furrow of perplexity. He crossed pensively to the settee in the corner and addressed the group of Eggs and Crumpets assembled there.

'I say,' he said, 'in re Freddie Widgeon, do any of you chaps happen to know if he's gone off his rocker?'

An Egg asked what made him think so.

'Well, he's out in the bar, drinking Lizard's Breaths...'

'Nothing unbalanced about that.'

'No, but his manner is strange. It so happens that at the seminary where he and I were educated they are getting up a fund for some new racquets courts, and when I tackled Freddie just now and said that he ought to chip in and rally round the dear old school, he replied that he was fed to the tonsils with dear old schools and never wished to hear anyone talk about dear old schools again.'

'Rummy,' agreed the Egg.

'He then gave a hideous laugh and added that, if anybody was interested in his plans, he was going to join the Foreign Legion, that Cohort of the Damned in which broken men may toil and die and, dying, forget.'

'Beau Widgeon?' said the Egg, impressed. 'What ho!'

A Crumpet shook his head.

'You won't catch Freddie joining any Foreign Legion, once he gets on to the fact that it means missing his morning cup of tea. All the same, I can understand his feeling a bit upset at the moment, poor old blighter. Tragedy has come into his life. He's just lost the only girl in the world.'

'Well, he ought to be used to that by this time.'

'Yes. But he also got touched for his only tenner in the world, and on top of that his uncle, old Blicester, has cut his allowance in half.'

'Ah,' said the Egg understandingly.

'It was at Cannes that it all happened,' proceeded the Crumpet. 'Old Blicester had been ordered there by his doctor, and he offered to take Freddie along, paying all expenses. A glittering prospect, of course, for there are few juicier spots than the South of France during the summer season: nevertheless, I warned the poor fish not to go. I told him no good could come of it, pointing out the unexampled opportunities he would have of making some sort of a bloomer and alienating the old boy, if cooped up with him at a foreign resort for a matter of six weeks. But he merely blushed prettily and said that, while nobody was more alive to that possibility than himself, he was jolly well going to go, because this girl was at Cannes.'

'Who was this girl?'

'I forget her name. Drusilla something. Never met her myself. He described her to me, and I received the impression of a sort of blend of Tallulah Bankhead and a policewoman. Fascinating exterior, I mean to say, but full of ideas at variance with the spirit of modern progress. Apparently she sprang from a long line of Bishops and Archdeacons and what not, and was strongly opposed to all forms of gambling, smoking, and cocktail-drinking. And Freddie had made an excellent first impression on her owing to the fact that he never gambled, never smoked, and looked on cocktails as the curse of the age.'

'Freddie?' said the Egg, startled.

'That was what he had told her, and I consider it a justifiable stratagem. I mean to say, if you don't kid the delicately nurtured along a bit in the initial stages, where are you?'

'True,' said the Egg.

Well, that is how matters stood when Freddie arrived at Cannes, and as he sauntered along the Croisette on the fourth or fifth day of his visit I don't suppose there was a happier bloke in all that gay throng. The sun was shining, the sea was blue, the girl had promised to have tea with him that afternoon at the Casino, and he knew he was looking absolutely his best. Always a natty dresser, today he had eclipsed himself. The glistening trousers, the spotless shirt, the form-fitting blue coat . . . all these combined to present an intoxicating picture. And this picture he had topped off with a superb tie which he had contrived to pinch overnight from his uncle's effects. Gold and lavender in its general colour scheme, with a red stripe thrown in for good measure. Lots of fellows, he tells me, couldn't have carried it off, but it made him look positively godlike.

Well, when I tell you that he hadn't been out on the Croisette ten minutes before a French bloke came up and offered him five hundred francs to judge a Peasant Mothers Baby Competition down by the harbour, where they were having some sort of local fete or jamboree in honour of a saint whose name has escaped me, you will admit that he must have looked pretty impressive. These knowledgeable Gauls don't waste their money on tramps.

Now, you might have thought that as old Blicester, the world's greatest exponent of the one-way pocket, consistently refused to slip him so much as a franc for current expenses, Freddie would have jumped at this chance of making a bit. But it so happened that he had recently wired to a staunch pal in London for a tenner and had received intimation that the sum would be arriving by that afternoon's post. He had no need, accordingly, for the gold the chap was dangling before his eyes. However, he was pleased by the compliment, and said he would most certainly look in, if he could, and lend the binge the prestige of his presence, and they parted on cordial terms.

It was almost immediately after this that the bird in the shabby reach-me-downs accosted him.

His watch having told him that the afternoon post would be in any minute now, Freddie, in his perambulations, had not moved very far from the Carlton, which was the hotel where he and his uncle and also the girl were stopping, and he was manœuvring up and down about opposite it when a voice at his elbow, speaking in that sort of surprised and joyful manner in which one addresses an old friend encountered in a foreign spot, said:

'Why, hullo!'

And, turning, he perceived the above-mentioned bird in the reach-me-downs as described. A tallish, thinnish chap.

'Well, well, well!' said the bird.

Freddie goggled at him. As far as memory served, he didn't know the blighter from Adam.

'Hullo,' he said, playing for time.

'Fancy running into you,' said the chap.

'Ah,' said Freddie.

'It's a long time since we met.'

'Absolutely,' said Freddie, the persp. beginning to start out a bit on the brow. Because if there's one thing that makes a man feel a chump it is this business of meeting ancient cronies and not being able to put a name to them.

'I don't suppose you see any of the old crowd now?' said the chap.

'Not many,' said Freddie.

'They scatter.'

'They do scatter.'

'I came across Smith a few weeks ago.'

'Oh, yes?'

'T. T. Smith, I mean.'

'Oh, T. T. Smith?'

'Yes. Not J. B. I hear J. B.'s gone to the Malay States. T. T.'s in some sort of agency business. Rather prosperous.'

'That's good.'

'You seem to be doing pretty well, yourself.'

'Oh, fairly.'

'Well, I'm not surprised,' said the chap. 'One always knew you would, even at school.'

The word, Freddie tells me, was like a lifebelt. He grabbed at it. So this was a fellow he had known at school. That narrowed it down a lot. Surely now, he felt, the old brain would begin to function. Then he took another look at the chap, and the momentary exhilaration ebbed. He had not known him from Adam, and he still did not know him from Adam. The situation had thus become more awkward than ever, because the odds were that in the end this fellow was going to turn out to be someone he had shared a study with and ought to be falling on the neck of and swopping reminiscences of the time when old Boko Jervis brought the white rabbit into chapel and what not.

'Yes,' said the chap. 'Even then one could tell that you were bound to go up and up. Gosh, how I used to admire you at the dear old school. You were my hero.'

'What!' yipped Freddie. He hadn't the foggiest that he had been anyone's hero at school. His career there hadn't been so dashed distinguished as all that. He had scraped into the cricket team in his last year, true: but even so he couldn't imagine any of his contemporaries looking up to him much.

'You were,' said the chap. 'I thought you a marvel.'

'No, really?' said Freddie, suffused with coy blushes. 'Well, well, well, fancy that. Have a cigarette?'

'Thanks,' said the chap. 'But what I really want is a meal. I'm right on my uppers. We aren't all like you, you see. While you've been going up and up, some of us have been going down and down. If I don't get a meal today, I don't know what I shall do.'

Freddie tells me the thing came on him as a complete surprise. You might have supposed that a wary bird like him, who has been a member of this club since he came down from Oxford, would have known better, but he insists that he had absolutely no suspicion that a touch was in the air till it suddenly hit him like this. And his first impulse, he says, was to mumble something at the back of his throat and slide off.

And he was just going to when a sudden surge of generous emotion swept over him. Could he let a fellow down who had not only been at school with him but who, when at school, had looked upon him as a hero? Imposs., felt Freddie. There had been six hundred and forty-seven chaps at the old school. Was he to hand the callous mitten to the only one of those six hundred and forty-seven who had admired him? Absolutely out of the q., was Freddie's verdict. A *mille* was the dickens of a sum of money, of course – present rate of exchange a bit more than a tenner – but it would have to be found somehow. *Noblesse oblige*, he meant to say.

And just when the fervour was at its height he recollected this cheque which was arriving by the afternoon post. In the stress of emotion it had quite slipped his mind.

'By Jove!' he said. 'Yes, I can fix you up. Suppose we meet at the Casino a couple of hours from now.'

'God bless you,' said the chap.

'Not at all,' said Freddie.

It was with mixed feelings that he went into the hotel to see if the post had come. On the one hand, there was the solemn anguish of parting with a tenner which he had earmarked for quite a different end. On the other, there was the quiet chestiness induced by the realization that here he had been jogging along through the world, not thinking such a frightful lot of himself, and all the while in the background was this bloke treasuring his memory and saying to himself: 'Ah, if we could all be like Freddie Widgeon!' Cheap at a tenner, he told himself, the sensation of spiritual yeastiness which this reflection gave him.

All the same, he wished the chap could have done with five, because there was a bookie in London to whom he had owed a fiver for some months now and recent correspondence had shown that this hell-hound was on the verge of becoming a bit unpleasant. Until this episode had occurred, he had fully intended to send the man thirty bob or so, to sweeten him. Now, of course, this was out of the question. The entire sum must go unbroken to this old school-fellow whose name he wished he could remember.

Spivis? . . . Brent? . . . Jerningham? . . . Fosway? . . .
No.

Brewster?...Goggs?...Bootle?...Finsbury?...

No.

He gave it up and went to the desk. The letter was there, and in it the cheque. The very decent johnny behind the counter cashed it for him without a murmur, and he was just gathering up the loot when somebody behind him said 'Ah!'

Now, in the word 'Ah!' you might say that there is nothing really to fill a fellow with a nameless dread. Nevertheless, that is what this 'Ah!' filled Freddie with. For he had recognized the voice. It was none other than that of the bookie to whom he owed the fiver. That is the trouble about Cannes in August – it becomes very mixed. You get your Freddie Widgeons there – splendid chaps who were worshipped by their schoolmates – and you also get men like this bookie. All sorts, if you follow me, from the highest to the lowest.

From the moment when he turned and gazed into the fellow's steely eyes, Freddie tells me he hadn't a hope. But he did his best.

'Hullo, Mr McIntosh!' he said. 'You here? Well, well, well! Ha, ha!'

'Yes,' said the bookie.

'I never thought I should run into you in these parts.'

'You have,' the bookie assured him.

'Come down here for a nice holiday, what? Taking a perfect rest, eh? Going to bask in the lovely sunshine and put all thoughts of business completely out of your head, yes?'

'Well, not quite all,' said the bookie, producing the little black book. 'Now, let me see, Mr Widgeon....Ah, yes, five pounds on Marmalade to cop in the second at Ally Pally. Should have won by the form-book, but ran third. Well, that's life, isn't it? I think it comes to a little more than four hundred and fifty francs, really, but we'll call it four-fifty. One doesn't want any haggling among friends.'

'I'm awfully sorry,' said Freddie. 'Some other time, what? I can't manage it just at the moment. I haven't any money.'

'No?'

'I mean to say, I want this for a poor man.'

'So do I,' said the bookie.

And the upshot and outcome, of course, was that poor old Freddie had to brass up. You can't appeal to a bookie's better feelings, because he hasn't any. He pushed over the four hundred and fifty.

'Oh, very well,' he said. 'Here you are. And let me tell you, Mr McIntosh, that the curse of the Widgeons goes with it.'

'Right,' said the bookie.

So there Freddie was with five hundred and fifty francs in his kick, and needing a thousand.

I must say I wouldn't have blamed him if, in these circs., he had decided to give a miss to the old school-friend. Allowing fifty francs for lushing up the girl Drusilla at the tea-table, he would in that case have had a cool five hundred with which to plunge into the variegated pleasures of Cannes in the summer-time. A very nice sum, indeed.

But, though tempted, he was strong. This old admirer of his – Muttlebury?...Jukes?...Ferguson?...Braithwaite?... – had said that he needed a *mille*, and a *mille* he must have.

But how to raise the other five hundred? That was the prob.

For some moments he toyed with mad schemes like trying to borrow it from his uncle. Then it suddenly flashed upon him that the sum he required was the exact amount which the intelligent Gaul had offered him if he would come down to the jamboree by the harbour and judge the Peasant Mothers Baby Competition.

Now, Freddie's views on babies are well defined. He is prepared to cope with them singly, if all avenues of escape are blocked and there is a nurse or mother standing by to lend aid in case of sudden hiccoughs, retchings, or nauseas. Under such conditions he has even been known to offer his watch to one related by ties of blood in order that the little stranger might listen to the tick-tick. But it would be paltering with the truth to say that he likes babies. They give him, he says, a sort of grey feeling. He resents their cold stare and the supercilious and up-stage way in which they dribble out of the corner of their mouths on seeing him. Eyeing them, he is conscious of doubts as to whether Man can really be Nature's last word.

This being so, you will readily understand that, even for so stupendous a fee as five hundred francs, he shrank from being closeted with a whole platoon of the little brutes. And I think it is greatly to his credit that after only the shortest of internal struggles he set his teeth, clenched his fists, and made for the harbour with a steady step. How different it would all have been, he felt wistfully, if he were being called upon to judge a contest of Bathing Belles.

There was the possibility, of course, that in the interval since he had met the intelligent Gaul the post of judge would have been filled. But no. The fellow welcomed him with open arms and led him joyfully into a sort of marquee place crowded with as tough-looking a bunch of mothers and as hard-boiled a gaggle of issue as anybody could wish to see. He made a short speech in French which was much too rapid for Freddie to follow, and the mothers all applauded, and the babies all yelled, and then he was conducted along the line, with all the mothers glaring at him in an intimidating way, as much as to warn him that if he dared give the prize to anybody else's offspring he had jolly well better look out for himself. Dashed unpleasant, the whole thing, Freddie tells me, and I see his view-point.

He kept his head, however. This was the first time he had ever been let in for anything of this nature, but a sort of instinct told him to adopt the policy followed by all experienced judges at these affairs – viz. to ignore the babies absolutely and concentrate entirely on the mothers. So many points for ferocity of demeanour, that is to say, and so many for possibility of knife concealed in stocking, and so on and so forth. You ask any curate how he works the gaff at the annual Baby Competition in his village, and he will tell you that these, broadly, are the lines on which he goes.

There were, it seemed, to be three prizes and about the first one there could be no question at all. It went automatically to a heavy-weight mother with beetling eyebrows who looked as if she had just come from doing a spot of knitting at the foot of the guillotine. Just to see those eyebrows, Freddie tells me, was to hear the heads dropping into the basket, and he had no hesitation, as I say, in declaring her progeny the big winner.

The second and third prizes were a bit more difficult, but after some consideration he awarded them to two other female plug-uglies with suspicious bulges in their stockings. This done, he sidled up to the intelligent Gaul to receive his wage, doing his best not to listen to the angry mutterings from the losers which were already beginning to rumble through the air.

The brand of English which this bird affected was not of the best, and it took Freddie some moments to get his drift. When he did, he reeled and came very near clutching for support at the other's beard. Because what the Gaul was endeavouring to communicate was the fact that, so far from being paid five hundred francs for his services, Freddie was expected to cough up that sum.

It was an old Cannes custom, the man explained, for some rich visiting milord to take on the providing of the prizes on this occasion, his reward being the compliment implied in the invitation.

He said that when he had perceived Freddie promenading himself on the Croisette he had been so struck by his appearance of the most elegant and his altogether of a superbness so unparalleled that he had picked him without another look at the field.

Well, dashed gratifying, of course, from one point of view and a handsome tribute to the way Freddie had got himself up that day: but it was not long before he was looking in a tentative sort of manner at the nearest exit. And I think that, had that exit been just a shade closer, he would have put his fortune to the test, to win or lose it all.

But to edge out and leg it would have taken that ten seconds or so which make all the difference. Those mothers would have been on his very heels, and the prospect of sprinting along the streets of Cannes under such conditions was too much for him. Quite possibly he might have shown a flash of speed sufficient to shake off their challenge, but it would have been a very close thing, with nothing in it for the first five hundred yards or so, and he could not have failed to make himself conspicuous.

So, with a heavy sigh, he forked out the five h., and tottered into the open. So sombre was his mood that he scarcely heard the mutterings of the disappointed losers, who were now calling him an *espèce de* something and hinting rather broadly in the local *patois* that he had been fixed.

And the thing that weighed so heavily upon him was the thought that, unless some miracle occurred, he would now be forced to let down his old chum Bulstrode, Waters, Parsloe, Bingley, Murgatroyd, or whatever the blighter's name might be.

He had told the fellow to meet him outside the Casino – which in summer at Cannes is, of course, the Palm Beach at the far end of the Croisette – so he directed his steps thither. And jolly halting steps they were, he tells me. The urge to give the school-chum his *mille* had now become with Frederick Widgeon a regular obsession. He felt that his honour was involved. And he shuddered at the thought of the meeting that lay before him. Up the chap would come frisking, with his hand outstretched and the light of expectation in his eyes, and what would ensue? The miss-in-baulk.

He groaned in spirit. He could see the other's pained and disillusioned look. He could hear him saying to himself: 'This is not the old Widgeon form. The boy I admired so much in the dear old days of school would not have foozled a small loan like this. A pretty serious change for the worse there must have been in Frederick W. since the time when we used to sport together in the shade of the old cloisters.' The thought was agony.

All the way along the Croisette he pondered deeply. To the gay throng around him he paid no attention. There were girls within a biscuit-throw in bathing-suits which began at the base of the spine and ended two inches lower down, but he did not give them so much as a glance. His whole being was absorbed in this reverie of his.

By the time he reached the Casino, he had made up his mind. Visionary, chimerical though the idea would have seemed to anybody who knew the latter and his views on parting with cash, he had resolved to make the attempt to borrow a thousand francs from his uncle. With this end, therefore, he proceeded to the Baccarat rooms. The other, he knew, was always to be found at this hour seated at one of the three-louis chemmy tables. For, definite though the Earl of Blicester's creed was on the subject of his nephew gambling, he himself enjoyed a modest flutter.

He found the old boy, as expected, hunched up over the green cloth. At the moment of Freddie's arrival he was just scooping in three pink counters with a holy light of exaltation on his face. For there was nothing spacious and sensational about Lord Blicester's methods of play. He was not one of those punters you read about in the papers who rook the Greek Syndicate of three million francs in an evening. If he came out one-and-sixpence ahead of the game, he considered his day well spent.

It looked to Freddie, examining the counters in front of his relative, as if the moment were propitious for a touch. There must have been fully five bob's worth of them, which meant that the other had struck one of those big winning streaks which come to all gamblers sooner or later. His mood, accordingly, ought to be sunny.

'I say, uncle,' he said, sidling up.

'Get to hell out of here,' replied Lord Blicester, not half so sunny as might have been expected. 'Banco!' he cried, and a second later was gathering in another sixty francs.

'I say, Uncle...'

'Well, what is it?'

'I say, Uncle, will you lend me...'

'No.'

'I only want...'

'Well, you won't get it.'

'It's not for myself...'

'Go to blazes,' said old Blicester.

Freddie receded. Though he had never really expected any solid results, his heart was pretty well bowed down with weight of care. He had shot his bolt. His last source of supply had proved a wash-out.

He looked at his watch. About now, the old schoolmate would be approaching the tryst. He would be walking – so firm would be his faith in his hero – with elastic steps. Possibly he would even be humming some gay air. Had he a stick? Freddie could not remember. But if he had he would be twirling it.

And then would come the meeting . . . the confession of failure . . . the harsh awakening and the brutal shattering of dreams . . .

It was at this moment that he was roused from his meditations by the one word in the French language capable of bringing him back to the world.

'*Un mille.*'

It was the voice of the croupier, chanting his litany.

'*Cinquante louis à la banque. Un banco de mille.*'

I can't do the dialect, you understand, but what he meant was that somebody holding the bank had run it up to a thousand francs. And Freddie, waking with a start, perceived that a pile of assorted counters, presumably amounting to that sum, now lay in the centre of the board.

Well, a thousand francs isn't much, of course, to the nibs at the big tables, but among the three-louis-minimum lizards if you run a bank up to a *mille* you make a pretty big sensation. There was quite a crowd round the table now, and over their heads Freddie could see that pile of counters, and it seemed to smile up at him.

For an instant he hesitated, while his past life seemed to flit before him as if he had been a drowning man. Then he heard a voice croak '*Banco*' and there seemed something oddly familiar about it, and he suddenly realized that it was his own. He had taken the plunge.

It was a pretty agonizing moment for old Freddie, as you may well imagine. I mean to say, he had bancoed this fellow, whoever he was, and if he happened to lose the *coup* all he would have to offer him would be fifty francs and his apologies. There would, he could not conceal it from himself, be the devil of a row. What exactly, he wondered, did they do to you at these French Casinos if you lost and couldn't pay up? Something sticky, beyond a question. Hardly the guillotine, perhaps, and possibly not even Devil's Island. But something nasty, undoubtedly. With a dim recollection of a movie he had once seen, he pictured himself in the middle of a hollow square formed by punters and croupiers with the managing director of the place snipping off his coat-buttons.

Or was it trouser-buttons? No, in a mixed company like this it would hardly be trouser-buttons. Still, even coat-buttons would be bad enough.

And, if the moment was agonizing for Freddie, it was scarcely less so for his uncle, Lord Blicester. It was his bank which had been running up to such impressive proportions, and he was now faced with the problem of whether to take a chance on doubling his loot or to pass the hand.

Lord Blicester was a man who, when in the feverish atmosphere of the gaming-rooms, believed in small profits and quick returns. He was accustomed to start his bank at the minimum, run it twice with his heart in his mouth, and then pass. But on the present occasion he had been carried away to such an extent that he had worked the kitty up to a solid *mille*. It was a fearful sum to risk losing. On the other hand, suppose he didn't lose?

Someone in the crowd outside his line of vision had said, 'Banco!' and with a bit of luck he might be two *mille* up instead of one, just like that.

What to do? It was a man's cross-roads.

In the end, he decided to take the big chance. And it was as the croupier pushed the cards along the table and the crowd opened up a bit to let the challenger get at them that he recognized in the individual leaning forward his nephew Frederick.

'Brzzghl!' gasped Lord Blicester. 'Gor! Woosh!'

What he meant was that the deal was off because the young hound who had just come into the picture was his late sister's son Frederick Fotheringay Widgeon, who had never had a penny except what he allowed him and certainly hadn't a hundredth part of the sum necessary for cashing in if he lost. But he hadn't made himself clear enough. The next moment, with infinite emotion, Freddie was chucking down a nine and the croupier was pushing all old Blicester's hard-earned at him.

It was as he was gathering it up that he caught the old boy's eye. The effect of it was to cause him to spill a hundred-franc counter, two louis counters, and a five-franc counter. And he had just straightened himself after picking these up, when a voice spoke.

'Good afternoon, Mr Widgeon,' said the girl Drusilla.

'Oh, ah,' said Freddie.

You couldn't say it was a frightfully bright remark, but he considers it was dashed good going to utter even as much as that. In the matter of eyes, he tells me, there was not much to choose between this girl's and his uncle's. Their gazes differed in quality, it is true, because, whereas old Blicester's had been piping hot and had expressed hate, fury and the desire to skin, the girl

Drusilla's was right off the ice and conveyed a sort of sick disillusionment and a loathing contempt. But as to which he would rather have met on a dark night down a lonely alley, Freddie couldn't have told you.

'You appear to have been lucky,' said this Drusilla.

'Oh, ah,' said Freddie.

He looked quickly away, and ran up against old Blicester's eye again. Then he looked back and caught Drusilla's. The whole situation, he tells me, was extraordinarily like that of an African explorer who, endeavouring to ignore one of the local serpents, finds himself exchanging glances with a man-eating tiger.

The girl was now wrinkling her nose as if a particularly foul brand of poison-gas had begun to permeate the Casino and she was standing nearest it.

'I must confess I am a little surprised,' she said, 'because I was under the impression that you had told me that you never gambled.'

'Oh, ah,' said Freddie.

'If I remember rightly, you described gambling as a cancer in the body politic.'

'Oh, ah,' said Freddie.

She took a final sniff, as if she had been hoping against hope that he was not a main sewer and was now reluctantly compelled to realize that he was.

'I am afraid I shall not be able to come to tea this afternoon. Goodbye, Mr Widgeon.'

'Oh, ah,' said Freddie.

He watched her go, knowing that she was going out of his life and that any chance of the scent of orange-blossoms and the amble up the aisle with the organ playing 'O perfect Love' was now blue round the edges; and it was as if there was a dull weight pressing on him.

And then he found that there was a dull weight pressing on him, viz. that of all the counters he was loaded down with. And it was at this point that it dawned upon him that, though he had in prospect an interview with old Blicester which would undoubtedly lower all previous records, and though a life's romance had gone phut, he was at least in a position to satisfy the *noblesse oblige* of the Widgeons.

So he tottered to the cashier's desk and changed the stuff into a pink note, and then he tottered out of the Casino, and was tottering down the steps when he perceived the school-friend in the immediate offing, looking bright and expectant.

'Here I am,' said the school-friend.

'Oh, ah,' said Freddie.

And with a supreme gesture of resignation he pressed the *mille* into the man's hand.

There was never any doubt about the chap taking it. He took it like a trout sucking down a may-fly and shoved it away in a pocket at the back of his costume. But what was odd was that he seemed stupefied. His eyes grew round, his jaw fell, and he stared at Freddie in awe-struck amazement.

'I say,' he said, 'don't think I'm raising any objections or anything of that sort, because I'm not. I am heart and soul in this scheme of giving me a *mille*. But it's an awful lot, isn't it? I don't mind telling you that what I had been sketching out as more or less the sum that was going to change hands was something in the nature of fifty francs.'

Freddie was a bit surprised too. He couldn't make this out.

'But you said you had to have a *mille*.'

'And a meal is just what I'm going to have,' replied the chap, enthusiastically. 'I haven't had a bite to eat since breakfast.'

Freddie was stunned. He isn't what you would call a quick thinker, but he was beginning to see that there had been a confusion of ideas.

'Do you mean to tell me,' he cried, 'that when you said a *mille* what you meant was a meal?'

'I don't suppose anyone ever meant a meal more,' said the chap. He stood awhile in thought. 'Hors d'œuvres, I think, to start with,' he went on, passing his tongue meditatively over his lips. 'Then perhaps a touch of clear soup, followed by some fish of the country and a good steak *minute* with fried potatoes and a salad. Cheese, of course, and the usual etceteras, and then coffee, liqueur, and a cigar to wind up with. Yes, you may certainly take it as official that I intend to have a meal. Ah, yes, and I was forgetting. A bot. of some nice, dry wine to wash things down. Yes, yes, yes, to be sure. You see this stomach?' he said, patting it. 'Here stands a stomach that is scheduled in about a quarter of an hour to get the surprise of its young life.'

Freddie saw it all now, and the irony of the situation seemed to hit him like a bit of lead-piping on the base of the skull. Just because of this footling business of having words in one language which meant something quite different in another language – a thing which could so easily have been prevented by the responsible heads of the French and English nations getting together across a round table and coming to some sensible arrangement – here he was deeper in the soup than he had ever been in the whole course of his career.

He tells me he chafed, and I don't blame him. Anybody would have chafed in the circs. For about half a minute he had half a mind to leap at the chap and wrench the *mille* out of him and substitute for it the fifty francs which he had been anticipating.

Then the old *noblesse oblige* spirit awoke once more. He might be in the soup, he might be a financial wreck, he might be faced with a *tête-à-tête* with his uncle, Lord Blicester, in the course of which the testy old man would in all probability endeavour to bite a piece out of the fleshy part of his leg, but at least he had done the fine, square thing. He had not let down a fellow who had admired him at school.

The chap had begun to speak again. At first, all he said was a brief word or two revising that passage in his previous address which had dealt with steak *minute*. A steak *minute*, he told Freddie, had among its obvious merits one fault – to wit, that it was not as filling as it might be. A more prudent move, he considered, and he called on Freddie to endorse this view, would be a couple of chump chops. Then he turned from that subject.

'Well, it was certainly a bit of luck running into you, Postle-thwaite,' he said.

Freddie was a trifle stymied.

'Postlethwaite?' he said. 'How do you mean, Postlethwaite?'

The chap seemed surprised.

'How do you mean, how do I mean Postlethwaite?'

'I mean, why Postlethwaite? How has this Postlethwaite stuff crept in?'

'But, Postlethwaite, your name's Postlethwaite.'

'My name's Widgeon.'

'Widgeon?'

'Widgeon.'

'*Not* Postlethwaite?'

'Certainly not.'

The chap uttered an indulgent laugh.

'Ha, ha. Still the same old jovial, merry, kidding Postle-thwaite, I see.'

'I'm not the same old jovial, merry, kidding Postlethwaite,' said Freddie, with heat. 'I never was the jovial, merry, kidding Postlethwaite.'

The chap stared.

'You aren't the Postlethwaite I used to admire so much at dear old Bingleton?'

'I've never been near dear old Bingleton in my life.'

'But you're wearing an Old Bingletonian tie.'

Freddie reeled.

'Is this beastly thing an Old Bingletonian tie? It's one I sneaked from my uncle.'

The chap laughed heartily.

'Well, of all the absurd mix-ups! You look like Postlethwaite and you're wearing an O.B. tie. Naturally, I thought you *were* Postlethwaite. And all the time we were thinking of a couple of other fellows! Well, well, well! However, it's all worked out for the best, what? Goodbye,' he added hastily, and was round the corner like a streak.

Freddie looked after him dully. He was totting up in his mind the final returns. On the debit side, he had lost Drusilla what-ever-her-name-was. He had alienated his uncle, old Blicester. He was down a tenner. And, scaliest thought of all, he hadn't been anybody's hero at school. On the credit side, he had fifty francs.

At the Palm Beach Casino at Cannes you can get five Martini cocktails for fifty francs. Freddie went and had them.

Then, wiping his lips with the napkin provided by the management, he strode from the bar to face the hopeless dawn.

In order that they might enjoy their afternoon luncheon coffee in peace, the Crumpet had taken the guest whom he was entertaining at the Drones Club to the smaller and less frequented of the two smoking-rooms. In the other, he explained, though the conversation always touched an exceptionally high level of brilliance, there was apt to be a good deal of sugar thrown about.

The guest said he understood.

'Young blood, eh?'

'That's right. Young blood.'

'And animal spirits.'

'And animal, as you say, spirits,' agreed the Crumpet. 'We get a fairish amount of those here.'

'The complaint, however, is not, I observe, universal.'

'Eh?'

The other drew his host's attention to the doorway, where a young man in form-fitting tweeds had just appeared. The aspect of this young man was haggard. His eyes glared wildly and he sucked at an empty cigarette-holder. If he had a mind, there was something on it. When the Crumpet called to him to come and join the party, he merely shook his head in a distraught sort of way and disappeared, looking like a character out of a Greek tragedy pursued by the Fates.

The Crumpet sighed. 'Poor old Pongo!'

'Pongo?'

'That was Pongo Twistleton. He's all broken up about his Uncle Fred.'

'Dead?'

'No such luck. Coming up to London again tomorrow. Pongo had a wire this morning.'

'And that upsets him?'

'Naturally. After what happened last time.'

'What was that?'

'Ah!' said the Crumpet.

'What happened last time?'

'You may well ask.'

'I do ask.'

'Ah!' said the Crumpet.

Poor old Pongo (said the Crumpet) has often discussed his Uncle Fred with me, and if there weren't tears in his eyes when he did so, I don't know a tear in the eye when I see one. In round numbers the Earl of Ickenham, of Ickenham Hall, Ickenham, Hants, he lives in the country most of the year, but from time to time has a nasty way of slipping his collar and getting loose and descending upon Pongo at his flat in the Albany. And every time he does so, the unhappy young blighter is subjected to some soul-testing experience. Because the trouble with this uncle is that, though sixty if a day, he becomes on arriving in the metropolis as young as he feels – which is, apparently, a youngish twenty-two. I don't know if you happen to know what the word 'excesses' means, but those are what Pongo's Uncle Fred from the country, when in London, invariably commits.

It wouldn't so much matter, mind you, if he would confine his activities to the club premises. We're pretty broad-minded here, and if you stop short of smashing the piano, there isn't much that you can do at the Drones that will cause the raised eyebrow and the sharp intake of breath. The snag is that he will insist on lugging Pongo out in the open and there, right in the public eye, proceeding to step high, wide and plentiful.

So when, on the occasion to which I allude, he stood pink and genial on Pongo's hearth-rug, bulging with Pongo's lunch and wreathed in the smoke of one of Pongo's cigars, and said: 'And now, my boy, for a pleasant and instructive afternoon,' you will readily understand why the unfortunate young clam gazed at him as he would have gazed at two-penn'orth of dynamite, had he discovered it lighting up in his presence.

'A what?' he said, giving at the knees and paling beneath the tan a bit.

'A pleasant and instructive afternoon,' repeated Lord Ickenham, rolling the words round his tongue. 'I propose that you place yourself in my hands and leave the programme entirely to me.'

Now, owing to Pongo's circumstances being such as to necessitate his getting into the aged relative's ribs at intervals and shaking him down for an occasional much-needed tenner or what not, he isn't in a position to use the iron hand with the old buster. But at these words he displayed a manly firmness.

'You aren't going to get me to the dog races again.'

'No, no.'

'You remember what happened last June.'

'Quite,' said Lord Ickenham, 'quite. Though I still think that a wiser magistrate would have been content with a mere reprimand.'

'And I won't—'

'Certainly not. Nothing of that kind at all. What I propose to do this afternoon is to take you to visit the home of your ancestors.'

Pongo did not get this.

'I thought Ickenham was the home of my ancestors.'

'It is one of the homes of your ancestors. They also resided rather nearer the heart of things, at a place called Mitching Hill.'

'Down in the suburbs, do you mean?'

'The neighbourhood is now suburban, true. It is many years since the meadows where I sported as a child were sold and cut up into building lots. But when I was a boy Mitching Hill was open country. It was a vast, rolling estate belonging to your great-uncle, Marmaduke, a man with whiskers of a nature which you with your pure mind would scarcely credit, and I have long felt a sentimental urge to see what the hell the old place looks like now. Perfectly foul, I expect. Still, I think we should make the pious pilgrimage.'

Pongo absolutely-ed heartily. He was all for the scheme. A great weight seemed to have rolled off his mind. The way he looked at it was that even an uncle within a short jump of the loony bin couldn't very well get into much trouble in a suburb. I mean, you know what suburbs are. They don't, as it were, offer the scope. One follows his reasoning, of course.

'Fine!' he said. 'Splendid! Topping!'

'Then put on your hat and rompers, my boy,' said Lord Ickenham, 'and let us be off. I fancy one gets there by omnibuses and things.'

Well, Pongo hadn't expected much in the way of mental uplift from the sight of Mitching Hill, and he didn't get it. Alighting from the bus, he tells me, you found yourself in the middle of rows and rows of semi-detached villas, all looking exactly alike, and you went on and you came to more semi-detached villas, and those all looked exactly alike, too. Nevertheless, he did not repine. It was one of those early spring days which suddenly change to mid-winter and he had come out without his overcoat, and it looked like rain and he hadn't an umbrella, but despite this his mood was one of sober ecstasy. The hours were passing and his uncle had not yet made a goat of himself. At the Dog Races the other had been in the hands of the constabulary in the first ten minutes.

It began to seem to Pongo that with any luck he might be able to keep the old blister pottering harmlessly about here till nightfall, when he could shoot a bit of dinner into him and put him to bed. And as Lord Ickenham had specifically stated that his wife, Pongo's Aunt Jane, had expressed her intention of scalping him with a blunt knife if he wasn't back at the Hall by lunchtime on the morrow, it really looked as if he might get through this visit without perpetrating a single major outrage on the public weal. It is rather interesting to note that as he thought this Pongo smiled, because it was the last time he smiled that day.

All this while, I should mention, Lord Ickenham had been stopping at intervals like a pointing dog and saying that it must have been just about here that he plugged the gardener in the trousers seat with his bow and arrow and that over there he had been sick after his first cigar, and he now paused in front of a villa which for some unknown reason called itself The Cedars. His face was tender and wistful.

'On this very spot, if I am not mistaken,' he said, heaving a bit of a sigh, 'on this very spot, fifty years ago come Lammas Eve, I . . . Oh, blast it!'

The concluding remark had been caused by the fact that the rain, which had held off until now, suddenly began to buzz down like a shower-bath. With no further words, they leaped into the porch of the villa and there took shelter, exchanging glances with a grey parrot which hung in a cage in the window.

Not that you could really call it shelter. They were protected from above all right, but the moisture was now falling with a sort of swivel action, whipping in through the sides of the porch and tickling them up properly. And it was just after Pongo had turned up his collar and was huddling against the door that the door gave way. From the fact that a female of general-servant aspect was standing there he gathered that his uncle must have rung the bell.

This female wore a long mackintosh, and Lord Ickenham beamed upon her with a fairish spot of suavity.

'Good afternoon,' he said.

The female said good afternoon.

'The Cedars?'

The female said yes, it was The Cedars.

'Are the old folks at home?'

The female said there was nobody at home.

'Ah? Well, never mind. I have come,' said Lord Ickenham, edging in, 'to clip the parrot's claws. My assistant, Mr Walkinshaw, who applies the anaesthetic,' he added, indicating Pongo with a gesture.

'Are you from the bird shop?'

'A very happy guess.'

'Nobody told me you were coming.'

'They keep things from you, do they?' said Lord Ickenham, sympathetically. 'Too bad.'

Continuing to edge, he had got into the parlour by now, Pongo following in a sort of dream and the female following Pongo.

'Well, I suppose it's all right,' she said. 'I was just going out. It's my afternoon.'

'Go out,' said Lord Ickenham cordially. 'By all means go out. We will leave everything in order.'

And presently the female, though still a bit on the dubious side, pushed off, and Lord Ickenham lit the gas-fire and drew a chair up.

'So here we are, my boy,' he said. 'A little tact, a little address, and here we are, snug and cosy and not catching our deaths of cold. You'll never go far wrong if you leave things to me.'

'But, dash it, we can't stop here,' said Pongo.

Lord Ickenham raised his eyebrows.

'Not stop here? Are you suggesting that we go out into that rain? My dear lad, you are not aware of the grave issues involved. This morning, as I was leaving home, I had a rather painful disagreement with your aunt. She said the weather was treacherous and wished me to take my woolly muffler. I replied that the weather was not treacherous and that I would be dashed if I took my woolly muffler. Eventually, by the exercise of an iron will, I had my way, and I ask you, my dear boy, to envisage what will happen if I return with a cold in the head. I shall sink to the level of a fifth-class power. Next time I came to London, it would be with a liver pad and a respirator. No! I shall remain here, toasting my toes at this really excellent fire. I had no idea that a gas-fire radiated such warmth. I feel all in a glow.'

So did Pongo. His brow was wet with honest sweat. He is reading for the Bar, and while he would be the first to admit that he hasn't yet got a complete toe-hold on the Law of Great

Britain he had a sort of notion that oiling into a perfect stranger's semi-detached villa on the pretext of pruning the parrot was a tort or misdemeanour, if not actual barratry or soccage in fief or something like that. And apart from the legal aspect of the matter there was the embarrassment of the thing. Nobody is more of a whale on correctness and not doing what's not done than Pongo, and the situation in which he now found himself caused him to chew the lower lip and, as I say, perspire a goodish deal.

'But suppose the blighter who owns this ghastly house comes back?' he asked. 'Talking of envisaging things, try that one over on your pianola.'

And, sure enough, as he spoke, the front door bell rang.

'There!' said Pongo.

'Don't say "There!" my boy,' said Lord Ickenham reprovingly. 'It's the sort of thing your aunt says. I see no reason for alarm. Obviously this is some casual caller. A ratepayer would have used his latchkey. Glance cautiously out of the window and see if you can see anybody.'

'It's a pink chap,' said Pongo, having done so.

'How pink?'

'Pretty pink.'

'Well, there you are, then. I told you so. It can't be the big chief. The sort of fellows who own houses like this are pale and sallow, owing to working in offices all day. Go and see what he wants.'

'You go and see what he wants.'

'We'll both go and see what he wants,' said Lord Ickenham.

So they went and opened the front door, and there, as Pongo had said, was a pink chap. A small young pink chap, a bit moist about the shoulder-blades.

'Pardon me,' said this pink chap, 'is Mr Roddis in?'

'No,' said Pongo.

'Yes,' said Lord Ickenham. 'Don't be silly, Douglas – of course I'm in. I am Mr Roddis,' he said to the pink chap. 'This, such as he is, is my son Douglas. And you?'

'Name of Robinson.'

'What about it?'

'My name's Robinson.'

'Oh, *your* name's Robinson? Now we've got it straight. Delighted to see you, Mr Robinson. Come right in and take your boots off.'

They all trickled back to the parlour, Lord Ickenham pointing out objects of interest by the wayside to the chap, Pongo gulping for air a bit and trying to get himself abreast of this new twist in the scenario. His heart was becoming more and more bowed down with weight of woe. He hadn't liked being Mr Walkinshaw, the anaesthetist, and he didn't like it any better being Roddis Junior. In brief, he feared the worst. It was only too plain to him by now that his uncle had got it thoroughly up his nose and had settled down to one of his big afternoons, and he was asking himself, as he had so often asked himself before, what would the harvest be?

Arrived in the parlour, the pink chap proceeded to stand on one leg and look coy.

'Is Julia here?' he asked, simpering a bit, Pongo says.

'Is she?' said Lord Ickenham to Pongo.

'No,' said Pongo.

'No,' said Lord Ickenham.

'She wired me she was coming here today.'

'Ah, then we shall have a bridge four.'

The pink chap stood on the other leg.

'I don't suppose you've ever met Julia. Bit of trouble in the family, she gave me to understand.'

'It is often the way.'

'The Julia I mean is your niece Julia Parker. Or, rather, your wife's niece Julia Parker.'

'Any niece of my wife is a niece of mine,' said Lord Ickenham heartily. 'We share and share alike.'

'Julia and I want to get married.'

'Well, go ahead.'

'But they won't let us.'

'Who won't?'

'Her mother and father. And Uncle Charlie Parker and Uncle Henry Parker and the rest of them. They don't think I'm good enough.'

'The morality of the modern young man is notoriously lax.'

'Class enough, I mean. They're a haughty lot.'

'What makes them haughty? Are they earls?'

'No, they aren't earls.'

'Then why the devil,' said Lord Ickenham warmly, 'are they haughty? Only earls have a right to be haughty. Earls are hot stuff. When you get an earl, you've got something.'

'Besides, we've had words. Me and her father. One thing led to another, and in the end I called him a perishing old— Coo!' said the pink chap, breaking off suddenly.

He had been standing by the window, and he now leaped lissomely into the middle of the room, causing Pongo, whose nervous system was by this time definitely down among the wines and spirits and who hadn't been expecting this *adagio* stuff, to bite his tongue with some severity.

'They're on the doorstep! Julia and her mother and father. I didn't know they were all coming.'

'You do not wish to meet them?'

'No, I don't!'

'Then duck behind the settee, Mr Robinson,' said Lord Ickenham, and the pink chap, weighing the advice and finding it good, did so. And as he disappeared the door bell rang.

Once more, Lord Ickenham led Pongo out into the hall.

'I say!' said Pongo, and a close observer might have noted that he was quivering like an aspen.

'Say on, my dear boy.'

'I mean to say, what?'

'What?'

'You aren't going to let these bounders in, are you?'

'Certainly,' said Lord Ickenham. 'We Roddises keep open house. And as they are presumably aware that Mr Roddis has no son, I think we had better return to the old layout. You are the local vet, my boy, come to minister to my parrot. When I return, I should like to find you by the cage, staring at the bird in a scientific manner. Tap your teeth from time to time with a pencil and try to smell of iodoform. It will help to add conviction.'

So Pongo shifted back to the parrot's cage and stared so earnestly that it was only when a voice said 'Well!' that he became aware that there was anybody in the room. Turning, he perceived that Hampshire's leading curse had come back, bringing the gang.

It consisted of a stern, thin, middle-aged woman, a middle-aged man and a girl.

You can generally accept Pongo's estimate of girls, and when he says that this one was a pippin one knows that he uses the term in its most exact sense. She was about nineteen, he thinks, and she wore a black beret, a dark-green leather coat, a shortish tweed skirt, silk stockings and high-heeled shoes. Her eyes were large and lustrous and her face like a dewy rosebud at daybreak on a June morning. So Pongo tells me. Not that I suppose he has ever seen a rosebud at daybreak on a June morning, because it's generally as much as you can do to lug him out of bed in time for nine-thirty breakfast. Still, one gets the idea.

'Well,' said the woman, 'you don't know who I am, I'll be bound. I'm Laura's sister Connie. This is Claude, my husband. And this is my daughter Julia. Is Laura in?'

'I regret to say, no,' said Lord Ickenham.

The woman was looking at him as if he didn't come up to her specifications.

'I thought you were younger,' she said.

'Younger than what?' said Lord Ickenham.

'Younger than you are.'

'You can't be younger than you are, worse luck,' said Lord Ickenham. 'Still, one does one's best, and I am bound to say that of recent years I have made a pretty good go of it.'

The woman caught sight of Pongo, and he didn't seem to please her, either.

'Who's that?'

'The local vet, clustering round my parrot.'

'I can't talk in front of him.'

'It is quite all right,' Lord Ickenham assured her. 'The poor fellow is stone deaf.'

And with an imperious gesture at Pongo, as much as to bid him stare less at girls and more at parrots, he got the company seated.

'Now, then,' he said.

There was silence for a moment, then a sort of muffled sob, which Pongo thinks proceeded from the girl. He couldn't see, of course, because his back was turned and he was looking at the parrot, which looked back at him – most offensively, he says, as parrots will, using one eye only for the purpose. It also asked him to have a nut.

The woman came into action again.

'Although,' she said, 'Laura never did me the honour to invite me to her wedding, for which reason I have not communicated with her for five years, necessity compels me to cross her threshold today. There comes a time when differences must be forgotten and relatives must stand shoulder to shoulder.'

'I see what you mean,' said Lord Ickenham. 'Like the boys of the old brigade.'

'What I say is, let bygones be bygones. I would not have intruded on you, but needs must. I disregard the past and appeal to your sense of pity.'

The thing began to look to Pongo like a touch, and he is convinced that the parrot thought so, too, for it winked and cleared its throat. But they were both wrong. The woman went on.

'I want you and Laura to take Julia into your home for a week or so, until I can make other arrangements for her. Julia is studying the piano, and she sits for her examination in two weeks' time, so until then she must remain in London. The trouble is, she has fallen in love. Or thinks she has.'

'I know I have,' said Julia.

Her voice was so attractive that Pongo was compelled to slew round and take another look at her. Her eyes, he says, were shining like twin stars and there was a sort of Soul's Awakening expression on her face, and what the dickens there was in a pink chap like the pink chap, who even as pink chaps go wasn't much of a pink chap, to make her look like that, was frankly, Pongo says, more than he could understand. The thing baffled him. He sought in vain for a solution.

'Yesterday, Claude and I arrived in London from our Bexhill home to give Julia a pleasant surprise. We stayed, naturally, in the boarding-house where she has been living for the past six weeks. And what do you think we discovered?'

'Insects.'

'Not insects. A letter. From a young man. I found to my horror that a young man of whom I knew nothing was arranging to marry my daughter. I sent for him immediately, and found him to be quite impossible. He jellies eels!'

'Does what?'

'He is an assistant at a jellied eel shop.'

'But surely,' said Lord Ickenham, 'that speaks well for him. The capacity to jelly an eel seems to me to argue intelligence of a high order. It isn't everybody who can do it, by any means. I know if someone came to me and said, "Jelly this eel!" I should be nonplussed. And so, or I am very much mistaken, would Ramsay MacDonald and Winston Churchill.'

The woman did not seem to see eye to eye.

'Tchah!' she said. 'What do you suppose my husband's brother Charlie Parker would say if I allowed his niece to marry a man who jellies eels?'

'Ah!' said Claude, who, before we go any further, was a tall, drooping bird with a red soup-strainer moustache.

'Or my husband's brother, Henry Parker.'

'Ah!' said Claude. 'Or Cousin Alf Robbins, for that matter.'

'Exactly. Cousin Alfred would die of shame.'

The girl Julia hiccoughed passionately, so much so that Pongo says it was all he could do to stop himself nipping across and taking her hand in his and patting it.

'I've told you a hundred times, Mother, that Wilberforce is only jellying eels till he finds something better.'

'What is better than an eel?' asked Lord Ickenham, who had been following this discussion with the close attention it deserved. 'For jellying purposes, I mean.'

'He is ambitious. It won't be long,' said the girl, 'before Wilberforce suddenly rises in the world.'

She never spoke a truer word. At this very moment, up he came from behind the settee like a leaping salmon.

'Julia!' he cried.

'Wilby!' yipped the girl.

And Pongo says he never saw anything more sickening in his life than the way she flung herself into the blighter's arms and clung there like the ivy on the old garden wall. It wasn't that he had anything specific against the pink chap, but this girl had made a deep impression on him and he resented her glueing herself to another in this manner.

Julia's mother, after just that brief moment which a woman needs in which to recover from her natural surprise at seeing eel-jelliers pop up from behind sofas, got moving and plucked her away like a referee breaking a couple of welter-weights.

'Julia Parker,' she said, 'I'm ashamed of you!'

'So am I,' said Claude.

'I blush for you.'

'Me, too,' said Claude. 'Hugging and kissing a man who called your father a perishing old bottle-nosed Gawd-help-us.'

'I think,' said Lord Ickenham, shoving his oar in, 'that before proceeding any further we ought to go into that point. If he called you a perishing old bottle-nosed Gawd-help-us, it seems to me that the first thing to do is to decide whether he was right, and frankly, in my opinion...'

'Wilberforce will apologize.'

'Certainly I'll apologize. It isn't fair to hold a remark passed in the heat of the moment against a chap...'

'Mr Robinson,' said the woman, 'you know perfectly well that whatever remarks you may have seen fit to pass don't matter one way or the other. If you were listening to what I was saying you will understand...'

'Oh, I know, I know. Uncle Charlie Parker and Uncle Henry Parker and Cousin Alf Robbins and all that. Pack of snobs!'

'What!'

'Haughty, stuck-up snobs. Them and their class distinction. Think themselves everybody just because they've got money. I'd like to know how they got it.'

'What do you mean by that?'

'Never mind what I mean.'

'If you are insinuating—'

'Well, of course, you know, Connie,' said Lord Ickenham mildly, 'he's quite right. You can't get away from that.'

I don't know if you have ever seen a bull-terrier embarking on a scrap with an Airedale and just as it was getting down nicely to its work suddenly having an unexpected Kerry Blue sneak up behind it and bite it in the rear quarters. When this happens, it lets go of the Airedale and swivels round and fixes the butting-in animal with a pretty nasty eye. It was exactly the same with the woman Connie when Lord Ickenham spoke these words.

'What!'

'I was only wondering if you had forgotten how Charlie Parker made his pile.'

'What are you talking about?'

'I know it is painful,' said Lord Ickenham, 'and one doesn't mention it as a rule, but, as we are on the subject, you must admit that lending money at two hundred and fifty per cent interest is not done in the best circles. The judge, if you remember, said so at the trial.'

'I never knew that!' cried the girl Julia.

'Ah,' said Lord Ickenham. 'You kept it from the child? Quite right, quite right.'

'It's a lie!'

'And when Henry Parker had all that fuss with the bank it was touch and go they didn't send him to prison. Between ourselves, Connie, has a bank official, even a brother of your husband, any right to sneak fifty pounds from the till in order to put it on a hundred to one shot for the Grand National? Not quite playing the game, Connie. Not the straight bat. Henry, I grant you, won five thousand of the best and never looked back afterwards, but, though we applaud his judgment of form, we must surely look askance at his financial methods. As for Cousin Alf Robbins...'

The woman was making rummy stuttering sounds. Pongo tells me he once had a Pommery Seven which used to express itself in much the same way if you tried to get it to take a hill on high. A sort of mixture of gurgles and explosions.

'There is not a word of truth in this,' she gasped at length, having managed to get the vocal cords disentangled. 'Not a single word. I think you must have gone mad.'

Lord Ickenham shrugged his shoulders.

'Have it your own way, Connie. I was only going to say that, while the jury were probably compelled on the evidence submitted to them to give Cousin Alf Robbins the benefit of the doubt when charged with smuggling dope, everybody knew that he had been doing it for years. I am not blaming him, mind you. If a man can smuggle cocaine and get away with it, good luck to him, say I. The only point I am trying to make is that we are hardly a family that can afford to put on dog and sneer at honest suitors for our daughters' hands. Speaking for myself, I consider that we are very lucky to have the chance of marrying even into eel-jellying circles.'

'So do I,' said Julia firmly.

'You don't believe what this man is saying?'

'I believe every word.'

'So do I,' said the pink chap.

The woman snorted. She seemed overwrought.

'Well,' she said, 'goodness knows I have never liked Laura, but I would never have wished her a husband like you!'

'Husband?' said Lord Ickenham, puzzled. 'What gives you the impression that Laura and I are married?'

There was a weighty silence, during which the parrot threw out a general invitation to join it in a nut. Then the girl Julia spoke.

'You'll have to let me marry Wilberforce now,' she said. 'He knows too much about us.'

'I was rather thinking that myself,' said Lord Ickenham. 'Seal his lips, I say.'

'You wouldn't mind marrying into a low family, would you, darling?' asked the girl, with a touch of anxiety.

'No family could be too low for me, dearest, if it was yours,' said the pink chap.

'After all, we needn't see them.'

'That's right.'

'It isn't one's relations that matter: it's oneselves.'

'That's right, too.'

'Wilby!'

'Julia!'

They repeated the old ivy on the garden wall act. Pongo says he didn't like it any better than the first time, but his distaste wasn't in it with the woman Connie's.

'And what, may I ask,' she said, 'do you propose to marry on?'

This seemed to cast a damper. They came apart. They looked at each other. The girl looked at the pink chap, and the pink chap looked at the girl. You could see that a jarring note had been struck.

'Wilberforce is going to be a very rich man some day.'

'Some day!'

'If I had a hundred pounds,' said the pink chap, 'I could buy a half-share in one of the best milk walks in South London tomorrow.'

'If!' said the woman.

'Ah!' said Claude.

'Where are you going to get it?'

'Ah!' said Claude.

'Where,' repeated the woman, plainly pleased with the snappy crack and loath to let it ride without an encore, 'are you going to get it?'

'That,' said Claude, 'is the point. Where are you going to get a hundred pounds?'

'Why, bless my soul,' said Lord Ickenham jovially, 'from me, of course. Where else?'

And before Pongo's bulging eyes he fished out from the recesses of his costume a crackling bundle of notes and handed it over. And the agony of realizing that the old bounder had had all that stuff on him all this time and that he hadn't touched him for so much as a tithe of it was so keen, Pongo says, that before he knew what he was doing he had let out a sharp, whinnying cry which rang through the room like the yowl of a stepped-on puppy.

'Ah,' said Lord Ickenham. 'The vet wishes to speak to me. Yes, vet?'

This seemed to puzzle the cerise bloke a bit.

'I thought you said this chap was your son.'

'If I had a son,' said Lord Ickenham, a little hurt, 'he would be a good deal better-looking than that. No, this is the local veterinary surgeon. I may have said I *looked* on him as a son. Perhaps that was what confused you.'

He shifted across to Pongo and twiddled his hands enquiringly. Pongo gaped at him, and it was not until one of the hands caught him smartly in the lower ribs that he remembered he was deaf and started to twiddle back. Considering that he wasn't supposed to be dumb, I can't see why he should have twiddled, but no doubt there are moments when twiddling is about all a fellow feels himself equal to. For what seemed to him at least ten hours Pongo had been undergoing great mental stress, and one can't blame him for not being chatty. Anyway, be that as it may, he twiddled.

'I cannot quite understand what he says,' announced Lord Ickenham at length, 'because he sprained a finger this morning and that makes him stammer. But I gather that he wishes to have a word with me in private. Possibly my parrot has got something the matter with it which he is reluctant to mention even in sign language in front of a young unmarried girl. You know what parrots are. We will step outside.'

'*We* will step outside,' said Wilberforce.

'Yes,' said the girl Julia. 'I feel like a walk.'

'And you,' said Lord Ickenham to the woman Connie, who was looking like a female Napoleon at Moscow. 'Do you join the hikers?'

'I shall remain and make myself a cup of tea. You will not grudge us a cup of tea, I hope?'

'Far from it,' said Lord Ickenham cordially. 'This is Liberty Hall. Stick around and mop it up till your eyes bubble.'

Outside, the girl, looking more like a dewy rosebud than ever, fawned on the old buster pretty considerably.

'I don't know how to thank you!' she said. And the pink chap said he didn't, either.

'Not at all, my dear, not at all,' said Lord Ickenham.

'I think you're simply wonderful.'

'No, no.'

'You are. Perfectly marvellous.'

'Tut, tut,' said Lord Ickenham. 'Don't give the matter another thought.'

He kissed her on both cheeks, the chin, the forehead, the right eyebrow, and the tip of the nose, Pongo looking on the while in a baffled and discontented manner. Everybody seemed to be kissing this girl except him.

Eventually the degrading spectacle ceased and the girl and the pink chap shoved off, and Pongo was enabled to take up the matter of that hundred quid.

'Where,' he asked, 'did you get all that money?'

'Now, where did I?' mused Lord Ickenham. 'I know your aunt gave it to me for some purpose. But what? To pay some bill or other, I rather fancy.'

This cheered Pongo up slightly.

'She'll give you the devil when you get back,' he said, with not a little relish. 'I wouldn't be in your shoes for something. When you tell Aunt Jane,' he said, with confidence, for he knew his Aunt Jane's emotional nature, 'that you slipped her entire roll to a girl, and explain, as you will have to explain, that she was an extraordinarily pretty girl – a girl, in fine, who looked like something out of a beauty chorus of the better sort, I should think she would pluck down one of the ancestral battle-axes from the wall and jolly well strike you on the mazzard.'

'Have no anxiety, my dear boy,' said Lord Ickenham. 'It is like your kind heart to be so concerned, but have no anxiety. I shall tell her that I was compelled to give the money to you to enable you to buy back some compromising letters from a Spanish *demi-mondaine*. She will scarcely be able to blame me for rescuing a fondly-loved nephew from the clutches of an adventuress. It may be that she will feel a little vexed with you for a while, and that you may have to allow a certain time to elapse before you visit Ickenham again, but then I shan't be wanting you at Ickenham till the ratting season starts, so all is well.'

At this moment, there came toddling up to the gate of The Cedars a large red-faced man. He was just going in when Lord Ickenham hailed him.

'Mr Roddis?'

'Hey?'

'Am I addressing Mr Roddis?'

'That's me.'

'I am Mr J. G. Bulstrode from down the road,' said Lord Ickenham. 'This is my sister's husband's brother, Percy Frensham, in the lard and imported-butter business.'

The red-faced bird said he was pleased to meet them. He asked Pongo if things were brisk in the lard and imported-butter business, and Pongo said they were all right, and the red-faced bird said he was glad to hear it.

'We have never met, Mr Roddis,' said Lord Ickenham, 'but I think it would be only neighbourly to inform you that a short while ago I observed two suspicious-looking persons in your house.'

'In my house? How on earth did they get there?'

'No doubt through a window at the back. They looked to me like cat burglars. If you creep up, you may be able to see them.'

The red-faced bird crept, and came back not exactly foaming at the mouth but with the air of a man who for two pins would so foam.

'You're perfectly right. They're sitting in my parlour as cool as dammit, swigging my tea and buttered toast.'

'I thought as much.'

'And they've opened a pot of my raspberry jam.'

'Ah, then you will be able to catch them red-handed. I should fetch a policeman.'

'I will. Thank you, Mr Bulstrode.'

'Only too glad to have been able to render you this little service, Mr Roddis,' said Lord Ickenham. 'Well, I must be moving. I have an appointment. Pleasant after the rain, is it not? Come, Percy.'

He lugged Pongo off.

'So that,' he said, with satisfaction, 'is that. On these visits of mine to the metropolis, my boy, I always make it my aim, if possible, to spread sweetness and light. I look about me, even in a foul hole like Mitching Hill, and I ask myself – How can I leave this foul hole a better and happier foul hole than I found it? And if I see a chance, I grab it. Here is our omnibus. Spring aboard, my boy, and on our way home we will be sketching out rough plans for the evening. If the old Leicester Grill is still in existence, we might look in there. It must be fully thirty-five years since I was last thrown out of the Leicester Grill. I wonder who is the bouncer there now.'

Such (concluded the Crumpet) is Pongo Twistleton's Uncle Fred from the country, and you will have gathered by now a rough notion of why it is that when a telegram comes announcing his impending arrival in the great city Pongo blenches to the core and calls for a couple of quick ones.

The whole situation, Pongo says, is very complex. Looking at it from one angle, it is fine that the man lives in the country most of the year. If he didn't, he would have him in his midst all the time. On the other hand, by living in the country he generates, as it were, a store of loopiness which expends itself with frightful violence on his rare visits to the centre of things.

What it boils down to is this – Is it better to have a loopy uncle whose loopiness is perpetually on tap but spread out thin, so to speak, or one who lies low in distant Hants for three hundred and sixty days in the year and does himself proud in London for the other five? Dashed moot, of course, and Pongo has never been able to make up his mind on the point.

Naturally, the ideal thing would be if someone would chain the old hound up permanently and keep him from Jan. One to Dec. Thirty-one where he wouldn't do any harm – viz. among the spuds and tenantry. But this, Pongo admits, is a Utopian dream. Nobody could work harder to that end than his Aunt Jane, and she has never been able to manage it.

'THIS here Socialism,' said a Pint of Bitter thoughtfully. 'You see a lot of that about nowadays. Seems to be all the go.' Nothing in the previous conversation – we had been speaking of mangel-wurzels – had led up to the remark, but in the matter of debate we of the bar-parlour of the Angler's Rest are quick movers. We range. We flit. We leap from point to point. As an erudite Gin and Angostura once put it, we are like Caesar's wife, ready for anything. Rapidly adjusting our minds, we prepared to deal with this new topic.

'Ah,' agreed a Small Bass, 'you may well say that.'

'You well may,' said a Light Lager. 'Spreading all the time, Socialism is. May be something in it, too. What I mean is, it doesn't seem hardly right somehow that you and I should be living off the fat of the land, as the saying is, while there's others, in humbler circumstances, who don't know where to turn for their next half-pint.'

Mr Mulliner nodded.

'That,' he said, 'was precisely how my nephew Archibald felt.'

'He was a Socialist, was he?'

'He became one temporarily.'

The Small Bass wrinkled his forehead.

'Seems to me you've told us about your nephew Archibald before. Was he the one who had the trouble with the explorer?'

'That was Osbert.'

'The one who stammered?'

'No. That was George.'

'You seem to have so many nephews.'

'I have been singularly blessed in that respect,' agreed Mr Mulliner. 'But, as regards Archibald, it may serve to recall him to you if I mention that he was generally considered to be London's leading exponent of the art of imitating a hen laying an egg.'

'Of course, yes. He got engaged to a girl named Aurelia Cammarleigh.'

'At the time when my story begins, he was still engaged to her and possibly the happiest young man in the whole W.1. postal district. But the storm-clouds, I regret to say, were only just over the horizon. The tempest which was so nearly to wreck the bark of Love had already begun to gather.'

Few fashionable engagements (said Mr Mulliner) have ever started with fairer prospects of success than that of my nephew Archibald and Aurelia Cammarleigh. Even cynical Mayfair had to admit that for once a really happy and enduring marriage appeared to be indicated. For such a union there is no surer basis than a community of taste, and this the young couple possessed in full measure. Archibald liked imitating hens, and Aurelia liked listening to him. She used to say she could listen to him all day, and she sometimes did.

It was after one of these sessions – when, hoarse but happy, he was walking back to his rooms to dress for dinner, that he found his progress impeded by a man of seedy aspect who, without any preamble but a short hiccough, said that he had not been able to taste bread for three days.

It puzzled Archibald a little that a complete stranger should be making him the recipient of confidences which might more reasonably have been bestowed upon his medical adviser: but it so happened that only recently he himself had not been able to taste even Stilton cheese. So he replied as one having knowledge.

'Don't you worry, old thing,' he said. 'That often happens when you get a cold in the head. It passes off.'

'I have not got a cold in the head, sir,' said the man. 'I have got pains in the back, weak lungs, a sick wife, stiff joints, five children, internal swellings, and no pension after seven years in His Majesty's army owing to jealousy in high quarters, but not a cold in the head. Why I can't taste bread is because I have no money to buy it. I wish, sir, you could hear my children crying for bread.'

'I'd love to,' said Archibald civilly. 'I must come up and see you some time. But tell me about bread. Does it cost much?'

'Well, sir, it's this way. If you buy it by the bottle, that's expensive. What I always say is, best to get in a cask. But then, again, that needs capital.'

'If I slipped you a fiver, could you manage?'

'I'd try, sir.'

'Right ho,' said Archibald.

This episode had a singular effect on Archibald Mulliner. I will not say that it made him think deeply, for he was incapable of thinking deeply. But it engendered a curious gravity, an odd sense that life was stern and life was earnest, and he was still in the grip of this new mood when he reached his rooms and

Meadowes, his man, brought him a tray with a decanter and syphon upon it.

'Meadowes,' said Archibald, 'are you busy for the moment?'

'No, sir.'

'Then let us speak for a while on the subject of bread. Do you realize, Meadowes, that there are blokes who can't get bread? They want it, their wives want it, their children are all for it, but in spite of this unanimity what is the upshot? No bread. I'll bet you didn't know that, Meadowes.'

'Yes, sir. There is a great deal of poverty in London.'

'Not really?'

'Oh, yes, indeed, sir. You should go down to a place like Bottleton East. That is where you hear the Voice of the People.'

'What people?'

'The masses, sir. The martyred proletariat. If you are interested in the martyred proletariat, I could supply you with some well-written pamphlets. I have been a member of the League for the Dawn of Freedom for many years, sir. Our object, as the name implies, is to hasten the coming revolution.'

'Like in Russia, do you mean?'

'Yes, sir.'

'Massacres and all that?'

'Yes, sir.'

'Now, listen, Meadowes,' said Archibald firmly. 'Fun's fun, but no rot about stabbing me with a dripping knife. I won't have it, do you understand?'

'Very good, sir.'

'That being clear, you may bring me those pamphlets. I'd like to have a look at them.'

*

Knowing Archibald as I do (said Mr Mulliner), I find it difficult to believe that the remarkable change which at this point took place in what for want of a better term one may call his mental outlook could have come entirely from reading pamphlets. Indeed, I cannot bring myself to think that he ever read one of those compositions in its entirety. You know what pamphlets are. They ramble. They go into sections and subsections. If they can think of a phrase like 'the basic fundamentals of the principles governing distribution,' they shove it in. It seems far more likely that he was influenced by hearing Meadowes speak in the Park. Meadowes, on his days off, had the third rostrum from the left as you enter by the Marble Arch gate, and in addition to an impressive delivery enjoyed a considerable gift of invective.

However, of one thing there is no doubt. Before the end of the second week Archibald had become completely converted to the gospel of the Brotherhood of Man: and, as this made him a graver, deeper Archibald, it was not long, of course, before Aurelia noticed the change. And one night, when they were dancing at the Mottled Earwig, she took him to task in her forthright way, accusing him in set terms of going about the place looking like an uncooked haddock.

'I'm sorry, old girl,' replied Archibald apologetically. 'The fact is, I'm brooding a bit at the moment on the situation in Bottleton East.'

Aurelia stared at him.

'Archibald,' she said, for she was a girl of swift intuitions, 'you've had one over the eight.'

'No, I haven't, honestly. It's simply that I'm brooding. And I was wondering if you would mind if I toddled home fairly shortly. All this sort of thing jars on me a goodish bit. All this dancing and so forth, I mean. I mean to say, so different from the home-life of Bottleton East. I don't think a chap ought to be dancing at a time when the fundamental distribution of whatever-it-is is so dashed what-d'you-call-it. You don't find Stalin dancing. Nor Maxton. Nor, for the matter of that, Sidney, Lord Passfield.'

Aurelia refused to be mollified.

'I don't know what's come over you,' she said petulantly. 'You seem absolutely to have changed this last couple of weeks. You used to be one of the cheeriest old bounders that ever donned a spat, and now you're a sort of emperor of the Glooms. You don't even do your hen-imitation any more.'

'Well, the thing is, you can't imitate a hen laying an egg properly if your heart's bleeding for the martyred proletariat.'

'The what?'

'The martyred proletariat.'

'What's that?'

'Well...er...it's – how shall I put it?...it's the martyred proletariat.'

'You wouldn't know a martyred proletariat if they brought it to you on a skewer with Béarnaise sauce.'

'Oh, yes, I should. Meadowes has been giving me all the inside stuff. What it all boils down to, if you follow me, is that certain blokes – me, for example – have got much too much of the ready, while certain other blokes – the martyred proletariat, for instance – haven't got enough. This makes it fairly foul for the m.p., if you see what I mean.'

'I don't see what you mean at all. Oh, well, let's hope you'll have slept all this off by tomorrow. By the way, where are you taking me to dine tomorrow?'

Archibald looked embarrassed.

'I'm awfully sorry, old prune, but I had rather planned to buzz down to Bottleton East tomorrow, to take a dekko at the martyred p.'

'Listen,' said Aurelia tensely, 'do you know what you're really doing to do tomorrow? You're coming round to my house and you're going to render that hen-imitation of yours...'

'But it seems so shallow. Sir Stafford Cripps doesn't imitate hens.'

'...and render it,' continued Aurelia, 'with even more than ordinary brio, gusto and zip. Otherwise, everything is over.'

'But don't you realize that one four four oh point oh oh six families in Bottleton East...'

'That will be all about Bottleton East,' said Aurelia coldly. 'I've said all I am going to say. You understand the position. If, by closing-time tomorrow, you are not round at Number 36A, Park Street, imitating hens till your eyes bubble, you may seek elsewhere for a mate. Because, as far as I am concerned, my nomination will be cancelled. I don't think anybody could call me an unreasonable girl. I am not capricious, not exacting. But I'm positively dashed if I'm going to marry a man who is beginning to be hailed on all sides as London's leading living corpse.'

It was a thoughtful Archibald Mulliner who rose towards evening of the following day and rang the bell for Meadowes, his man. This expedition to Bottleton East was very near his heart. What he felt, he meant to say, was that it's not much good a chap loving the Masses if he never goes near them. He wanted to dash about and fraternize, and show the Masses that in Archibald Mulliner they had a bird whose heart bled for them. And unless he went and looked them up every now and then, they couldn't know that there was an Archibald Mulliner in existence.

No, come what might, he could not forgo this trip. He put it to Meadowes when he entered, explaining all the circumstances, and Meadowes felt the same.

'There must always be martyrs to the Cause, Comrade Mulliner,' said Meadowes.

'Yes, I suppose there must, when you come right down to it,' agreed Archibald moodily. 'Though I'd a dashed sight rather it was a couple of other fellows. All right, then, I'll go. And if that's a drink you've got there, my dear old Third Internationalist, pour it out. There are moments when a chap needs a stiff one.'

'Say when, Comrade Mulliner.'

'Not all the soda, Comrade Meadowes,' said Archibald.

My nephew Archibald, like all the Mulliners, is of an honest and candid disposition, incapable of subterfuge, and there is no doubt that if you had asked him his opinion of Bottleton East as he paced its streets that night he would have confessed frankly that he was just a bit disappointed in the place. Too bright, would have been his verdict, too bally jovial. Arriving in the expectation of finding a sort of grey inferno, he appeared to have been plunged into a perfect maelstrom of gaiety.

On every side, merry matrons sat calling each other names on doorsteps. Cheery cats fought among the garbage-pails. From the busy public-houses came the sound of mouth-organ and song. While, as for the children, who were present in enormous quantities, so far from crying for bread, as he had been led to expect, they were playing hop-scotch all over the pavements. The whole atmosphere, in a word, was, he tells me, more like that of Guest Night at the National Liberal Club than anything he had ever encountered.

But a Mulliner is not easily discouraged. Archibald had come to Bottleton East to relieve the sufferings of the tortured Masses, and he intended to do so if it took all night. Surely, he felt, somewhere among these teeming, pleasure-seeking children there must be one who could do with a bit of bread. And presently it seemed to him that he had found such a one. He had turned down a side-street, and there, coming towards him, kicking a tin can in a preoccupied manner, was a small boy who looked just about in the right vein for a slice or two. His face was grave, his manner sombre and introspective. If he was not actually crying for the stuff at the moment, it was simply, Archibald felt, because he was taking time off.

To seize this child by the hand and drag him to the nearest confectioner and baker was with Archibald Mulliner the work of a moment. He pulled out his note-case and was soon in possession of a fine quartern loaf. He thrust it into the child's hands.

'Bread,' he said, cordially.

The child recoiled. The look of pain on his face had deepened.

'It's all right,' Archibald assured him. 'Nothing to pay. This is on me. A free gift. One loaf, with comps. of A. Mulliner.'

Gently patting the stripling's head, he turned away, modestly anxious to be spared any tearful gratitude, and he had hardly gone a couple of steps when something solid struck him a violent blow on the nape of the neck. For an instant, he thought of thunderbolts, falling roofs, and explosions which kill ten. Then, looking down, he perceived the quartern loaf rolling away along the gutter.

The fact was, the child had been a little vexed. At first, when Archibald had started steering him towards the shop, he had supposed my nephew unbalanced. Then, observing that among the objects for sale at the emporium were chocolate bars, jujubes, and all-day suckers, he had brightened a little. Still dubious as to his companion's sanity, he had told himself that an all-day sucker tastes just as good, even if it proceeds from a dotty donor. And then, just as hope had begun to rise high, this man had fobbed him off with a loaf of bread.

Little wonder that he had chafed. His mood was bitter. And when moods are bitter in Bottleton East direct action follows automatically.

Well, Archibald did what he could. Stooping and picking up the loaf, he darted after the child with bared teeth and flaming eyes. It was his intention to overtake him and fill him up with bread, regardless of his struggles and protests. The thing seemed to him a straight issue. This child needed bread, and he was jolly well going to get it – even if it meant holding him with one hand and shoving the stuff down his throat with the other. In all the history of social work in London's East End there can seldom have been an instance of one of the philanthropic rich being more firmly bent on doing good and giving of his abundance.

His efforts, however, were fruitless. Life in Bottleton East tends to make the young citizen nippy on his feet. Archibald cut out quite a nice pace, but a knowledge of the terrain stood the little fellow in good stead. Presently he had vanished into the night from which he had come, and Archibald, for the weather was sultry and the going had been fast, was left standing – all other emotions swept away in an imperious desire for a cool drink.

There is something about the atmosphere of the tap-room of a public-house that never fails to act like magic on ruffled feelings. The rich smell of mixed liquors, the gay clamour of carefree men arguing about the weather, the Government, the Royal Family, greyhound racing, the tax on beer, pugilism, religion, and the price of bananas – these things are medicine to the bruised soul. Standing in the doorway of the Goose and Gherkin, Archibald became immediately conscious of a restored benevolence.

He had been wrong, he saw, to allow the unpleasant personality of a single child to colour his views on the Masses. Probably that blighted kid had been in no sense representative of the Masses. If one did but know, he told himself, the little beast was very likely thoroughly unpopular in the neighbourhood, if not actually cut by the Bottleton East equivalent of the County. Judging the martyred proletariat by that child was like coming to Mayfair and forming your opinion of the West End of London after meeting somebody like Clarence ('Pot of Poison') Greaseley.

No, the Masses were all right. Once more his heart bled for them, and it seemed to him that the least he could do was to stand them drinks all round. With this humane object in view, he advanced to the counter and, with recollections of old Western films in his mind, addressed the shirt-sleeved man behind it.

'Set 'em up!' he said.

'What's that?' asked the shirt-sleeved man.

'Set 'em up. Ask these gentlemen to name their poison.'

'I don't follow you at all,' said the shirt-sleeved man.

'Dash it,' said Archibald, a little nettled, 'it's quite simple, isn't it? I want these martyred chaps to join me in a spot. Serve out noggins to the multitude and chalk it up to me.'

'Ah!' said the shirt-sleeved man. 'Now I see. Now I understand.'

The information, rapidly flashed about the room, that a human drinking-fountain was in their midst, had the usual effect on the gathering. Their already marked geniality became intensified, and Archibald, as the founder of the feast, was soon the centre of a loving group. They all seemed to look to him for guidance on the various topics of discussion, and with each minute his favourable opinion of the Masses grew. A young man who, when among his peers, generally experienced a certain difficulty in obtaining an audience for his views – his fellow-members of the Drones Club being too prone, whenever he opened his mouth, to urge him to put a sock in it – he found this novel deference enchanting. In the Masses, it seemed to him, he had found his spiritual mates.

Madame Récamier or any other of the hostesses of the old-time *salon* would have recognized and understood his emotions. They knew how agreeable it is to be the focal point of a brilliant gathering. His first half-hour in the tap-room of the Goose and Gherkin was, I should imagine, the happiest of my nephew Archibald's life.

They seemed so anxious to make it plain to him, these honest fellows, that in him they recognized not only the life and soul of the party but the Master Mind. Draining and refilling their glasses at his expense, they hung on his words and made him the unquestioned arbiter of their little disputes. Scarcely had he reassured one as to the chances of the rain holding off, when he was informing another that the Government, though fat-headed, on the whole meant well. He told a man in a cloth cap how to address a Duchess at an informal lunch. He put a man with a broken nose right on the subject of the Apostolic Claims of the Church of Abyssinia.

Each dictum that he uttered was received with murmurs of assent and approval, while at intervals some hearty soul would have his glass recharged and the expense debited to Archibald's account in order that he might drink Archibald's health. I have heard my nephew describe the scene again and again, and each time he described it I could see more clearly how closely the whole affair must have approximated to a love-feast.

But the pleasantest of functions must come to an end, and it seemed to Archibald that the time had come to be pushing along. Much as he liked these tortured bimbos, there were other tortured bimbos in Bottleton East and it was only fair that he should give those, too, a little happiness. So, having ordered a final round, he asked for his account and, thrusting a hand into his pocket, brought it out empty. His note-case was not there. Presumably, when paying for the loaf of bread, he must have left it on the counter of the baker's shop, and the baker, one of those strong, silent men who give the Englishman his reputation for reticence the world over, had not thought it worth while to call his attention to the lapse.

As a psychologist, I found it interesting when Archibald told me that his immediate reaction to this discovery was not dismay. So uplifted was he by the atmosphere of adulation in which he had been basking for the past half-hour that all he felt for the moment was a sort of humorous self-reproach. The laugh, he recognized, was on him. He would have to be prepared, he foresaw, to become the butt of a certain amount of good-natured chaff. With a deprecatory titter he informed the shirt-sleeved man of the position of affairs, and he was just about to add his name and address, in order to facilitate the forwarding of the bill by post, when there broke out something which in its general aspect, he felt dimly, closely paralleled that social revolution of which Meadowes had often spoken so feelingly. And through a sort of mist he saw the shirt-sleeved man vaulting over the counter, moistening the palms of his hands in a purposeful manner.

One can see the situation through the eyes of this shirt-sleeved man. From boyhood up, his views on bilking had been hard and bigoted. Even a mere snitched half-pint had been, in the past, enough to rouse his worst passions. And here before him he saw a man who had bilked on a scale so stupendous, so – as one might say – epic, that history had been made that night in Bottleton East.

Archibald's assertion that the shirt-sleeved man had six arms I discount as due to his not unnatural perturbation at the moment. He bases it on the fact that someone – he assumes it to have been the shirt-sleeved man – seized him by the collar, the right arm, the left arm, the right leg, the left leg, and the seat of the trousers simultaneously. However, be that as it may, my nephew passed the next few moments of his career being shaken like some patent medicine until he could feel his contents frothing within him. Then, just as he had begun to realise that, if this continued, he must reluctantly come unstuck, something seemed to give and he was shooting through the night air – to hit the pavement, bounce, hit it again, bounce for the second time, ricochet along the polished surface for a considerable distance, and eventually come to a halt in the gutter with his head resting against what in its prime must have been part of a good-sized fish. A halibut, Archibald thinks, or a cod.

*

He did not remain there long. In relating to you these little family reminiscences of mine, I have often been struck by a curious thing. I refer to the manner in which a Mulliner, when the crisis arrives, always proves himself a Mulliner – a man, that is to say, of sagacity, resource and initiative. It would be paltering with the truth to say that my nephew Archibald was one of the most quick-witted of the clan, but even he, on observing the shirt-sleeved man heading in his direction, followed by an incensed mob of his recent guests, knew enough to jump to his feet and disappear into the darkness like a hare. Panic lent him wings. There was a moment or two when he heard footsteps clattering in his rear, and once a hard-boiled egg missed him by a hair's-breadth, but eventually he won to a clear lead, and presently was at leisure to halt and give himself up to his meditations.

These, as you may readily imagine, were not of the kindliest. Sir Stafford Cripps would not have liked them. Stalin, could he have been aware of them, would have pursed his lips. For they were definitely hostile to the Masses. All his pitying love for the martyred proletariat had vanished. He has specifically informed me since that in those black moments he wished the martyred proletariat would choke. And the same went for the tortured Masses. He tells me that when he reflected how he had, to all intents and purposes, spurned Aurelia's love and broken her gentle heart just for the sake of doing a bit of good to these tortured bounders he could have laid his head against a lamp-post and wept.

At length, rested and refreshed by his halt, he resumed his progress. He desired above all else to find a way out of this ghastly locality, to return to the civilized amenities of Mayfair, W.1., where men are men and where, if one of those men finds himself short of cash in a place of refreshment, he can simply call for a pencil and sign the bill. Imagine, he meant to say, Ferraro at the Berkeley taking a fellow by the seat of the trousers and playing quoits with him along Piccadilly.

Yes, as I say, my nephew Archibald yearned for Mayfair as the hart pants for cooling streams when heated in the chase. But the problem was: How to get there. He had steeled himself to the prospect of having to walk. All he wanted to know was in what direction to walk. He asked a policeman the way to Piccadilly Circus, but you cannot ask a question like that in Bottleton East without exciting unpleasant suspicions. The policeman merely gave Archibald a narrow look and told him to pass along. Upon which, Archibald passed along and the episode concluded.

It was possibly some twenty minutes after this that he became conscious of a great hunger.

It had been his intention, on setting out for Bottleton East, to take his evening meal there. He had not supposed that the place would run to anything luxurious, but he rather enjoyed the prospect of roughing it as a sort of graceful gesture towards the Masses. And, after all, he was no hog. A little clear soup, with possibly a touch of smoked salmon or a bit of melon in front of it, followed by – say – *truite bleue* and the wing of a chicken and some sort of *soufflé* would do him nicely. And he had been about to look around him for a suitable restaurant when the affair of the anti-bread child had distracted his thoughts. And after that there had been all the *salon* stuff and then the race for life. The consequence was that he was now extremely peckish.

And it was at this moment that he found himself outside one of the myriad public-houses of the locality, staring through an open window into a room with two oilcloth-covered tables in it.

At one there sat a dishevelled man, asleep with his head on his arms. The other was unoccupied, except for a knife and fork which gave promise of rich entertainment.

For a while he stood, staring wolfishly. As he had no money, the situation seemed an *impasse*. But, as I said before, the crisis always brings out the Mulliner in a member of my family. Suddenly, like a flash, there shot into Archibald's mind the recollection that round his neck, carefully adjusted so that it should lie exactly over his heart, he always wore a miniature of Aurelia Cammarleigh in a neat little platinum case.

He hesitated. His spiritual side told him that it would be sacrilege to hand over the outer covering of that sweet girl's miniature in exchange for a meal. But his material self wanted steak and beer, and had him charging through the doorway like a mustang before the hesitation had lasted ten seconds.

Half an hour later, Archibald Mulliner was pushing back his plate and uttering a deep sigh.

It was a sigh of repletion, not of regret. And yet in it there was, perhaps, something of regret as well – for, his hunger now satisfied, kindlier feelings had once more begun to burgeon within him, and he was feeling a little remorseful that he should have allowed himself to think such hard thoughts about the Masses.

After all, reasoned Archibald, sipping his beer and glowing with the broad-minded charity of repletion, you had to admit that at the time of all that unpleasantness there had been something to be said for the view-point of the Masses. He meant to say, a nasty jar it must have been for those poor old proletarians, after having been martyred like the dickens since they were slips of boys, to suck down what they had been led to suppose were free drinks and then suddenly to realize that, owing to the donor having no money, they were in ghastly danger of having to pay for them themselves.

And the shirt-sleeved man. Yes, he could follow the shirt-sleeved man's thought-processes. Perfect stranger comes in and starts strewing drinks all over the place... Can't pay for them... What to do? What to do?... Yes, attitude of shirt-sleeved man quite intelligible. Whole episode, Archibald considered, well calculated to cause a spot of alarm and despondency.

In fact, he had reached at this juncture such a pitch of sweetness and light that, had he been able at that moment to transport himself to his cosy rooms in Cork Street, W.1., it is highly probable that he would still be the same lover of the Masses who had set out that night with such benevolence for Bottleton East.

But more was to happen to my nephew Archibald in Bottleton East that night, and that which happened ruined the Masses' chances of winning his esteem finally.

I have mentioned, I think, that at the other table in this eating-room there was seated – or, rather, reclining – a dishevelled man who slept. He now awoke with a start and, hoisting himself up, blinked beerily at Archibald. He had been doing himself well that night, and the process known as sleeping it off was not yet quite completed. It was, therefore, a rather fishy and inflamed eye that now rested on my nephew. And as the dishevelled man was one of those people who are always a little cross on waking, there was in this eye nothing of the genial, the kindly, or the beaming. He looked at Archibald as if he disliked him, and it is extremely probable that he did. For one thing, Archibald was wearing a collar – slightly soiled after the experiences through which he had passed, but nevertheless a collar – and a sturdy distaste for collars was part of this awakened sleeper's spiritual make-up.

'Wot you doin' there?' he demanded.

Archibald replied cordially enough that he had just been enjoying a medium-grilled steak and fried.

'R!' said the other. 'And took it out of the mouth of the widow and the orphan, like as not.'

'Absolutely no,' replied Archibald. 'The waitress brought it on a tray.'

'So you say.'

'I give you my solemn word,' said Archibald. 'I wouldn't dream of eating a steak that had been in the mouth of a widow or an orphan. I mean to say, in any case, what a beastly idea.'

'And flaunting a collar,' grumbled the man.

'Oh, no, dash it,' objected Archibald. 'Would you say flaunting?'

'Flaunting,' insisted the other.

Archibald was embarrassed.

'Well, I'm awfully sorry,' he said. 'If I'd only known we were going to meet and you would take it like this, I wouldn't have worn a collar. It isn't a stiff collar,' he added, more hopefully. 'Just flannel, soft, gent's one. But, if you like, I'll take it off.'

'Wear it while you can,' advised the dishevelled man. 'The day's coming when collars'll run in streams down Park Lane.'

This puzzled Archibald.

'You don't mean collars, do you? Blood, surely?'

'Blood, too. Blood *and* collars.'

'We'll be able to play boats,' suggested Archibald brightly.

'*You* won't,' said the man. 'And why? Because you'll be inside one of them collars and outside all that blood. Rivers of blood there'll be. Great flowing, bubbling rivers of spouting blood.'

'I say, old lad,' begged Archibald, who was a little squeamish, 'not quite so soon after dinner, if you don't mind.'

'Eh?'

'I say I've just finished dinner, and . . .'

'Dinner! And took it out of the mouth of the widow and the . . .'

'No, no. We went into all that before.'

'Well, get on with it,' said the man, with a moody gesture. Archibald was perplexed.

'Get on with it?'

'Your dinner. You ain't got much time. Because soon you'll be flowing down Park Lane.'

'But I've finished my dinner.'

'No, you ain't.'

'Yes, I have.'

'No, you ain't. That's just where you make your ruddy error. If you've finished your dinner, what's all that fat doing there on the side of the plate?'

'I never eat fat.'

The man had risen. He was now scowling menacingly at Archibald.

'You don't eat fat?'

'No, never.'

The man banged the table.

'You eat that fat,' he bellowed. 'That's what you do. I was taught when I was a nipper to always eat my fat.'

'But, I say . . .'

'You eat that fat!'

'No, but listen, laddie . . .'

'You eat that FAT!'

It was a difficult situation, and my nephew Archibald

recognized it as such. It was not easy to see how two individuals of such conflicting views as this dishevelled man and himself could ever find a formula. Where he liked collars and disliked fat, the other had this powerful anti-collar complex and, apparently, an equally strong fat-urge. He was glad when, presumably attracted by the voice of his companion, who for the last minute and a half had been shouting 'Fat! Fat! Fat!' at the extreme limit of his lungs, somebody came hurrying along the corridor outside and burst into the room.

I say he was glad, but I must add that his gladness was of very brief duration. For the newcomer was none other than his old acquaintance, the shirt-sleeved man.

Yes, gentlemen, like all travellers lost in strange, desert lands, my nephew Archibald, after leaving the Goose and Gherkin, had been wandering round in a circle. And at long last his footsteps had taken him back to the Goose and Gherkin once more. And here he was, face to face again with the one man who, he had hoped, had passed permanently out of his life.

'Wot's all this?' demanded the shirt-sleeved man.

The dishevelled customer had undergone a sudden change of mood. No longer meancing, he was now crying quietly into an ashtray.

'He won't eat his fat,' he sobbed. 'His fat, that's what he won't eat, and it's breakin' his poor father's heart.' He gulped. 'Wears a blinkin' collar, goes runnin' in streams down Park Lane, and won't eat his fat. Make him eat his fat,' he begged, brushing away with a piece of potato the tears that coursed over his face.

'Don't you pay no attention to him . . .' the shirt-sleeved man had begun to say to Archibald. And then the ingratiating note of host to customer faded from his voice. He stopped, stared, uttered a strangled gulp, stared again.

'Gor-blimey!' he whispered, awed. '*You* again?'

He raised a hand, moistened it slightly: raised the other, and moistened that.

'I say, listen . . .' begged Archibald.

'I'm listenin',' said the dishevelled man. He was now in his old position, with head sunk on arms. 'I'm listenin'. That's right,' he said, as a fearful crashing resounded through the room. 'Make him eat his fat.'

It was as the hands of such clocks as were right by Greenwich time were pointing to five minutes past three on the following morning that an at first faint, then swelling 'Charawk-chawk-chawk' made itself heard beneath the window of Aurelia Cammarleigh's bedroom at Number 36A, Park Street. Weary, footsore, remorseful, emptied of his love for the Masses, but full once more of passion for the girl he adored, Archibald Mulliner was fulfilling her behest and imitating for her the hen laying an egg. She had ordered him to come round to her house and give of his best, and here he was, doing it.

For a while, physical fatigue had rendered the performance a poor one. But gradually, as, artist-like, he became absorbed in his task, Archibald's voice gained in volume, in expression, and in all those qualities which make a hen-imitation a thing of beauty. Soon windows all along the street were opening, heads were being thrust out, and complaining voices calling for the police. All the world loves a lover, but not when imitating hens outside their bedroom windows at three in the morning.

The force manifested itself in the person of Constable C-44.

'What,' he asked, 'is all this?'

'Charawk,' cried Archibald.

'Pardon?' said the constable.

'Charawk,' fluted Archibald. 'Charawk.'

And now, having reached the point where it was necessary for the purposes of his art to run round in a circle, holding the sides of his coat, and finding the officer's hand on his shoulder an impediment, he punched the latter smartly in the wind and freed himself. And it was at this moment that Aurelia's window flew open. The lovely girl was a sound sleeper, and, at first, even when the mellow clucking had reached her ears, she had thought it but a dream.

But now she was awake, and her heart was filled with an ecstasy of relief and love.

'Archibald!' she cried. 'Is that really you, you old leper?'

'In person,' replied Archibald, suspending his rendition for an instant.

'Come in and have a spot.'

'Thanks. I'd like to. No, sorry,' added Archibald, as the hand of the Law fell on his shoulder once more. 'I'm afraid I can't.'

'Why not?'

'I've just been pinched by a bally policeman.'

'And you'll stay pinched,' said Officer C-44 in a none too genial voice. His abdomen was still paining him.

'And he says I'll stay pinched,' added Archibald. 'Indeed, it looks very much as if I were even now off to chokey... for about how long would you say, Officer?'

'For about fourteen days without the op.,' replied the other, rubbing his waistband with his disengaged hand. 'Charged with resisting and assaulting the police in the execution of their duty, that's what you'll be.'

'Fourteen days or two weeks, it begins to look like,' shouted Archibald, as he was dragged away. 'Call it a fortnight.'

'I will be waiting for you when you come out,' cried Aurelia.

'You'll be what?' asked Archibald. His voice was barely audible to her now, for the officer was cutting out a good pace.

'Waiting for you . . . When you come out,' shrieked Aurelia.

'Then you love me still?'

'Yes.'

'What?'

'Yes!!'

'Sorry. I didn't get it.'

'YES!!!' roared Aurelia.

And, as she stopped to ease her tortured throat, from round the corner there came to her ears a faint, barely audible 'Charawk', and she knew that he understood.

Park Street closed its windows and went to sleep again.

Our little group of serious thinkers in the bar-parlour of the Angler's Rest had been discussing a breach of promise case to which the papers were giving a good deal of prominence at the moment: and a Whisky Sour had raised the question of how these fellows did it.

'Tell a girl it's all off, I mean,' said the Whisky Sour. 'It must take the courage of a lion. I was a daring sort of young chap in my prime, but if you had told me to go to my dear wife – Miss Bootle she was then, one of the East Balham Bootles – and cast her aside like a soiled glove, I'd never have had the nerve. Yet apparently it's happening every day. Odd.'

A thoughtful Eggnogg said that he understood that the telephone was a great help on these occasions. A Gin and Ginger preferred what he called the good old false beard method.

'It solves the whole problem,' said the Gin and Ginger. 'You get your false beard, then you write the girl a letter, then you slap on the beard and go to Nova Scotia.'

A Half of Stout said that wasn't British. The Gin and Ginger said: Yes, it was, very British. The Half of Stout appealed to Mr Mulliner.

'Would you do that, Mr M.? If you were engaged to a girl and wanted to break it off, would you buy a false beard?'

Mr Mulliner smiled indulgently.

'In my case, as in that of any member of my family,' he said, sipping his hot Scotch and lemon, 'the question of how to break off an engagement could never arise. We may be wrong, we may be foolishly jealous of the *noblesse oblige* of an ancient name, but the code of the Mulliners is that an engagement cannot be broken off by the male contracting party. When a Mulliner plights his troth, it stays plighted. It was this scrupulous sense of chivalry, handed down to him by a long line of ancestors, that so complicated matters for my nephew Archibald when he wished to be free of his honourable obligations to Aurelia Cammarleigh.'

We were stunned.

'Archibald?' we cried. 'Your nephew Archibald? The one who imitated hens? But we thought he worshipped the girl with the utmost fervour.'

'He did.'

'Then why did he want to break the engagement?'

'I need scarcely say that his motives, as the motives of any nephew of mine could not fail to be, were in the last degree praiseworthy and altruistic. He conceived himself to be acting entirely in Aurelia's best interests. But perhaps you would care to hear the story?'

You remarked just now (said Mr Mulliner) that my nephew Archibald worshipped Aurelia Cammarleigh with the utmost fervour, and that is precisely what he did worship her with. Her lightest word was law to him. A smile from her made his day. When I tell you that not once but on three separate occasions he sent his man, Meadowes, out into the Park with instructions to carve his, Archibald's, initials and those of Miss Cammarleigh on the nearest convenient tree with a heart round them, you will understand something of the depths of his feelings. And you will also understand why, when after they had been betrothed some six weeks he found her manner towards him growing definitely cold, he was shaken to the core.

Now, mere temporary and fleeting demonstrations of frigidity on the part of the adored object are, of course, not unusual. Girls affect them simply in order to enjoy the luxury of melting again. But this was different. This had all the earmarks of the real stuff. He would call her the lodestar of his life, and she would say 'Ho-hum.' He would enquire of her if she loved her little Archibald, and she would say 'Hi-ho.' He would speak of their coming wedding-day, and she would ask him if he had read any good books lately. Trifles, you may say... Nothing tangible, I grant... But, nevertheless, taking this with that and weighing all the evidence, Archibald Mulliner became convinced that for some mysterious reason his Aurelia had gone off the boil. And at length, as every young man should do when his heart is aching, he decided to go and ask advice of his mother.

Archibald's mother, since her widowhood, had taken up her abode in the neighbourhood of Kew. Between her and Aurelia there had sprung up a warm friendship, and it occurred to Archibald that in the course of one of their chats together the girl might possibly have let fall some remark which would provide a clue to the mystery. At any rate, it seemed a good speculative venture to pop round and enquire, so he unleashed his two-seater and presently was making his way through the little garden to the sunlit room at the back of the house where his mother liked to sit of an afternoon. And he was just about to step through the open french windows with a filial 'Pip-pip', when a sudden sight sent him back on his heels and he stood gaping – his eyeglass, cast adrift in his emotion, bobbing like some live thing on the end of its cord.

For there, gentlemen, in that sunlit room, stood Lady (Wilhelmina) Mulliner, relict of the late Sir Sholto Mulliner, M.V.O., with her tongue out like a dog's, panting in deep gasps with a sort of horrible 'ha-ha-ha-ha-ha' sound that turned the blood in Archibald's veins to ice. And then, as he watched, she suddenly stopped panting and began to utter a remark which, even by Archibald's not too exacting standards, seemed noticeably goofy. It consisted of the letters 'QX', repeated over and over again. And, as Archibald has often told me, it was the way she said them that got right in amongst a fellow.

The 'Q', he tells me, was an almost inaudible murmur, produced through pouting lips. That, he says, he could have endured. What made everything seem so sad and hopeless was the 'X'. As she emitted this, she drew her mouth back in a ghastly grin till the muscles of her neck stood out like ropes. And she went on and on and on. She refrained from Q-ing the 'Q' only to X the 'X', and when she wasn't X-ing to beat the band she was Q-ing away like a two-year-old. That was how my nephew Archibald described the scene to me, and I must admit that it conjures up a vivid picture.

Well, of course, Archibald understood now why Aurelia's manner towards him had changed of late. Obviously, she must have come upon the poor old parent unexpectedly in the middle of one of these spells of hers and perceived, as he did, that she was as loony as a coot. Enough to make any girl think a bit.

He turned away and staggered out of the garden with blind steps. One can, of course, appreciate his agony, poor lad. Few things are less pleasant for a young man in the spring-time of life than to have a well-loved mother suddenly go off her rocker: and

when such a tragedy involves also the breaking off of his engagement to the girl he worships, you have got something that
Somerset Maugham could make a three-act play out of without
conscious cerebration.

For he realized, of course, that his engagement would have to
be broken off. A man of nice scruples like Archibald Mulliner
could have no option. A chap, he meant to say, can't go lugging
girls off to the altar if there is insanity in his family. Apart
from anything else, this pottiness was probably catching. Quite
likely it would be coming out in himself, too, before he knew
where he was. And a nice thing it would be for Aurelia if, as
they stood side by side in the sacred edifice and the clergyman
said,'Wilt thou, Archibald?' he were to reply,'QX' or, worse, pant
like a dog with his tongue out. All sorts of remarks it would
cause. A girl in such circumstances could scarcely help but feel
pretty silly.

No, he must break the engagement at once...

And then, suddenly, even as he framed the thought, there
rose up before him the recollection of the code of the Mulliners,
and he saw that the whole affair was going to be a good deal
more difficult and complex than he had supposed. He could not
break the engagement. He would have to do something to make
Aurelia take that step. And what it now boiled down to was
What?

He mused. What girls of his acquaintance had broken off
their engagements? And why?

There was Jane Todmarsh. Her betrothed, taking her out for
a spin in the old Pommery Seven, had driven it, her, and himself
into a duck-pond out Hitchin way. She had given the young man
his freedom within two seconds of spitting the first newt out of
her mouth.

Suppose he were to take Aurelia for a drive and...No. He shrank from it. He couldn't say why exactly, but he shrank from it.

Milly Salt had returned her fiancé to store because of his habit of uttering a short, dry, nasty snigger every time she missed a shot in the mixed doubles. No help for Archibald here. Aurelia did not play tennis. Besides, he knew that in no circumstances could he bring himself to snigger drily and nastily at one who to him was more like some sort of a goddess than anything.

The case of Hypatia Sloggett was different. A former flame of the future lord and master had turned up in the middle of dinner one night at the Savoy and made a row.

This, Archibald felt, was the best bet yet. There was the difficulty that he had no former flames, but a moment's thought told him that he could easily go round to some theatrical agency and engage one. There were probably a hundred out-of-work actresses in the Strand neighbourhood who would be delighted to come in on the deal for a fiver.

And yet once again he found himself shrinking. That sort of thing happening in a crowded restaurant could not fail to make a fellow feel pretty dashed conspicuous, and he hated feeling conspicuous. If there was any other alternative, he would vastly prefer to take it.

And it was then that he remembered Dora Trevis. On the eve of becoming Mrs Aubrey Rochester-Wapshott, she had notified the *Morning Post* that the fixture was off, and the whole trouble, Archibald recalled, had been caused by poor old Aubrey getting a bit pie-eyed at the family dinner table and insulting her father.

There was the solution. He would insult old Cammarleigh and leave the rest to Aurelia.

*

Not but what, felt Archibald, it was going to take some doing. This father of Aurelia's was not one of those mild old men who make nice easy insulting. He was a tough, hard-bitten retired Colonial Governor of the type which comes back to England to spend the evening of its days barking at club waiters, and until now it had been Archibald's prudent policy to conciliate him to the utmost. With sedulous assiduity he had always bent himself to the task of giving Sir Rackstraw Cammarleigh the old oil. He had deferred to his opinions. He had smirked meekly, infusing into his manner a rather revolting reverence. Above all, he had listened raptly to his stories, caring little that a certain eccentricity of memory sometimes led the ex-proconsul to tell the same one four evenings in succession.

By these means, he had so succeeded in ingratiating himself with the old blighter that a sudden reversal of policy would have all the greater effect. One bold effort, and it seemed to Archibald that the whole subject of wedding-bells must inevitably be removed from the agenda-paper.

Pale but resolute, my nephew dressed himself with his usual care and set off to dine *en famille* at his loved one's home.

I do not know if any of you gentlemen have ever watched a retired Colonial Governor at his evening meal. I have not had the experience myself, but Archibald tells me it is one fraught with interest. He begins, it seems, in a spirit rather similar to that of the lion of the jungle at feeding-time, growling fiercely over his soup, absorbing his fish to the accompaniment of a series of muffled snarls. It is only with the entrée that a softer mood starts to manifest itself. Then, and onward through the joint and sweet, one is aware of a growing geniality. The first animal hunger has abated. Repletion has done its kindly work.

With the dessert and port, the now mellow subject leans back and starts to tell stories.

It was so that it happened tonight. Bagshot, the butler, filled his employer's glass and stepped back into the shadows: and Sir Rackstraw, grunting not unamiably, fixed Archibald with a bulging eye. Had he been a man to take notice of such phenomena, he would have seen that the young man was white and tense and wore a strung-up look. But if there was one thing in this world that did not interest Sir Rackstraw Cammarleigh it was the play of expression on the face of Archibald Mulliner. He was regarding him now purely in the light of a recipient of his story of old George Bates and the rhinoceros.

'What you say about there being a full moon tonight,' he began, for it was on this subject that Archibald had just hazarded a remark, 'reminds me of a curious thing that happened to an old friend of mine out in Bongo-Bongo. Old George Bates.'

He paused to sip at his glass, and Archibald saw that Aurelia's face had grown tired and hard. Her mother, too, a pale, worn woman, uttered a stifled little sigh. Somewhere in the background he could hear Bagshot stirring uneasily.

'At the time of the full moon,' resumed Sir Rackstraw, 'it is the custom in Bongo-Bongo to hunt the rhinoceros, and this friend of mine . . . George Bates his name was . . . by the way, stop me if I've told you this before . . .'

'Stop!' said Archibald.

There was a tense silence. Sir Rackstraw was quivering as if the word had been a bullet and he the rhinoceros which in his less cordial moods he somewhat resembled.

'What did you say?' he rasped.

'I said "Stop!",' replied Archibald. Though quaking inwardly, he preserved an outward firmness, even a sort of truculence. 'You told me to stop you if I had heard it before, and I stopped you. I have heard that story six times before. Even if it were good, I wouldn't like it. But it is not good. It is rotten. And I shall be extremely obliged, Cammarleigh, if you will refrain from inflicting it upon me either now or at any other time when you may feel the urge. I never wish to hear of Bates and his rhinoceros again. And I couple with the name of this rhinoceros the names of any other rhinoceri you or your friends may have encountered in your exceptionally tedious past. You understand me, Cammarleigh? Enough is enough.'

He stopped and helped himself to port. At the same moment, he pushed his chair back a little, prepared, should events so shape themselves as to render such a course advisable, to slide under the table and there defend himself with tooth and claw. A stoutish ex-Colonial Governor, he reasoned, would find it pretty hard to get at a fellow who had dug himself well in under a table.

It was as he reached this decision that Lady Cammarleigh spoke.

'Thank you, Archibald,' she said, and there were tears in her faded voice. 'It was about time some tough bimbo came along and spoke those brave words. You have said just what I have been wanting to say for years. This would have made the hundred and twenty-seventh time I have heard the story of George Bates and the rhinoceros.'

Aurelia's eyes were shining.

'I've heard it forty-three times,' she said.

There was a decorous cough in the shadows.

'And I,' said Bagshot, the butler, 'eighty-six. May I take the liberty of adding my humble tribute of gratitude to Mr Mulliner for the firm stand he has taken. I sometimes think that gentlemen do not realize how distressing it is for a butler to have to listen to their after-dinner stories. His official position, involving, as it does, the necessity of standing with his back against the sideboard, renders escape impossible. It makes a butler's life very wearing, very wearing. Thank you, Mr Mulliner.'

'Not at all,' said Archibald.

'Thank you, Archibald,' said Lady Cammarleigh.

'Don't mention it,' said Archibald.

'Thank you, dear,' said Aurelia.

'Only too pleased,' said Archibald.

'You see now, Father,' said Aurelia, turning to Sir Rackstraw, 'why you are shunned at the club.'

The proconsul started.

'I am not shunned at the club!'

'You are shunned at the club. It's all over London.'

'Well, upon my word, do you know, I believe you're right,' said Sir Rackstraw thoughtfully. 'Now you mention it, fellows have shunned me at the club. I see it all now. I was degenerating into a club bore. And, thanks to the fearless candour of this fine young fellow here, my eyes have been opened. I see the light. Bagshot, charge the glasses. My dear, have you port? Aurelia, you? Then I give you my future son-in-law, Archibald Mulliner, who has rendered me a service this night which I can never sufficiently repay. And now, Aurelia, my dear, as we have finished our simple evening meal, perhaps you and our young friend here would care to take a stroll round the square. As he so justly observed a moment ago,' chuckled Sir Rackstraw, 'there is a full moon.'

Out in the moonlit square, Aurelia was all remorse and worshipping admiration.

'Oh, Archibald,' she cried, as she pressed against his arm, 'I feel so awful. You must have noticed how cold I have been of late. It was because you were so meek and wormlike with Father. I recognized, of course, that he is a man who chews tenpenny nails and swallows broken bottles, but it revolted me to think that you should be afraid of him. You were my wonder-man, and it seemed during those awful days that I had been mistaken in you; that you had failed me. And all the while you were simply biding your time, preparatory to slipping it across him properly. I really do think, darling, that you are the most marvellous man on earth.'

Well, Archibald said, 'No, I say, really, thanks awfully,' but it was in a dull, toneless voice that he said it. The hideous irony of his position was weighing sorely on the young man. Here he was, adored – one might say fawned upon – by this lovely girl, and simple decency made it impossible that he should marry her. And if you could tie that, even in a Russian novel, he would like to know how.

'Tomorrow,' said Aurelia, 'you shall take me to dine at the Savoy, and we'll celebrate.'

'Right ho,' said Archibald absently.

He was wondering where the best theatrical agency was.

It was at eleven-thirty next morning that Archibald stood with reluctant feet half-way up the dark staircase that leads to the offices of Isadore McCallum, the well-known agent who has told more people that he will write and let them know if anything turns up than any other man of his profession in London. His mood was Hamlet-like – wavering, irresolute.

Reason told him that this thing had got to be done: but, as he told Reason, nobody was going to make him like it.

And so he hesitated. And it was while he was still hesitating that there came from above the sound of a slammed door and the noise of rushing feet. A moment later, a solid body had struck him, and in its company, inextricably entwined, he fell the half-flight of stairs that ended in the street door. It was only when this frail barrier had given way before their combined weights and he was sorting himself out upon the pavement that he perceived that what had caused all this activity was a stout young woman in pink with peroxide hair.

For a few moments she stood there panting, her demeanour that of one who has recently passed through some great ordeal. Then she spoke.

'Did I bump you, dearie? I'm sorry.'

'Not at all,' said Archibald courteously, straightening with his right hand a rib that seemed to have got a little bent.

'I wasn't looking where I was going.'

'It's quite all right.'

'And who would have been looking where they were going after being insulted by a worm?' demanded the woman.

Archibald, ever sympathetic, clicked his tongue.

'Did a worm insult you?'

'You bet a worm insulted me.'

'Worms will be worms,' suggested Archibald.

This tolerant view-point seemed to give offence.

'Not while I have my strength, they won't,' said the woman. 'Listen! What do you think that man up there said to me? Said I was too stout to play heroines in the Number Two towns!' She sniffed bitterly. 'Why, you can't be too stout for the Number Two towns. The thing isn't possible. They like their heroines stout. It makes them feel they've had their money's worth. "This buxom beauty" – *Leicester Argus*.'

'I beg your pardon?'

'I was saying what the *Leicester Argus* said about me. My "Geraldine" in *Twisted Lives*.'

Archibald's intellect, such as it was, began to assert itself. He had been a little shaken by his fall.

'Do you play heroines in melodramas?' he asked eagerly.

'Do *I* play heroines in melodramas?' she echoed. 'Do I play *heroines* in melodramas? Do I play heroines in *melodramas*? Why...'

Archibald saw that she did.

'I say,' he said, 'how about stepping up to the Bodega for a small port? I've a little business proposition I should like to put to you.'

She seemed suspicious. Her gaze, unlike her waist-measurement, was narrow.

'Business?'

'Strictly business.'

'You don't want to cover me with jewels?'

'Absolutely not.'

'Well, then, I don't mind if I do,' she said, relieved. 'You've no notion how careful a girl has got to be these days,' she added. 'I've had men in places like Huddersfield offer me guilty splendour on the strength of my having accepted a Bath bun and a small cocoa at their hands.'

'Baronets?' asked Archibald, for he had heard that there was a good deal of moral laxness among that class.

'I think so,' said his companion. 'Disguised.'

And so, chatting amiably, they passed into the fragrant coolness of the Bodega.

*

I have little or no acquaintance among the pure and beefy ladies who play heroines in our Number Two towns (said Mr Mulliner), so I am unable to say whether Miss Yvonne Maltravers – for such was the name on the professional card which she had handed to my nephew – was exceptionally gifted, or whether intelligence like hers is the rule or norm in those circles. Suffice it to say that she not only grasped his position, as he explained it, with lightning celerity, but seemed to find nothing unusual in a young man being in such a position. And Archibald, who had anticipated a good deal of tedious explanation, was enchanted by her quickness at the uptake.

'Then you follow the scenario?' he said. 'You see what I'm driving at? You really will breeze along to the Savoy tonight and play the role of a betrayed girl?'

Miss Maltravers coughed with a touch of rebuke.

'Not betrayed, dearie. I've always kept my Art clean and always shall. You don't read the *Bexhill Gazette*, do you? "She is purity personified," it said. I put it in my professional ads. for a time. That was when I was "Myrtle" in *The Hand of Doom*. If you will allow me to make a suggestion – we're all working for the good of the show – I'd say let me be someone unspotted who's bringing a breach of promise action against you.'

'That's just as good, you think?'

'It's better,' said Miss Maltravers firmly. 'It's the duty of all of us in these licentious post-war days to put our hands to the plough and quench the flame of this rising tide of unwholesome suggestiveness.'

'I've thought that a hundred times,' said Archibald.

'I've thought it a couple of hundred,' said Miss Maltravers.

'Then that's fine,' said Archibald, rising. 'I'll expect you at the Savoy Grill round about nine-fifteen. You come in—'

'Enter,' corrected Miss Maltravers.

'That's right.'

'Left. I always enter left. It shows up my best profile.'

'And you accuse me of having trifled with your affections—'

'In a nice way.'

'In a perfectly nice way... at ... where would you say?'

'Middlesbrough,' said Miss Maltravers with decision. 'And I'll tell you why. My affections actually were trifled with in Middlesbrough once, so it'll help me give colour and movement to the scene. When I remember Bertram, I mean to say. That was his name – Bertram Lushington. I put him over my knee and gave him a good spanking.'

'That won't be necessary tonight, will it?' asked Archibald, a little anxiously. 'Of course, I don't want to interfere with your conception of the role or whatever you call it—'

'It's how I *see* the part.'

'Dress trousers are dashed thin, you know.'

'Very well,' said Miss Maltravers regretfully. 'Just as you like. Cut business. Lines only.'

'Thanks awfully.'

'I'll tell you one thing that's going to be a great help,' said Miss Maltravers, brightening. 'The whole scene's very like my big second-act smash in *His Forgotten Bride*, except that that was at the altar rails. You wouldn't prefer to postpone production till we can get an altar-rails set?'

'No, I think we'd better rush the thing through tonight.'

'Just as you say. It'll mean making a few line cuts, but most of the speeches will fit in. You won't mind if I call you a heartless cur who should blush to think that he sullies the grand old name of Englishman?'

'Not at all.'

'It got a round at Eastbourne. All right, then. Nine-fifteen tonight.'

'Nine-fifteen on the dot,' said Archibald.

It might be supposed that, now that everything had been so satisfactorily arranged, my nephew Archibald would have felt relieved. But such was not the case. As he sat toying with his food at the Savoy that night, the reflection that he had done his duty like a Mulliner was not enough to keep him from experiencing a hideous depression and apprehension.

One paid dearly, he mused, for the traditions of his race. How simple it would have been for one who was not a Mulliner to write Aurelia a letter severing their relations and then go abroad somewhere and lie low till the thing had blown over. Instead of which, here he was, faced with the prospect of disgrace and shame in a restaurant filled with his friends and acquaintances.

He had always been so proud of his reputation. He had liked to think that, as he walked about London, people pointed him out and whispered 'That's Mulliner, the chap who imitates hens.' From tonight the formula would be changed. It would be, 'Look! See that bird? Mulliner. The fellow who was mixed up in that priceless scene at the Savoy Grill.' A bitter reflection, rendered none the more pleasant by the thought that it was quite possible that, carried away by her art, his accomplice might forget their gentleman's agreement and spank him after all.

It was with a distrait ear, therefore, that he listened to Aurelia's conversation. She was in lively mood, and her silvery laugh often rang out over the din and chatter. And every time it did so it seemed to go right through Archibald like an electric drill.

He looked about him, and shuddered at what he saw. Somehow, when he had first conceived this masquerade, he had visualized it as taking place in what Miss Maltravers would have described as a 'set' occupied only by himself and Aurelia. But tonight the whole muster-roll of his acquaintance seemed to be present. Over there sat the young Marquis of Hampshire, who did the Gossip for the *Daily Tribune*. Two tables beyond, he saw the young Duke of Datchet, who did the Gossip for the *Daily Post*. And, besides these, at least half a dozen more Earls, Barons, Viscounts, and Baronets, who did the Gossip for a half-dozen more journals. He would be sure of an extended, if not a good, Press.

And then suddenly there occurred something which seemed to him positively to put the saucepan cover on it. Through the door, accompanied by an elderly gentleman of military aspect, came his mother.

Archibald had reached the sardines-on-toast stage by this time, and he tells me that he distinctly felt those sardines turn to ashes in his mouth. He had always loved and respected his mother, even after circumstances had so arranged themselves as to convince him that she was leaky in the overhead valves, and the thought that she was to be a witness of tonight's scene gashed him like a knife.

Dimly, he realized that Aurelia was saying something to him. 'Eh?' he said.

'I said, "There's your mother".'

'I saw her.'

'She's looking ever so much better, don't you think?'

'Better?'

'She was worried,' explained Aurelia, 'because she was getting a double chin. I found her in floods of tears one afternoon, trying to work it off with a squeegee. Absolutely no good, of course, and I told her so. There's only one thing for a double chin, and that's this new method everybody's going in for these days. First, you stand and pant like a dog for twenty minutes. This hardens the throat muscles. Then you breathe deeply and keep saying "QX", "QX" over and over again. The "Q" isn't so important, but the "X" is the goods. It works directly on the chin and neck, tightening them up and breaking down the fatty tissues.'

The room seemed to be rocking about Archibald.

'What!'

'Absolutely,' said Aurelia. 'You've got to be careful, of course, at first, otherwise you're extremely apt to dislocate your neck, or something.'

'Do you mean to tell me,' demanded Archibald, choking, 'that all that "QX" stuff I saw her doing was simply one of these bally modern beauty-drill things?'

'Oh, did you see her? It must have given you rather a shock, I should think. The first time I saw my aunt doing it, I was on the phone, ringing up doctors to come on the run and certify her, before you could say "What ho".'

Archibald leaned back in his chair, breathing heavily. For a moment, all he could feel was a sullen resentment against the Fate that wrecks our lives – as far as one can see, in a spirit of pure whimsicality. A fat lot of good it was, he felt, acting from the best motives in this world.

Then his resentment extended itself to Woman. Women, he felt, simply ought not to be allowed loose. You never knew what they were going to do next.

And then, correcting himself, he realized that he knew quite well what one woman, at least, was going to do next. Miss Yvonne Maltravers was going to come entering left and telling him that he was sullying the grand old name of Middlesbrough or whatever it was.

He looked at his watch. The hands pointed to fourteen minutes past nine.

'Of course, if it's a question of reducing the tummy,' said Aurelia, 'that's different. You have to go down on all fours and crawl round the room, saying "Oofa-oofa". I say,' she broke off, and her silvery laugh rang through the room once more, 'you do get all sorts in these eating-houses nowadays. Look at that weird female by the door.'

Archibald followed her gaze, and his heart did two double hand-springs. It was Miss Maltravers who stood on the threshold or, as she would no doubt have preferred to put it herself, in the downstage O.P. entrance. She was peering about her at the tables.

'Seems to be looking for someone,' said Aurelia.

If some sportive hand had suddenly introduced a bradawl into the seat of my nephew Archibald's trousers, he could not have risen with more celerity. There was, he told himself, just one hope. It might lead to a certain amount of talk, but if he were to place one hand over Miss Maltravers's mouth and, seizing the slack of her dress with the other, rush her out the way she had come, dump her into a cab, tell that cab to drive to Shepherd's Bush, and on the way thither drop the talented artiste out of window into a convenient basement, he might yet be saved.

The policy, as I say, might excite comment. Aurelia, no doubt, would raise her eyebrows in a mute demand for an explanation. But he could always say that it was one of these new slimming exercises, designed to strengthen the triceps muscles and remove superfluous fat from the upper chest.

More like a puma of the African hinterlands than a Mulliner, Archibald sped across the room. And Miss Maltravers, sighting him, spoke.

'Oh, Mr Mulliner, I was looking for you.'

To Archibald's surprise, she spoke in a whisper. At their previous meeting, in the Bodega, her voice had been full and robust – so much so that nervous fellow-customers had twice complained. But now she was more like a leaky gas-pipe than anything Archibald could think of. And even this novel method of delivery seemed to cause her pain. She winced distinctly.

'I wanted to tell you, dearie,' she proceeded, still in that same strange, hushed voice, 'that there's been a sort of hitch, if you know what I mean. The fact is, like a silly girl, taking those harsh words of Mr McCallum's too much to heart, I started trying one of these new exercises for reducing the chin this afternoon, that a lady friend happened to tell me of. You may have heard of it – it's the one where you say "QX", and it was all right for the first three "Q"s and the first two "X"s, but I wasn't more than half-way through the third "X" when something suddenly seemed to go crack in my throat, and now I can't speak except in a whisper without feeling as if I was being torn asunder with pincers. So there it is, dearie, I hate to disappoint my public, a thing I've never done in my life before – "This loyal artist." – *Wolverhampton Express* – so I'll go on, if you like, but I warn you it won't be the same thing. I shan't be able to do myself what you might call justice. That part wants playing, and a girl can't give of her best in a whisper. Why, once in Peebles I cracked a couple of footlights. Still, as I say, if you'd like me to walk the scene, I will.'

For a moment, Archibald could not speak. It was not so much that his mouth was still full of sardines on toast as that he was overpowered, unmanned by a rush of emotion such as he had not experienced since the day when Aurelia Cammarleigh had promised to be his.

'Don't dream of it,' he urged. 'It won't be necessary. Owing to unforeseen circumstances, the production is off. You go straight home, old soul, and rub liniment on yourself. I'll send you a cheque in the morning.'

'It's just about here that it seems to catch me.'

'I'll bet it does,' said Archibald. 'Well, pip-pip, toodle-oo, cheerio, and God bless you. I shall watch your future career with considerable interest.'

With feet that hardly seemed to touch the floor he returned to his table. Aurelia was puzzled and curious.

'Did you know her?' she asked.

'Oh, yes,' said Archibald. 'Old nurse of mine.'

'What did she want?'

'Just came to wish me many happy returns of the day.'

'But it isn't your birthday.'

'No, but you know what these old nurses are. Now, tell me, my precious angel dream-rabbit,' said Archibald, 'this wedding of ours. My idea is to rope in a couple of Bishops and do the thing right. Not one Bishop, if you see what I mean – two Bishops. Because, if you have a spare, nothing can go wrong. And nowadays, when you see people straining their throats on all sides, you can't afford to take any chances.'

THE Pint of Lager breathed heavily through his nose.

'Silly fathead!' he said. 'Ashtrays in every nook and cranny of the room – ashtrays staring you in the eye wherever you look – and he has to go and do a fool thing like that.'

He was alluding to a young gentleman with a vacant, fish-like face who, leaving the bar-parlour of the Angler's Rest a few moments before, had thrown his cigarette into the wastepaper basket, causing it to burst into a cheerful blaze. Not one of the little company of amateur fire-fighters but was ruffled. A Small Bass with a high blood pressure had had to have his collar loosened, and the satin-clad bosom of Miss Postlethwaite, our emotional barmaid, was still heaving.

Only Mr Mulliner seemed disposed to take a tolerant view of what had occurred.

'In fairness to the lad,' he pointed out, sipping his hot Scotch and lemon, 'we must remember that our bar-parlour contains no grand piano or priceless old walnut table, which to the younger generation are the normal and natural repositories for lighted cigarette-ends. Failing these, he, of course, selected the waste-paper basket. Like Mordred.'

'Like who?' asked a Whisky and Splash.

'Whom,' corrected Miss Postlethwaite.

The Whisky and Splash apologized.

'A nephew of mine. Mordred Mulliner, the poet.'

'Mordred,' murmured Miss Postlethwaite pensively. 'A sweet name.'

'And one,' said Mr Mulliner, 'that fitted him admirably, for he was a comely lovable sensitive youth with large, fawn-like eyes, delicately chiselled features and excellent teeth. I mention these teeth, because it was owing to them that the train of events started which I am about to describe.'

'He bit somebody?' queried Miss Postlethwaite, groping.

'No. But if he had had no teeth he would not have gone to the dentist's that day, and if he had not gone to the dentist's he would not have met Annabelle.'

'Annabelle whom?'

'Who,' corrected Miss Postlethwaite.

'Oh, shoot,' said the Whisky and Splash.

Annabelle Sprockett-Sprockett, the only daughter of Sir Murgatroyd and Lady Sprockett-Sprockett of Smattering Hall, Worcestershire. Impractical in many ways (said Mr Mulliner), Mordred never failed to visit his dentist every six months, and on the morning on which my story opens he had just seated himself in the empty waiting-room and was turning the pages of a three-months-old copy of the *Tatler* when the door opened and there entered a girl at the sight of whom – or who, if our friend here prefers it – something seemed to explode on the left side of his chest like a bomb. The *Tatler* swam before his eyes, and when it solidified again he realized that love had come to him at last.

Most of the Mulliners have fallen in love at first sight, but few with so good an excuse as Mordred. She was a singularly beautiful girl, and for a while it was this beauty of hers that enchained my nephew's attention to the exclusion of all else. It was only after he had sat gulping for some minutes like a dog with a chicken bone in its throat that he detected the sadness in her face. He could see now that her eyes, as she listlessly perused her four-months-old copy of *Punch*, were heavy with pain.

His heart ached for her, and as there is something about the atmosphere of a dentist's waiting-room which breaks down the barriers of conventional etiquette he was emboldened to speak.

'Courage!' he said. 'It may not be so bad, after all. He may just fool about with that little mirror thing of his, and decide that there is nothing that needs to be done.'

For the first time she smiled – faintly, but with sufficient breadth to give Mordred another powerful jolt.

'I'm not worrying about the dentist,' she explained. 'My trouble is that I live miles away in the country and only get a chance of coming to London about twice a year for about a couple of hours. I was hoping that I should be able to put in a long spell of window-shopping in Bond Street, but now I've got to wait goodness knows how long I don't suppose I shall have time to do a thing. My train goes at one-fifteen.'

All the chivalry in Mordred came to the surface like a leaping trout.

'If you would care to take my place—'

'Oh, I couldn't.'

'Please. I shall enjoy waiting. It will give me an opportunity of catching up with my reading.'

'Well, if you really wouldn't mind—'

Considering that Mordred by this time was in the market to tackle dragons on her behalf or to climb the loftiest peak of the

Alps to supply her with edelweiss, he was able to assure her that he did not mind. So in she went, flashing at him a shy glance of gratitude which nearly doubled him up, and he lit a cigarette and fell into a reverie. And presently she came out and he sprang to his feet, courteously throwing his cigarette into the wastepaper basket.

She uttered a cry. Mordred recovered the cigarette.

'Silly of me,' he said, with a deprecating laugh. 'I'm always doing that. Absent-minded. I've burned two flats already this year.'

She caught her breath.

'Burned them to the ground?'

'Well, not to the ground. They were on the top floor.'

'But you burned them?'

'Oh, yes. I burned them.'

'Well, well!' She seemed to muse. 'Well, goodbye, Mr—'

'Mulliner. Mordred Mulliner.'

'Goodbye, Mr Mulliner, and thank you so much.'

'Not at all, Miss—'

'Sprockett-Sprockett.'

'Not at all, Miss Sprockett-Sprockett. A pleasure.'

She passed from the room, and a few minutes later he was lying back in the dentist's chair, filled with an infinite sadness. This was not due to any activity on the part of the dentist, who had just said with a rueful sigh that there didn't seem to be anything to do this time, but to the fact that his life was now a blank. He loved this beautiful girl, and he would never see her more. It was just another case of ships that pass in the waiting-room.

Conceive his astonishment, therefore, when by the afternoon post next day he received a letter which ran as follows:

> Smattering Hall,
> > Lower Smattering-on-the-Wissel,
> > > Worcestershire.

Dear Mr Mulliner,

My little girl has told me how very kind you were to her at the dentist's today. I cannot tell you how grateful she was. She does so love to walk down Bond Street and breathe on the jewellers' windows, and but for you she would have had to go another six months without her little treat.

I suppose you are a very busy man, like everybody in London, but if you can spare the time it would give my husband and myself so much pleasure if you could run down and stay with us for a few days – a long week-end, or even longer if you can manage it.

> With best wishes,
> > Yours sincerely,
> > > Aurelia Sprockett-Sprockett.

Mordred read this communication six times in a minute and a quarter and then seventeen times rather more slowly in order to savour any *nuance* of it that he might have overlooked. He took it that the girl must have got his address from the dentist's secretary on her way out, and he was doubly thrilled – first, by this evidence that one so lovely was as intelligent as she was beautiful, and secondly because the whole thing seemed to him so frightfully significant. A girl, he meant to say, does not get her mother to invite fellows to her country home for long week-ends (or even longer if they can manage it) unless such fellows have made a pretty substantial hit with her. This, he contended, stood to reason.

He hastened to the nearest post-office, dispatched a telegram to Lady Sprockett-Sprockett assuring her that he would be with her on the morrow, and returned to his flat to pack his effects. His heart was singing within him. Apart from anything else, the invitation could not have come at a more fortunate moment, for what with musing on his great love while smoking cigarettes he had practically gutted his little nest on the previous evening, and while it was still habitable in a sense there was no gainsaying the fact that all those charred sofas and things struck a rather melancholy note and he would be glad to be away from it all for a few days.

It seemed to Mordred, as he travelled down on the following afternoon, that the wheels of the train, clattering over the metals, were singing 'Sprockett-Sprockett' – not 'Annabelle,' of course, for he did not yet know her name – and it was with a whispered 'Sprockett-Sprockett' on his lips that he alighted at the little station of Smattering-cum-Blimpstead-in-the-Vale, which, as his hostess's notepaper had informed him, was where you got off for the Hall. And when he perceived that the girl herself had come to meet him in a two-seater car the whisper nearly became a shout.

For perhaps three minutes, as he sat beside her, Mordred remained in this condition of ecstatic bliss. Here he was, he reflected, and here she was – here, in fact, they both were – together, and he was just about to point out how jolly this was and – if he could work it without seeming to rush things too much – to drop a hint to the effect that he could wish this state of affairs to continue through all eternity, when the girl drew up outside a tobacconist's.

'I won't be a minute,' she said. 'I promised Biffy I would bring him back some cigarettes.'

A cold hand seemed to lay itself on Mordred's heart.

'Biffy?'

'Captain Biffing, one of the men at the Hall. And Guffy wants some pipe-cleaners.'

'Guffy?'

'Jack Guffington. I expect you know his name, if you are interested in racing. He was third in last year's Grand National.'

'Is he staying at the Hall, too?'

'Yes.'

'You have a large house-party?'

'Oh, not so very. Let me see. There's Billy Biffing, Jack Guffington, Ted Prosser, Freddie Boot – he's the tennis champion of the county, Tommy Mainprice, and – oh, yes, Algy Fripp – the big-game hunter, you know.'

The hand on Mordred's heart, now definitely iced, tightened its grip. With a lover's sanguine optimism, he had supposed that this visit of his was going to be just three days of jolly sylvan solitude with Annabelle Sprockett-Sprockett. And now it appeared that the place was unwholesomely crowded with his fellow men. And what fellow men! Big-game hunters ... Tennis champions ... Chaps who rode in Grand Nationals ... He could see them in his mind's eye – lean, wiry, riding-breeched and flannel-trousered young Apollos, any one of them capable of cutting out his weight in Clark Gables.

A faint hope stirred within him.

'You have also, of course, with you Mrs Biffing, Mrs Guffington, Mrs Prosser, Mrs Boot, Mrs Mainprice and Mrs Algernon Fripp?'

'Oh, no, they aren't married.'

'None of them?'

'No.'

The faint hope coughed quietly and died.

'Ah,' said Mordred.

While the girl was in the shop, he remained brooding. The fact that none of these blisters should be married filled him with an austere disapproval. If they had had the least spark of civic sense, he felt, they would have taken on the duties and responsibilities of matrimony years ago. But no. Intent upon their selfish pleasures, they had callously remained bachelors. It was this spirit of *laissez-faire*, Mordred considered, that was eating like a canker into the soul of England.

He was aware of Annabelle standing beside him.

'Eh?' he said, starting.

'I was saying: "Have you plenty of cigarettes?"'

'Plenty, thank you.'

'Good. And of course there will be a box in your room. Men always like to smoke in their bedrooms, don't they? As a matter of fact, two boxes – Turkish and Virginian. Father put them there specially.'

'Very kind of him,' said Mordred mechanically.

He relapsed into a moody silence, and they drove off.

It would be agreeable (said Mr Mulliner) if, having shown you my nephew so gloomy, so apprehensive, so tortured with dark forebodings at this juncture, I were able now to state that the hearty English welcome of Sir Murgatroyd and Lady Sprockett-Sprockett on his arrival at the Hall cheered him up and put new life into him. Nothing, too, would give me greater pleasure than to say that he found, on encountering the dreaded Biffies and Guffies, that they were negligible little runts with faces incapable of inspiring affection in any good woman.

But I must adhere rigidly to the facts. Genial, even effusive, though his host and hostess showed themselves, their cordiality left him cold. And, so far from his rivals being weeds, they were one and all models of manly beauty, and the spectacle of their obvious worship of Annabelle cut my nephew like a knife.

And on top of all this there was Smattering Hall itself.

Smattering Hall destroyed Mordred's last hope. It was one of those vast edifices, so common throughout the countryside of England, whose original founders seem to have budgeted for families of twenty-five or so and a domestic staff of not less than a hundred. 'Home isn't home,' one can picture them saying to themselves, 'unless you have plenty of elbow room.' And so this huge, majestic pile had come into being. Romantic persons, confronted with it, thought of knights in armour riding forth to the Crusades. More earthy individuals felt that it must cost a packet to keep up. Mordred's reaction on passing through the front door was a sort of sick sensation, a kind of settled despair.

How, he asked himself, even assuming that by some miracle he succeeded in fighting his way to her heart through all these Biffies and Guffies, could he ever dare to take Annabelle from a home like this? He had quite satisfactory private means, of course, and would be able, when married, to give up the bachelor flat and spread himself to something on a bigger scale – possibly, if sufficiently *bijou*, even a desirable residence in the Mayfair district. But after Smattering Hall would not Annabelle feel like a sardine in the largest of London houses?

Such were the dark thoughts that raced through Mordred's brain before, during and after dinner. At eleven o'clock he pleaded fatigue after his journey, and Sir Murgatroyd accompanied him to his room, anxious, like a good host, to see that everything was comfortable.

'Very sensible of you to turn in early,' he said, in his bluff, genial way. 'So many young men ruin their health with late hours. Now you, I imagine, will just get into a dressing-gown and smoke a cigarette or two and have the light out by twelve. You have plenty of cigarettes? I told them to see that you were well supplied. I always think the bedroom smoke is the best one of the day. Nobody to disturb you, and all that. If you want to write letters or anything, there is lots of paper, and here is the wastepaper basket, which is always so necessary. Well, good night, my boy, good night.'

The door closed, and Mordred, as foreshadowed, got into a dressing-gown and lit a cigarette. But though, having done this, he made his way to the writing-table, it was not with any idea of getting abreast of his correspondence. It was his purpose to compose a poem to Annabelle Sprockett-Sprockett. He had felt it seething within him all the evening, and sleep would be impossible until it was out of his system.

Hitherto, I should mention, my nephew's poetry, for he belonged to the modern fearless school, had always been stark and rhymeless and had dealt principally with corpses and the smell of cooking cabbage. But now, with the moonlight silvering the balcony outside, he found that his mind had become full of words like 'love' and 'dove' and 'eyes' and 'summer skies.'

> *Blue eyes*, wrote Mordred...
> *Sweet lips*, wrote Mordred...
> *Oh, eyes like skies of summer blue*...
> *Oh, love*...
> *Oh, dove*...
> *Oh, lips*...

With a muttered ejaculation of chagrin he tore the sheet across and threw it into the wastepaper basket.

Blue eyes that burn into my soul,
  Sweet lips that smile my heart away,
Pom-pom, pom-pom, pom something whole (Goal?)
  And tiddly-iddly-umpty-ay (Gay? Say? Happy-day?)

Blue eyes into my soul that burn,
  Sweet lips that smile away my heart,
Oh, something something turn or yearn
  And something something something part.

You burn into my soul, blue eyes,
  You smile my heart away, sweet lips,
Short long short long of summer skies
  And something something something trips.
                              (Hips? Ships? Pips?)

He threw the sheet into the wastepaper basket and rose with a stifled oath. The wastepaper basket was nearly full now, and still his poet's sense told him that he had not achieved perfection. He thought he saw the reason for this. You can't just sit in a chair and expect inspiration to flow – you want to walk about and clutch your hair and snap your fingers. It had been his intention to pace the room, but the moonlight pouring in through the open window called to him. He went out on to the balcony. It was but a short distance to the dim, mysterious lawn. Impulsively he dropped from the stone balustrade.

The effect was magical. Stimulated by the improved conditions, his Muse gave quick service, and this time he saw at once that she had rung the bell and delivered the goods. One turn up and down the lawn, and he was reciting as follows:

TO ANNABELLE

Oh, lips that smile! Oh, eyes that shine
    Like summer skies, or stars above!
Your beauty maddens me like wine,
    Oh, umpty-pumpty-tumty love!

And he was just wondering, for he was a severe critic of his own work, whether that last line couldn't be polished up a bit, when his eye was attracted by something that shone like summer skies or stars above and, looking more closely, he perceived that his bedroom curtains were on fire.

Now, I will not pretend that my nephew Mordred was in every respect that cool-headed man of action, but this happened to be a situation with which use had familiarized him. He knew the procedure.

'Fire!' he shouted.

A head appeared in an upstairs window. He recognized it as that of Captain Biffing.

'Eh?' said Captain Biffing.

'Fire!'

'What?'

'Fire!' vociferated Mordred. 'F for Francis, I for Isabel...'

'Oh, fire?' said Captain Biffing. 'Right ho.'

And presently the house began to discharge its occupants.

In the proceedings which followed, Mordred, I fear, did not appear to the greatest advantage. This is an age of specialization, and if you take the specialist off his own particular ground he is at a loss. Mordred's genius, as we have seen, lay in the direction of starting fires. Putting them out called for quite different qualities, and these he did not possess. On the various occasions of holocausts at his series of flats, he had never attempted to play an active part, contenting himself with going downstairs and asking the janitor to step up and see what he could do about it. So now, though under the bright eyes of Annabelle Sprockett-Sprockett he would have given much to be able to dominate the scene, the truth is that the Biffies and Guffies simply played him off the stage.

His heart sank as he noted the hideous efficiency of these young men. They called for buckets. They formed a line. Freddie Boot leaped lissomely on to the balcony, and Algy Fripp, mounted on a wheel-barrow, handed up to him the necessary supplies. And after Mordred, trying to do his bit, had tripped up Jack Guffington and upset two buckets over Ted Prosser, he was advised in set terms to withdraw into the background and stay there.

It was a black ten minutes for the unfortunate young man. One glance at Sir Murgatroyd's twisted face as he watched the operations was enough to tell him how desperately anxious the fine old man was for the safety of his ancestral home and how bitter would be his resentment against the person who had endangered it. And the same applied to Lady Sprockett-Sprockett and Annabelle. Mordred could see the anxiety in their eyes, and the thought that ere long those eyes must be turned accusingly on him chilled him to the marrow.

Presently Freddie Boot emerged from the bedroom to announce that all was well.

'It's out,' he said, jumping lightly down. 'Anybody know whose room it was?'

Mordred felt a sickening qualm, but the splendid Mulliner courage sustained him. He stepped forward, white and tense.

'Mine,' he said.

He became the instant centre of attention. The six young men looked at him.

'Yours?'

'Oh, yours, was it?'

'What happened?'

'How did it start?'

'Yes, how did it start?'

'Must have started somehow, I mean,' said Captain Biffing, who was a clear thinker. 'I mean to say, must have, don't you know, what?'

Mordred mastered his voice.

'I was smoking, and I suppose I threw my cigarette into the wastepaper basket, and as it was full of paper...'

'Full of paper? Why was it full of paper?'

'I had been writing a poem.'

There was a stir of bewilderment.

'A what?' said Ted Prosser.

'Writing a what?' said Jack Guffington.

'Writing a *poem*?' asked Captain Biffing of Tommy Mainprice.

'That's how I got the story,' said Tommy Mainprice, plainly shaken.

'Chap was writing a poem,' Freddie Boot informed Algy Fripp.

'You mean the chap writes poems?'

'That's right. Poems.'

'Well, I'm dashed!'

'Well, I'm blowed!'

Their now unconcealed scorn was hard to bear. Mordred chafed beneath it. The word 'poem' was flitting from lip to lip, and it was only too evident that, had there been an 's' in the word, those present would have hissed it. Reason told him that these men were mere clods, Philistines, fatheads who would not recognize the rare and the beautiful if you handed it to them on a skewer, but that did not seem to make it any better. He knew that he should be scorning them, but it is not easy to go about scorning people in a dressing-gown, especially if you have no socks on and the night breeze is cool around the ankles. So, as I say, he chafed. And finally, when he saw the butler bend down with pursed lips to the ear of the cook, who was a little hard of hearing, and after a contemptuous glance in his direction speak into it, spacing his syllables carefully, something within him seemed to snap.

'I regret, Sir Murgatroyd,' he said, 'that urgent family business compels me to return to London immediately. I shall be obliged to take the first train in the morning.'

Without another word he went into the house.

In the matter of camping out in devastated areas my nephew had, of course, become by this time an old hand. It was rarely nowadays that a few ashes and cinders about the place disturbed him. But when he had returned to his bedroom one look was enough to assure him that nothing practical in the way of sleep was to be achieved here. Apart from the unpleasant, acrid smell of burned poetry, the apartment, thanks to the efforts of Freddie Boot, had been converted into a kind of inland sea. The carpet was awash, and on the bed only a duck could have made itself at home.

And so it came about that some ten minutes later Mordred

Mulliner lay stretched upon a high-backed couch in the library, endeavouring by means of counting sheep jumping through a gap in a hedge to lull himself into unconsciousness.

But sleep refused to come. Nor in his heart had he really thought that it would. When the human soul is on the rack, it cannot just curl up and close its eyes and expect to get its eight hours as if nothing had happened. It was all very well for Mordred to count sheep, but what did this profit him when each sheep in turn assumed the features and lineaments of Annabelle Sprockett-Sprockett and, what was more, gave him a reproachful glance as it drew itself together for the spring?

Remorse gnawed him. He was tortured by a wild regret for what might have been. He was not saying that with all these Biffies and Guffies in the field he had ever had more than a hundred to eight chance of winning that lovely girl, but at least his hat had been in the ring. Now it was definitely out. Dreamy Mordred may have been – romantic – impractical – but he had enough sense to see that the very worst thing you can do when you are trying to make a favourable impression on the adored object is to set fire to her childhood home, every stick and stone of which she has no doubt worshipped since they put her into rompers.

He had reached this point in his meditations, and was about to send his two hundred and thirty-second sheep at the gap, when with a suddenness which affected him much as an explosion of gelignite would have done, the lights flashed on. For an instant, he lay quivering, then, cautiously poking his head round the corner of the couch, he looked to see who his visitors were.

It was a little party of three that had entered the room. First came Sir Murgatroyd, carrying a tray of sandwiches. He was followed by Lady Sprockett-Sprockett with a syphon and glasses. The rear was brought up by Annabelle, who was bearing a bottle of whisky and two dry ginger ales.

So evident was it that they were assembling here for purposes of a family council that, but for one circumstance, Mordred, to whom anything in the nature of eavesdropping was as repugnant as it has always been to all the Mulliners, would have sprung up with a polite 'Excuse me' and taken his blanket elsewhere. This circumstance was the fact that on lying down he had kicked his slippers under the couch, well out of reach. The soul of modesty, he could not affront Annabelle with the spectacle of his bare toes.

So he lay there in silence, and silence, broken only by the swishing of soda-water and the *whoosh* of opened ginger-ale bottles, reigned in the room beyond.

Then Sir Murgatroyd spoke.

'Well, that's that,' he said, bleakly.

There was a gurgle as Lady Sprockett-Sprockett drank ginger ale. Then her quiet, well-bred voice broke the pause.

'Yes,' she said, 'it is the end.'

'The end,' agreed Sir Murgatroyd heavily. 'No good trying to struggle on against luck like ours. Here we are and here we have got to stay, mouldering on in this blasted barrack of a place which eats up every penny of my income when, but for the fussy interference of that gang of officious, ugly nitwits, there would have been nothing left of it but a pile of ashes, with a man from the Insurance Company standing on it with his fountain-pen, writing cheques. Curse those imbeciles! Did you see that young Fripp with those buckets?'

'I did, indeed,' sighed Lady Sprockett-Sprockett.

'Annabelle,' said Sir Murgatroyd sharply.

'Yes, Father?'

'It has seemed to me lately, watching you with a father's eye, that you have shown signs of being attracted by young Algernon Fripp. Let me tell you that if ever you allow yourself to be ensnared by his insidious wiles, or by those of William Biffing, John Guffington, Edward Prosser, Thomas Mainprice or Frederick Boot, you will do so over my dead body. After what occurred tonight, those young men shall never darken my door again. They and their buckets! To think that we could have gone and lived in London...'

'In a nice little flat...' said Lady Sprockett-Sprockett.

'Handy for my club...'

'Convenient for the shops...'

'Within a stone's throw of the theatres...'

'Seeing all our friends...'

'Had it not been,' said Sir Murgatroyd, summing up, 'for the pestilential activities of these Guffingtons, these Biffings, these insufferable Fripps, men who ought never to be trusted near a bucket of water when a mortgaged country-house has got nicely alight. I did think,' proceeded the stricken man, helping himself to a sandwich, 'that when Annabelle, with a ready intelligence which I cannot overpraise, realized this young Mulliner's splendid gifts and made us ask him down here, the happy ending was in sight. What Smattering Hall has needed for generations has been a man who throws his cigarette-ends into wastepaper baskets. I was convinced that here at last was the angel of mercy we required.'

'He did his best, Father.'

'No man could have done more,' agreed Sir Murgatroyd cordially. 'The way he upset those buckets and kept getting entangled in people's legs. Very shrewd. It thrilled me to see him. I don't know when I've met a young fellow I liked and respected more. And what if he is a poet? Poets are all right. Why, dash it, I'm a poet myself. At the last dinner of the Loyal Sons of Worcestershire I composed a poem which, let me tell you, was pretty generally admired. I read it out to the boys over the port, and they cheered me to the echo. It was about a young lady of Bewdley, who sometimes behaved rather rudely...'

'Not before Mother, Father.'

'Perhaps you're right. Well, I'm off to bed. Come along, Aurelia. You coming, Annabelle?'

'Not yet, Father. I want to stay and think.'

'Do what?'

'Think.'

'Oh, think? Well, all right.'

'But, Murgatroyd,' said Lady Sprockett-Sprockett, 'is there no hope? After all, there are plenty of cigarettes in the house, and we could always give Mr Mulliner another wastepaper basket...'

'No good. You heard him say he was leaving by the first train tomorrow. When I think that we shall never see that splendid young man again... Why, hullo, hullo, hullo, what's this? Crying, Annabelle?'

'Oh, Mother!'

'My darling, what is it?'

A choking sob escaped the girl.

'Mother, I love him! Directly I saw him in the dentist's waiting-room, something seemed to go all over me, and I knew that there could be no other man for me. And now...'

'Hi!' cried Mordred, popping up over the side of the couch like a jack-in-the-box.

He had listened with growing understanding to the conversation which I have related, but had shrunk from revealing his presence because, as I say, his toes were bare. But this was too much. Toes or no toes, he felt that he must be in this.

'You love me, Annabelle?' he cried.

His sudden advent had occasioned, I need scarcely say, a certain reaction in those present. Sir Murgatroyd had leaped like a jumping bean. Lady Sprockett-Sprockett had quivered like a jelly. As for Annabelle, her lovely mouth was open to the extent of perhaps three inches, and she was staring like one who sees a vision.

'You really love me, Annabelle?'

'Yes, Mordred.'

'Sir Murgatroyd,' said Mordred formally, 'I have the honour to ask you for your daughter's hand. I am only a poor poet . . .'

'How poor?' asked the other, keenly.

'I was referring to my Art,' explained Mordred. 'Financially, I am nicely fixed. I could support Annabelle in modest comfort.'

'Then take her, my boy, take her. You will live, of course' – the old man winced – 'in London?'

'Yes. And so shall you.'

Sir Murgatroyd shook his head.

'No, no, that dream is ended. It is true that in certain circumstances I had hoped to do so, for the insurance, I may mention, amounts to as much as a hundred thousand pounds, but I am resigned now to spending the rest of my life in this infernal family vault. I see no reprieve.'

'I understand,' said Mordred, nodding. 'You mean you have no paraffin in the house?'

Sir Murgatroyd started.

'Paraffin?'

'If,' said Mordred, and his voice was very gentle and winning, 'there had been paraffin on the premises, I think it possible that tonight's conflagration, doubtless imperfectly quenched, might have broken out again, this time with more serious results. It is often this way with fires. You pour buckets of water on them and think they are extinguished, but all the time they have been smouldering unnoticed, to break out once more in – well, in here, for example.'

'Or the billiard-room,' said Lady Sprockett-Sprockett.

'*And* the billiard-room,' corrected Sir Murgatroyd.

'And the billiard-room,' said Mordred. 'And possibly – who knows? – in the drawing-room, dining-room, kitchen, servants' hall, butler's pantry, and the usual domestic offices, as well. Still, as you say you have no paraffin . . .'

'My boy,' said Sir Murgatroyd, in a shaking voice, 'what gave you the idea that we have no paraffin? How did you fall into this odd error? We have gallons of paraffin. The cellar is full of it.'

'And Annabelle will show you the way to the cellar – in case you thought of going there,' said Lady Sprockett-Sprockett. 'Won't you, dear?'

'Of course, Mother. You will like the cellar, Mordred, darling. Most picturesque. Possibly, if you are interested in paraffin, you might also care to take a look at our little store of paper and shavings, too.'

'My angel,' said Mordred, tenderly, 'you think of everything.'

He found his slippers, and hand in hand they passed down the stairs. Above them, they could see the head of Sir Murgatroyd, as he leaned over the banisters. A box of matches fell at their feet like a father's benediction.

FROM

Mr Mulliner Speaking

The conversation in the bar-parlour of the Angler's Rest, which always tends to get deepish towards closing-time, had turned to the subject of the Modern Girl; and a Gin-and-Ginger-Ale sitting in the corner by the window remarked that it was strange how types die out.

'I can remember the days,' said the Gin-and-Ginger-Ale, 'when every other girl you met stood about six feet two in her dancing-shoes, and had as many curves as a Scenic Railway. Now they are all five foot nothing and you can't see them sideways. Why is this?'

The Draught Stout shook his head.

'Nobody can say. It's the same with dogs. One moment the world is full of pugs as far as the eye can reach; the next, not a pug in sight, only Pekes and Alsatians. Odd!'

The Small Bass and the Double-Whisky-and-Splash admitted that these things were very mysterious, and supposed we should never know the reason for them. Probably we were not meant to know.

'I cannot agree with you, gentlemen,' said Mr Mulliner. He had been sipping his hot Scotch and lemon with a rather abstracted air: but now he sat up alertly, prepared to deliver judgement. 'The reason for the disappearance of the dignified, queenly type of girl is surely obvious. It is Nature's method of ensuring the continuance of the species. A world full of the sort of young woman that Meredith used to put into his novels and du Maurier into his pictures in *Punch* would be a world full of permanent spinsters. The modern young man would never be able to summon up the nerve to propose to them.'

'Something in that,' assented the Draught Stout.

'I speak with authority on the point,' said Mr Mulliner, 'because my nephew, Archibald, made me his confidant when he fell in love with Aurelia Cammarleigh. He worshipped that girl with a fervour which threatened to unseat his reason, such as it was: but the mere idea of asking her to be his wife gave him, he informed me, such a feeling of sick faintness that only by means of a very stiff brandy and soda, or some similar restorative, was he able to pull himself together on the occasions when he contemplated it. Had it not been for . . . But perhaps you would care to hear the story from the beginning?'

People who enjoyed a merely superficial acquaintance with my nephew Archibald (said Mr Mulliner) were accustomed to set him down as just an ordinary pin-headed young man. It was only when they came to know him better that they discovered their mistake. Then they realised that his pinheadedness, so far from being ordinary, was exceptional. Even at the Drones Club, where the average of intellect is not high, it was often said of Archibald that, had his brain been constructed of silk, he would have been hard put to it to find sufficient material to make a canary a pair of cami-knickers. He sauntered through life with a cheerful insouciance, and up to the age of twenty-five had only once been moved by anything in the nature of a really strong emotion – on the occasion when, in the heart of

Bond Street and at the height of the London season, he discovered that his man, Meadowes, had carelessly sent him out with odd spats on.

And then he met Aurelia Cammarleigh.

The first encounter between these two has always seemed to me to bear an extraordinary resemblance to the famous meeting between the poet Dante and Beatrice Fortinari. Dante, if you remember, exchanged no remarks with Beatrice on that occasion. Nor did Archibald with Aurelia. Dante just goggled at the girl. So did Archibald. Like Archibald, Dante loved at first sight: and the poet's age at the time was, we are told, nine – which was almost exactly the mental age of Archibald Mulliner when he first set eyeglass on Aurelia Cammarleigh.

Only in the actual locale of the encounter do the two cases cease to be parallel. Dante, the story relates, was walking on the Ponte Vecchia, while Archibald Mulliner was having a thoughtful cocktail in the window of the Drones Club, looking out on Dover Street.

And he had just relaxed his lower jaw in order to examine Dover Street more comfortably when there swam into his line of vision something that looked like a Greek goddess. She came out of a shop opposite the club and stood on the pavement waiting for a taxi. And, as he saw her standing there, love at first sight seemed to go all over Archibald Mulliner like nettlerash.

It was strange that this should have been so, for she was not at all the sort of girl with whom Archibald had fallen in love at first sight in the past. I chanced, while in here the other day, to pick up a copy of one of the old yellowback novels of fifty years ago – the property, I believe, of Miss Postlethwaite, our courteous and erudite barmaid. It was entitled *Sir Ralph's Secret*, and its heroine, the Lady Elaine, was described as a superbly handsome girl, divinely tall, with a noble figure, the arched Montresor nose, haughty eyes beneath delicately pencilled brows, and that indefinable air of aristocratic aloofness which marks the daughter of a hundred Earls. And Aurelia Cammarleigh might have been this formidable creature's double.

Yet Archibald, sighting her, reeled as if the cocktail he had just consumed had been his tenth instead of his first.

'Golly!' said Archibald.

To save himself from falling, he had clutched at a passing fellow-member: and now, examining his catch, he saw that it was young Algy Wymondham-Wymondham. Just the fellow-member he would have preferred to clutch at, for Algy was a man who went everywhere and knew everybody and could doubtless give him the information he desired.

'Algy, old prune,' said Archibald in a low, throaty voice, 'a moment of your valuable time, if you don't mind.'

He paused, for he had perceived the need for caution. Algy was a notorious babbler, and it would be the height of rashness to give him an inkling of the passion which blazed within his breast. With a strong effort, he donned the mask. When he spoke again, it was with a deceiving nonchalance.

'I was just wondering if you happened to know who that girl is, across the street there. I suppose you don't know what her name is in rough numbers? Seems to me I've met her somewhere or something, or seen her, or something. Or something, if you know what I mean.'

Algy followed his pointing finger and was in time to observe Aurelia as she disappeared into the cab.

'That girl?'

'Yes,' said Archibald, yawning. 'Who is she, if any?'

'Girl named Cammarleigh.'

'Ah?' said Archibald, yawning again. 'Then I haven't met her.'

'Introduce you if you like. She's sure to be at Ascot. Look out for us there.'

Archibald yawned for the third time.

'All right,' he said, 'I'll try to remember. Tell me about her. I mean, has she any fathers or mothers or any rot of that description?'

'Only an aunt. She lives with her in Park Street. She's potty.'

Archibald started, stung to the quick.

'Potty? That divine...I mean that rather attractive-looking girl?'

'Not Aurelia. The aunt. She thinks Bacon wrote Shakespeare.'

'Thinks who wrote what?' asked Archibald, puzzled, for the names were strange to him.

'You must have heard of Shakespeare. He's well known. Fellow who used to write plays. Only Aurelia's aunt says he didn't. She maintains that a bloke called Bacon wrote them for him.'

'Dashed decent of him,' said Archibald, approvingly. 'Of course, he may have owed Shakespeare money.'

'There's that, of course.'

'What was the name again?'

'Bacon.'

'Bacon,' said Archibald, jotting it down on his cuff. 'Right.'

Algy moved on, and Archibald, his soul bubbling within him like a welsh rabbit at the height of its fever, sank into a chair and stared sightlessly at the ceiling. Then, rising, he went off to the Burlington Arcade to buy socks.

Also available in Arrow

The Clicking of Cuthbert

P.G. Wodehouse

A Golf collection

The Oldest Member knows everything that has ever happened
on the golf course – and a great deal more besides.

Take the story of Cuthbert, for instance. He's helplessly in love
with Adeline, but what use are his holes in one when she's in thrall
to Culture and prefers rising young writers to winners of the
French Open? But enter a Great Russian Novelist with a strange
passion, and Cuthbert's prospects are transformed. Then look at
what happens to young Mitchell Holmes, who misses short putts
because of the uproar of the butterflies in the adjoining meadows.
His career seems on the skids – but can golf redeem it?

The kindly but shrewd gaze of the Oldest Member picks out
some of the funniest stories Wodehouse ever wrote.

arrow books

Also available in Arrow

The World of Jeeves

P.G. Wodehouse

A Jeeves and Wooster omnibus

'Jeeves knows his place, and it is between the covers of a book.'

This is an omnibus of wonderful Jeeves and Wooster stories,
specially selected and introduced by Wodehouse himself, who
was struck by the size of his selection and described it as almost
the ideal paperweight. As he wrote:

'I find it curious, now that I have written so much about him, to
recall how softly and undramatically Jeeves first entered my
little world. Characteristically, he did not thrust himself
forward. On that occasion, he spoke just two lines.
The first was:
"Mrs Gregson to see you, sir."
The second:
"Very good, sir, which suit will you wear?"
It was only some time later that the man's qualities dawned
upon me. I still blush to think of the off-hand way I treated him
at our first encounter . . .'.

arrow books

Also available in Arrow

Summer Lightning

P.G. Wodehouse

A Blandings novel

The Empress of Blandings, prize-winning pig and all-consuming passion of Clarence, Ninth Earl of Emsworth, has disappeared.

Blandings Castle is in uproar and there are suspects a-plenty – from Galahad Threepwood (who is writing memoirs so scandalous they will rock the aristocracy to its foundations) to the Efficient Baxter, chilling former secretary to Lord Emsworth. Even Beach the Butler seems deeply embroiled. And what of Sir Gregory Parsloe-Parsloe, Clarence's arch-rival, and his passion for prize-winning pigs?

With the castle full of deceptions and impostors, will Galahad's memoirs ever see the light of day? And will the Empress be returned. . . ?

arrow books

The P G Wodehouse Society (UK)

The P G Wodehouse Society (UK) was formed in 1997 to promote the enjoyment of the writings of the twentieth century's greatest humorist. The Society publishes a quarterly magazine, *Wooster Sauce*, which includes articles, features, reviews, and current Society news. Occasional special papers are also published. Society events include regular meetings in central London, cricket matches and a formal biennial dinner, along with other activities. The Society actively supports the preservation of the Berkshire pig, a rare breed, in honour of the incomparable Empress of Blandings.

MEMBERSHIP ENQUIRIES

Membership of the Society is open to applicants from all parts of the world. The cost of a year's membership in 2008 is £15. Enquiries and requests for membership forms should be made to the Membership Secretary, The P G Wodehouse Society (UK), 26 Radcliffe Rd, Croydon, Surrey, CRO 5QE, or alternatively from info@pgwodehousesociety.org.uk

The Society's website can be viewed at
www.pgwodehousesociety.org.uk

Visit our special P.G. Wodehouse website
www.wodehouse.co.uk

Find out about P.G. Wodehouse's books now
reissued with appealing new covers

Read extracts from all your favourite titles

Read the exclusive extra content and immerse
yourself in Wodehouse's world

Sign up for news of future publications
and upcoming events